THREE BACHELORS
THREE PERSONAL ADS

Kevin Costner look-alike, the last of the great romantics, loves horseback riding, moonlit nights aboard my yacht and bungee jumping, looking for the perfect Valentine. Must be beautiful, witty, daring, fun-loving, free-spirited. If you're my Valentine, I promise to take you out on the date of a lifetime. And after that...anything's possible.

Your Heart's Desire

WANTED
A warm woman for a cold knight.

This SWM, or knight in frozen armor, doesn't want to be stuck by himself in a Minnesota snowbank on Valentine's Day. That's why I'm looking for a SWF to melt my heart. If you're looking for a Valentine who believes that romance should be the most important part of any fantasy, write and tell me what you'd like to do on the most romantic night of the year with me.

Mr. Romance

Want your feet rubbed?
Want a bedtime story?
Want your libido stroked?
Be my fantasy Valentine d

Dear Reader,

Valentine's Day is the most romantic day of the year. What better way to celebrate than with *Valentine Bachelors*, a brand-new collection of romantic short stories. Written by three bestselling Harlequin authors— Elise Title, Pamela Bauer and Tiffany White—these delightful tales will warm your heart!

Valentine Bachelors follows the adventures of three sexy, footloose hunks looking for their very own Valentine sweetheart. Enjoy the fun as Nicholas, Tristan and Alec each advertise for a fantasy date for February 14—with unexpected results!

Valentine Bachelors is our special treat for you. Have a wonderful Valentine's Day, and may it be filled with love, laughter and romance.

Sincerely,

Birgit Davis-Todd
Senior Editor
Harlequin Books

P.S. We love to hear from our readers!

Valentine
BACHELORS

ELISE TITLE
PAMELA BAUER
TIFFANY WHITE

Harlequin Books

TORONTO • NEW YORK • LONDON
AMSTERDAM • PARIS • SYDNEY • HAMBURG
STOCKHOLM • ATHENS • TOKYO • MILAN
MADRID • WARSAW • BUDAPEST • AUCKLAND

HARLEQUIN BOOKS

VALENTINE BACHELORS

Copyright © 1995 by Harlequin Enterprises B.V.

ISBN 0-373-83319-9

The publisher acknowledges the copyright holders of the individual works as follows:

YOUR HEART'S DESIRE
Copyright © 1995 by Elise Title

MR. ROMANCE
Copyright © 1995 by Pamela Muelhbauer

SLEEPLESS IN ST. LOUIS
Copyright © 1995 by Anna Eberhardt

This edition published by arrangement with Harlequin Enterprises B.V.

® and TM are trademarks of the publisher. Trademarks indicated with ® are registered in the United States Patent and Trademark Office, the Canadian Trade Marks Office and in other countries.

Printed in U.S.A.

ABOUT THE AUTHORS

Elise Title

One of Harlequin's most prolific and talented authors, Elise has written twenty-six books. She's a regular on the Waldenbooks bestseller list and has received several awards from *Romantic Times* magazine. Elise's first mainstream release, *Hot Property,* is available in January 1995 from Mira Books.

Pamela Bauer

This popular Superromance author began writing in 1986 and hasn't looked back since. Pamela is the recipient of two awards from *Affaire de Coeur,* and *The Honey Trap* was named Best Superromance by *Romantic Times* magazine. Her books often appear on bestseller lists. Watch for Pamela's next Superromance novel, a romantic Christmas story, in bookstores December 1995.

Tiffany White

With the publication of her first book, *Open Invitation,* in 1989, Tiffany's writing career took off. Now working on her tenth romance, she's known for her nineties characters and sizzling sensuality. No wonder this St. Louis resident has been nominated Most Sensual Writer by *Romantic Times* three years running! Look for Tiffany's latest Temptation novel, part of the Secret Fantasies promotion, in fall 1995.

To Rebecca and Tom
Happy Valentine's Day
—Elise Title

For my husband, Gerr,
my "Mr. Romance,"
the man I love
even more than chocolate. Honest.
—Pamela Bauer

For Joel Meyer,
World Series baseball player in training.
—Tiffany White

Contents

Contents

Prologue

New Year's Eve—Boston

"I'M A CURIOUS KIND of guy. Why are you three sitting in here instead of dancing over there?" Fred, a burly bartender, gestured to the ballroom across the hall where a party was in full swing. "*You* tell me why," he said, pointing at the dark-haired man seated in front of him.

"Blame it on the women of this world, Fred," Tristan Talbot answered, his two college buddies thumping their champagne flutes down hard on the bar top, in agreement.

"You're not going to tell me that three smart guys like you couldn't get dates? Give me a break!"

"Hard to believe. Three hot, happening, handsome guys couldn't get dates on New Year's Eve," Tristan said with a self-deprecating grin. "Women." He sighed loudly. "I have a good excuse, though. I'm from out of town."

"Wait a minute. I'm from out of town, too, and I had a date. It just didn't work out." Alec McCord, a tall, blond, muscular baseball pitcher, said, in self-defense.

"Translation. He was stood up," Nicholas Santiago told the bartender. Cramped from sitting at the bar, he stretched his arms over his head and then smoothed back his light brown hair.

"So instead of romance, he got us, lucky guy! A night on the town with Nick and me," Tristan said smugly.

Alec moaned, his moan accenting his dimples. "I can't believe I'm spending New Year's Eve in a bar with you two."

"But a damn good bar it is," Fred said proudly in his barrel-like voice as he refilled their champagne flutes with the bubbly liquid.

All three men raised their glasses while Alec proposed the toast.

"Here's to the New Year—may it be filled with single women looking for good-looking, fun-loving men."

As they clinked their glasses together, Tristan added, "To women who want romance."

"I think we should say, 'To women whose definition of romance agrees with ours.'"

Nick's amendment brought cheers from his friends. "Always the lawyer," Alec said, teasing.

"That might be a tough order to fill," Fred remarked as he swiped at a spot on the counter. "The way I see it, the world is a dance floor, and pushy broads are telling us men we no longer can lead," he proclaimed with an authority gained from thirty-five years of tending bar.

Tristan made a disgruntled sound. "Lead? I'm not sure women even want us on the same floor."

"Times have changed, that's for sure," Nick stated philosophically. "When Alex McCord gets stood up, it's a bad sign for all of us."

"It's probably a good thing it happened. I'm tired of dating women who only want to go out with me because I play ball for the Cardinals," Alec admitted.

"And I'm tired of women who only go out with men to prove their superiority," Tristan added. "There must be women out there who are more interested in romancing than in male bashing."

"The problem is finding them," Nick said.

"You could always advertise," Fred suggested. "You know, put an ad in the Personals."

"Uh-uh."

"Not in this lifetime."

Alec stared at his friends. "Why not?"

"Why not?" Tristan and Nicholas echoed in disbelief. "We're not in college anymore," Tristan said. "We don't want to be looking for love in all the wrong places."

"What's wrong with the Personals?" Alec asked.

"Well, it worked for one of my regular customers," Fred said. "He put an ad in the paper, met a real knockout, and had what he called the fantasy date of his life."

Alec swirled the champagne in his glass. "A night of romance just for a couple of lines in the paper."

"It sounds like something we would have done when we were at Boston College," Tristan said with disdain.

"Except if we had done it in college, we would have turned it into a challenge," Nick said. "Which one of us would end up with the best fantasy date?"

"No doubt Mr. Romance would have won," Tristan boasted shamelessly, clearly feeling the effects of several glasses of champagne. Alec and Nick hooted with laughter.

"You may have been nicknamed Mr. Romance at B.C., but what about now?" Alec mocked. "Still think you could score as easily?"

Tristan chuckled. "From a want ad? You've got to be kidding."

"I say we give it a try," Alec pressed on. "Valentine's Day is coming up. Maybe we should each put an ad in our local newspaper and see which one of us has the best luck in getting a date? Or isn't Mr. Romance up to the challenge?"

"And when have I ever walked away from a challenge?"

"All right, we're back in business," Alec exclaimed, slapping a high five with Tristan. "Now all we need to do is set the terms."

"Wait a minute. I didn't agree to anything," Nick protested.

"Aw, come on. Tris and I flew all the way to Boston so the three of us could be together. You can't back out on us now," Alec pleaded.

"It'll be just like old times," Tristan added, signaling for the bartender to open another bottle of champagne. "Say you'll do it."

"I have the feeling I'm going to regret this," Nick said as his glass filled with champagne.

"You'd regret it more if Tris and I left you out of this deal," Alec assured him.

Tristan raised his glass. "Another toast. To Valentine Bachelors. May we get the fantasy date of our dreams. And..." He paused dramatically before adding, "May the best bachelor win."

Pamela Bauer

YOUR HEART'S DESIRE

Elise Title

A Note from Elise Title

In my story, both figuratively and literally, love makes the world go round. Sometimes we go in search of love; sometimes love seeks us out; and sometimes it just comes upon us, hitting us like that proverbial "ton of bricks." That's one of the magical, mysterious things about love. When we experience love, no matter how we came to that feeling, we often find there are really no words that quite explain what it's like. Poets, writers, philosophers, bricklayers, bus drivers, doctors, homemakers and on and on, have all searched for ways to express what it's like to experience that emotion.

I've been writing about people falling in love for over ten years now. Each time I start a new romance novel, I'm newly awed by the wonders of this incredible phenomenon. Each of my couples that embarks on the road to love provides me (and I truly hope you) with new surprises, delights, wonder and magic.

Many of my stories—my Valentine's tale in this anthology no exception—are meant to put a smile on your face, maybe to make you giggle a little, make you want to cheer. I love a story that gives you, my reader, some of that same giddy feeling that my couples experience as they fall in love.

Yes, romance stories are fairy tales in a way. If there are frustrations, heartache, anxiety, insecurities (and my Valentine pair may take the cake here) thankfully, they're all resolved before you get to the last page. There's always a happy ending. Well, that's my gift to you. Something I hope you take with you when the story's done. A Valentine present whatever the day of the year.

I wish you all love. And happy endings.

Chapter One

"SORRY TO DISTURB YOU, Mr. Santiago. I thought you'd have left for your office already," Emma said, dust mop in hand.

Nicholas Santiago's eyes were glued to a paper lying on his large, sturdy oak desk. Suddenly he frowned. Emma, thinking the frown was meant for her, quickly apologized again. Only then did he look up from the paper he'd been staring at so intently.

"What?" he asked distractedly.

"I was saying that I didn't mean to disturb—"

Instantly, his expression softened. Nicholas gazed at Emma, a plump gray-haired woman who'd been his housekeeper since his divorce four years back. He flashed her a half-apologetic, half roguish grin. "You didn't disturb me, Emma." He lifted up the sheet and waved it in the air. "It's this. I can't believe I wrote this dumb thing."

"Oh, I'm sure nothing you wrote could be dumb, Mr. Santiago," Emma demurred. She was certainly not alone in thinking that her employer was a brilliant lawyer. He'd successfully handled the divorces of some of the biggest names in Boston. Not in a showy way; never seeking any of the limelight himself. Nicholas Santiago preferred maintaining a low profile. *Especially* since his own divorce.

"You're a great ego booster, Emma," Nick said with a smile so charming and engaging, it made the housekeeper once again wonder how it was that a man as smart, handsome and appealing as Nicholas Santiago had never found himself another wife, and why his ex-wife had walked out on him and their two children.

"I can dust in here later if you'd rather," Emma said.

Nick checked his watch. "Damn. I've got to be in court in twenty minutes. Where's my head?"

Emma grinned. "Right there square on your shoulders like always, Mr. Santiago."

"It got a little off-kilter this weekend," Nick said sheepishly as he rose, his head still pulsating from that damn hangover. He hardly ever drank. And it wasn't just the hangover that you woke up with the next morning. It was the idiotic things you got to thinking and doing—well, almost doing—when you had one too many.

Once more he stared down at the scribbled note on his desk. What the hell had he been thinking, writing a dumb personal ad like that? The answer was simple. He hadn't been thinking.

Shaking his head slowly, he picked up the ad, crumpled it into a wad and tossed it across the room in the direction of his wicker wastebasket about ten feet away, right near where Emma was standing by the door. Clean shot. Reminded him for an instant of the good old days when he'd been a point guard at Boston College. Nice to see he hadn't lost the old touch. When it came to making baskets, anyway.

He flashed his housekeeper another smile, this one more subdued but no less appealing, as he slipped on his classic-cut navy suit jacket and adjusted his red-and-blue striped power tie. Casting his eyes in the direction of the wastebasket, he tapped his head. "Now it's on straight again."

Emma gave him a baffled look as he headed for the door. Before exiting he glanced over at her. "Are the kids off to school already?"

"Ethan shot out of here about twenty minutes ago," the housekeeper told him. "He'd have come in to say goodbye, but like I said, we thought you'd gone already. Annie's still got a bit of a fever so I thought she ought to stay home today. Unless you think—" Emma didn't like to overstep her authority. Even though she'd been with the Santiagos full-time for the past four years, feeling almost like a grandmother to now ten-year-old Ethan and fourteen-year-old Annie, Emma believed their father should be the one to "rule the roost."

Nick felt instantly guilty. While he'd been out carousing with his old college buddies, Tristan and Alec, this New Year's Eve weekend at the Boston Harborside Hotel, his poor daughter had come down with a whopper of a cold. Emma should have called him. He'd have scooted right on home on the double. Which, he knew, was precisely why his housekeeper hadn't phoned. It was a conspiracy, that's what it was. Annie and Emma had both determined that he wasn't to spend another New Year's Eve home alone....

"Is Annie still up in her room?" he asked with fatherly concern. "I'll just check in on her. I should have done that an hour ago." He frowned. "I should have been here when she got sick."

Emma sighed. Her boss was so hard on himself. And here he was, probably one of the most loving and involved fathers she'd ever had the good fortune to know. His bad luck that the one time in over a year he took a little break and went off and had some fun, his kid came down with a case of the sniffles. You'd think Annie had pneumonia or something, the way he worried over her.

"Hi, Dad," came a cheery voice from the foot of the stairs.

Nick's gaze shot over to his petite blond-haired daughter who looked lost in his oversize gray plaid flannel shirt that hung down past her knees. Every time he cleaned out his closet and prepared to get rid of some of his old clothes, Annie invariably confiscated them. It seemed his daughter, like all her friends, liked to dress in baggy throwaways.

"Emma says you're running a fever," Nick said, crossing the beige-carpeted foyer and walking over to his daughter. The carpet as well as all the other blandly traditional and somewhat somber furnishings in the two-story Newbury Street town house the Santiagos had called home for the past nine years were just as his ex-wife, Beth Santiago, had left them. Not that Nick had any sentimental feelings about either Beth's decorating or Beth herself, for that matter. He simply had been too involved with raising his kids and with his law practice these past four years to give much thought to the house. One of these days, though, he'd get around to hiring a decorator and giving the place a much-needed face-lift.

"I don't feel all that bad," Annie said as her father placed his palm against her forehead.

"You are a little warm," Nick said, smoothing back his daughter's jagged bangs. "And paler than usual," he added with a close scrutiny, also noting that Annie was looking more and more like her mom every day. Not that he thought that a negative. Beth was a strikingly beautiful woman with her fair, flawless complexion, petite yet curvy body, wavy ash-blond hair and piercing blue eyes. He was glad, though, that when it came to dispositions, Annie's was as different from her mother's as day was from night. Beth had always been so critical, so burdened, so guarded. Annie was just the opposite—open and eager to tackle every problem that came along, albeit sometimes a bit too impulsively. In many ways, she was a lot like him. Or at least a lot like him when he was young and carefree. Now he had many responsibilities and had felt obliged to settle down. Or, as Annie sometimes teased, he was getting stodgy in his "old age."

His only real gripe with Annie was that she was always on his case about getting out more—which, translated, meant dating. Oh, she'd have been all for his putting that dumb personal ad in the newspaper.

"What's wrong?" Annie asked, noticing the scowl on her father's face.

He gave her a little hug. "Nothing, kiddo. Nothing at all. Tell you what, I'll come straight home after court— Oh, wait, I forgot. I've got a meeting with a new client."

"Hey, stop worrying," Annie said brightly. "I'll be fine."

He wasn't convinced. "Your nose is running."

She grinned. A pure Santiago grin. "Well, then, I'd better go catch it."

He relaxed a little and ruffled her hair. Emma handed Annie a tissue from her apron pocket and handed her boss his briefcase, reminding him that he was going to be late for court if he didn't step on it.

"I'll phone you when we're in recess," he called as he headed out the door.

As the door shut after him Annie and Emma shared a look.

"He thinks I look pale," Annie said with a grin. "I wonder if he caught a look at himself in the mirror this morning."

"Your father got home late and had to get up early this—"

Annie rolled her eyes. "I'm not a child, Emma. He had a hangover."

Emma frowned. "Of all the nonsense. What in heaven's name would give you such a notion? When have you ever seen your father so much as have a...a cocktail?"

"Never," Annie said blithely. "But it was New Year's Eve and he was with his old buddies and they were all probably drowning their sorrows."

"And what sorrows might those be?" Emma asked skeptically.

"Oh, come on, Emma. If I was a single guy in my thirties and I didn't have a date for New Year's Eve..."

"I'm sure if your father had wanted a date he could have had his pick of the lot," Emma countered.

"I know," Annie said with a sigh. "That's his problem in a nutshell. He's afraid of women."

"Nonsense. He has plenty of women clients," Emma said, heading for the den to do the dusting.

"Plenty more of them are men," Annie argued, following the housekeeper and leaning against the doorjamb. "Ever since he and Mom split, Dad's been hell-bent on not getting his heart broken again. I really think it's tragic."

"There you go with your Sarah Bernhardt routine again," Emma teased.

"Besides," Annie said, undeterred, "I just don't think it's good for him to be alone."

"He's not alone," Emma said, dusting the built-in bookshelves behind the desk. "He's got you and Ethan, a busy law practice—"

"You know what I mean," Annie said, giving the housekeeper a conspiratorial look.

Emma flushed. "Oh, go on, now. Why don't you empty out the wastebasket for me and then hop back into bed and I'll bring you up a nice hot cup of tea when I get finished in here."

Annie puffed her cheeks out, then exhaled slowly as she snatched up the wicker wastebasket by the door. On her way across the foyer, a crumpled paper fell out of the basket. She bent to scoop it up. Just as she was about to toss it back into the basket a word in her father's handwriting caught her eye. "Valentine."

"I DON'T GET IT," Ethan said, as he sat on the edge of Annie's bed, scratching his short, straw-colored hair.

Annie snatched the wrinkled paper from her brother's hands. "What don't you get?" She read aloud from the sheet. "Thirty-six-year-old divorced lawyer with two children seeks warm, friendly, intelligent woman for a Valentine's date. I'm pretty much a homebody but I thought we could visit an art museum, go out for dinner, take in a movie." She looked up at her brother who was already taller than her by several inches. "Signed, 'Just a nice guy.'"

"Why'd Dad write it?"

"Isn't that obvious?"

"He threw it away," Ethan reminded. "Maybe it was just a joke."

"Oh, Ethan. Don't you see? Dad was going to put this into one of those Personal columns in the newspaper, only he lost his nerve." Her blue eyes flashed. "Good thing he did. Can you just imagine the kind of responses an ad like this would have got him?"

Ethan pursed his lips. He really couldn't imagine. Nor was he all that interested in making the effort.

"It's all wrong," Annie said emphatically. "Every last bit of it. You don't announce right off that you're divorced and you have two kids. That's something you work your way into after you get the ball rolling."

"What ball?"

"Oh, Ethan. Come on. Use your imagination."

"Okay, if you're so smart, what *should* Dad's ad say?"

Two weeks later, Annie's best friend, Deirdre, scanned the circled ad in the Personals column of the Sunday paper as she lay on the beige carpet in the Santiago living room. "I don't get it."

Annie heaved one of her dramatic sighs. "Now you sound like Ethan. Read it aloud," she urged, hugging her knees as she sat in a chintz-covered wing chair.

Deirdre squinted at the small print.

"Oh, put on your glasses," Annie said, looking down at Deirdre. "There's no one here but me." She squirmed impatiently and then flung one leg over the armrest.

Deirdre, a plump, pretty redhead with a face full of freckles, sat up and reluctantly extracted a pair of glasses from the pocket of her denim overalls. "I can't wait until I finally get my contacts," she muttered, putting the gold-framed glasses on, and now having no trouble reading the ad.

She cleared her throat. "'Kevin Costner look-alike, the last of the great romantics, loves horseback riding, moonlit nights aboard my yacht...'" She eyed Annie. "What yacht? Your dad doesn't own a yacht. He doesn't even own a rowboat. I thought you told me he gets seasick on a ferry."

"It's called literary license," Annie said blithely. "One of the other lawyers in my dad's firm's got a yacht. I heard him talking about it. Anyway, they're not going to go boating in February. Keep reading."

"'Bungee jumping...'" Deirdre glanced up over the rims of her glasses. "Bungee jumping? Your dad?"

"Okay, so I got a little carried away. Just finish it."

Deirdre shrugged. "'Looking for the perfect Valentine. Must be beautiful, witty, daring, fun-loving, free-spirited. If you're my Valentine, I promise to take you out on the date of a lifetime. And after that...anything's possible. Your Heart's Desire.'"

Deirdre lowered the newspaper, then tapped Annie's leg with it. "Wow."

"Pretty good, huh?" Annie said with pride in her voice.

"Your Heart's Desire? Your dad wrote this?"

"No, silly. What my dad wrote was... Well, let's just say I punched it up a little, as Mr. Freedman calls it when he wants us to redo our compositions in English."

Deirdre removed her glasses and tucked her stick-straight red hair behind her ears. "What did your dad say when he saw this punchy version?"

Annie smiled sheepishly. "Well, actually..."

"Annie, you didn't? You didn't put your version in without his permission."

"Obviously I did, Deirdre. There it is in black-and-white," Annie said defensively. Okay, so she was feeling a tad guilty about what she'd done, but she quickly rationalized for the umpteenth time that it was for her dad's own good. When his perfect Valentine did appear, he'd thank her. She knew he would.

"Now what?" Deirdre asked.

"Now," Annie said, regaining her confidence, "all we have to do is pick up the replies after school each day at this post-office box I rented and pick out the one that's my dad's perfect Valentine."

"You mean I get to help choose?" Deirdre asked excitedly.

"Absolutely. This is a big decision to make and, well, you've read even more romance novels than I have." She paused, making a face. "Oh, Ethan gets to put his two cents in, too, since he paid for the post-office box. I don't know how that kid manages to hoard away so much of his allowance—"

"What about your dad, Annie? I mean, is he going to get a say?"

Annie's blue eyes sparkled. "All in good time, Deirdre."

"And exactly what time is that?"

Annie grinned. "When it's too late for him to back out."

ON A SATURDAY MORNING, exactly one week before Valentine's Day, Annie, Deirdre and Ethan sat in a circle on the floor in Annie's bedroom. In the center of the circle were three mountainous piles of opened letters—all replies from women claiming to be Nicholas Santiago's perfect Valentine.

With V-Day only a week away, they quickly got down to brass tacks, first dividing the letters into definite rejects, definite maybes and maybe defi-

nites. Then they eliminated all but the maybe defi-
nites. Not that that made choosing that much
easier. Ethan had his two favorites, Deirdre and
Annie agreed on three others and neither of them
liked either of Ethan's choices, and then the two
girls each had a single favorite that neither could
agree on.

In the midst of their arguing, there was a knock
on the door.

"Oh, no!" Ethan shrieked. "What if it's Dad?"

Deirdre shot Annie a look. "You still haven't told
him?"

"Just a sec," Annie called out, ignoring her
friend's question and grabbing a crocheted throw
from her bed. The bedroom door opened just as
Annie spread the throw over the pile of letters.

It was Emma at the door. Emma holding an envelope. Emma with a knowing smile on her face.

"You dropped this one on the landing. I'd give
it a look. If you ask me..." The housekeeper
paused, her smile turning wry. "I'd give it a close
look. She just might be your father's 'heart's desire.'" Did they really think they could put one over
on her?

Emma grinned as Annie sheepishly took the letter from her.

When Annie read the reply aloud, amazingly it
received a unanimous vote.

Now all they had to do was plan their father's
perfect Valentine's date.

Well, that wasn't all they had to do. There was still the matter of breaking the news to "Your Heart's Desire."

Annie, Ethan, Deirdre and Emma voted as to who would have the "honor." Annie won. It was three to one.

Chapter Two

"ANNIE, YOU'VE got to tell him now," Deirdre said in a mounting panic. She began pacing back and forth in Annie's bedroom. "The limo's gonna be here in, like, a half hour. You swore you'd tell him last night."

"She got cold feet," Ethan said with a gleeful smile, sitting cross-legged on the bed. It wasn't often he got the chance to see his big sister sweat.

"He was sort of grumpy last night," Annie defended herself. She stood looking out the window. "I think he just lost a case or something."

Emma popped her head into Annie's room. "He's thinking of changing his clothes and going out for a jog."

Annie turned and rushed over to the housekeeper. "Emma, you wouldn't—"

The housekeeper didn't let her finish. "You started this, Annie. It's up to you to see it through," she said, sympathetically yet firmly.

"Besides," Ethan piped in, "you won the vote."

"Okay, okay," Annie said. "I'm going."

Clutching the reply from "Your Perfect Valentine Dream," Annie reluctantly headed down the stairs to her father's den. The others all followed after her. No way they were going to miss the fireworks.

NICK STARED AT HIS daughter in utter disbelief. "You *are* joking."

Annie blinked several times. "I thought you'd be...happy." In hindsight, she realized that it was a pretty dumb thought.

"Well, I'm not happy, Annie. I'm anything but happy."

Annie studied the floor. "I know that now. But, Dad..."

"There are no buts about it," Nick said severely. "I threw that stupid ad away and you had no right to put it in the newspaper—"

"I didn't put *your* ad in." No sooner were the words out of her mouth than Annie wished more than anything in the world that she could take them back.

Nick folded his arms across his chest. "How's that again?"

Before Annie had to "fess up," a horn blasted outside the house. Nick glanced out the window, did a double take, then turned his green-eyed gaze slowly back to his daughter.

"There's a limousine parked at our curb."

Annie swallowed hard. "I know."

"And may I ask how—"

"Deirdre. Well, Deirdre's dad. Well, actually Deirdre's dad's brother. Which I guess is Deirdre's uncle. Her uncle on her father's side—"

"Annie."

"Her uncle owns a limo service. He gave us a great deal. Well, he gave Deirdre a great deal. Not that she's paying for it. I worked out a payment plan."

"A payment plan?"

"He's not even charging me interest. And I can pay it out over the year from my allowance and baby-sitting money."

Nick could only stand there shaking his head.

"Anyway, it's yours for...the whole day." She gritted her teeth. "And...night."

Nick stared at his daughter, feeling at a complete loss as to how to handle the situation.

"She's...waiting, Dad."

"Who's waiting?"

Annie gingerly showed him the envelope. "Why don't you just read her reply, Dad? I'm sure once you do—"

"No," Nick said adamantly.

Ethan popped his head inside the room. "But, Dad, you've got to go. I blew half of my savings on that dumb post-office box and all of us picked her for you...."

Nick squinted at Ethan and then at Annie. "All of you?"

"Please, Dad, just read her note," Annie pleaded.

"Absolutely not," Nick huffed. "I am not going ahead with this insane plan. I am not going to have any part in it. Do I make myself clear?"

The chauffeur behind the wheel of the limo out front loudly tooted his horn.

"Think of that poor woman, Dad," Annie pleaded. "Why, if you don't show up, she'll be devastated. I mean, here she is, on Valentine's Day, no less, thinking she's got a date with this incredible guy, and then he doesn't even show up? Who knows how she'll take it?"

"Maybe she'll slit her wrists or something," Ethan piped in.

"I did see something like that in a movie once," came Deirdre's voice from just outside the den.

Then Emma made an appearance at the door. "I know it was wrong of the children to do something like this behind your back, Mr. Santiago, but even if their heads weren't in the right place, their hearts were," she said softly.

Nick opened his mouth to argue, but then realized it was four against one. He crossed the room and snatched the envelope from Annie's hand.

"Okay," he said gruffly, "I'll go over there and explain what happened. I suppose it is the decent thing to do. But that's the extent of it," he told them all resolutely. "You can expect me home within the hour. And if you ever—"

"I won't, Dad," Annie said quickly. "I promise."

"Me neither," Ethan said.

"Me three," Deirdre added.

Emma smiled faintly. "Why don't we make it unanimous?"

THE GLASS PARTITION SLID down as Nick, feeling ridiculous, sat in the back of the posh black limo with its spiffy white leather interior.

"Where to, Mr. Santiago?" the chauffeur, a ruddy faced, middle-aged fellow, asked politely.

"Good question," Nick muttered, glancing at the envelope. The return address had gotten watermarked and was slightly smudged. He scrutinized it for a minute. "Is there a...Milburne Place somewhere in Boston?"

"Right in the South End," the chauffeur said. "What number?"

Again, Nick had to study the envelope. "Looks like number eleven."

"Eleven Milburne Place it is," the chauffeur said cheerily. "Have you there in a jiffy."

"Fine," Nick said, eager to get this over with. He took one more glimpse at the envelope. The woman's last name was completely blurred and he could only make out the first few letters of her first name. *S-a*—and then it was either an *n* or an *m*. He opted for *n. S-a-n...* Sandra. That was probably her name. Of course, he could check it out easily enough by reading her reply tucked inside the envelope, but he decided against it. The less he knew about the woman, the better.

At least the apartment number was clear enough. His "valentine" resided in apartment 4A.

SAMANTHA LOVEJOY, who resided at 11 Milburne Place, apartment 4A, lay sprawled out across her still-unmade bed in her small two-bedroom apartment. It was ten-fifteen in the morning and she was in the midst of a heated phone argument with her older sister Jennifer.

"It's not a matter of cold feet," Samantha argued. "I have a headache and I think I'm coming down with a cold or even a flu."

"Are you dressed? What are you wearing? For heaven's sake, Sam, don't wear that drab gray wool pantsuit you bought a century ago. How can someone who has such a fabulous sense of color and style when it comes to interior decorating, ever put on anything as drab and shapeless as that gray pantsuit?"

The drab, shapeless gray pantsuit was precisely what Sam was wearing. "I bought it a couple of years ago. You said at the time that you liked it," she said a touch defensively. She hadn't always been so colorless in her attire.

"I'd have said I liked a sackcloth at that particular time," Jennifer replied glibly. "You felt rotten enough with Teddy having walked out on you. Although I said it then and I'll say it again—"

"Don't," Samantha said quickly. "I know. He was a lying, cheating, rotten louse and Bridget and I are better off without him. Well, I am, anyway. Bridget loves her dad and that's fine with me. She's positively thrilled to be spending Valentine's Day with him."

"You're going to have a great Valentine's Day, too," Jennifer declared. "And who knows where it'll lead."

"It's going to lead nowhere," Samantha said stubbornly. "I'm not going. I'm sick."

"You're not sick. You're scared. You think just because you were once married to a jerk and he had a jerk of a divorce lawyer who put you through the wringer, that every other male creature out there's a jerk. Well, this one isn't."

"How do you know?" Samantha challenged. "You don't really know anything about the man."

"I do, too. I know he's rich, successful, suave, attractive...."

"Oh, I don't know why I ever let you talk me into this."

"You do too know why. Because in your heart of hearts you know you're lonely. You haven't been on a date in practically a year."

"Nine months," Samantha countered. "And it was a disaster."

"Admit it, Sam. Deep down you're yearning to feel loved and cherished."

"Give me a break, Jen. That's got nothing to do with reality. That's got nothing to do with this... this dumb blind date you talked me into."

"I know," Jen said. "Wear that red jersey knit dress. Red for Valentine's Day. What could be more perfect? And there are probably only a dozen women in all of Boston who have the body to wear a dress like that. And let your hair down, Sam. I'm talking literally and figuratively, here."

Samantha pulled the phone away from her ear for a second and grinned before she brought it back to her ear. "What do you have? X-ray vision?" She'd spent twenty minutes getting her hair into a sedate French twist.

"Do you know how many women would kill for hair like yours, Sam? Those wild, gypsy auburn curls—natural, yet."

"Jen, I just can't," Samantha said with an edge of desperation as she caught a glimpse of the time on the clock radio.

"Okay, okay. Wear your hair up if it makes you feel better. Once the two of you get comfy you can let him pull out the pins." Jennifer giggled, unable to resist adding, "With his teeth."

Samantha groaned as she got off the bed and walked over to her bedroom window. Her blind date would be arriving any minute.

"I'm kidding, Sam," Jennifer said when she heard the groan. "Far be it from me to suggest how far you should go on your first date."

"No, you don't get it," Samantha said. "I mean I can't go out with him. I'm not ready."

"So get ready. It'll take you two minutes to slip into that red dress—"

"No. I'm not ready emotionally."

"Sam, it's Valentine's Day."

"All the more reason why I don't want to go on this date. It just wouldn't be fair to him or to me. Valentine's Day. It's just so…romantic a time. And I don't feel romantic."

"Well, he hasn't even gotten there yet. How can you expect . . . ?"

Samantha wasn't listening to her sister. She was absorbed by the huge black limo pulling up to her curb. And even more absorbed by the tall, incredibly attractive man stepping out of the limo. Besides his good looks, she was struck by his casual dress—wool slacks, a bulky turtleneck sweater, a worn leather bomber jacket. Not exactly the kind of attire she'd have expected a guy who traveled by limo to wear. The incongruity held a certain appeal. But not enough to make her change her mind.

She ducked back from the window as she caught him looking up at her building as if he was making sure he had the right place.

"Sam, are you still there?" Jen asked on the other end of the line. "Are you listening to a word I'm saying?"

"What?" Samantha muttered.

"I knew it. You always tune people out when they're trying to give you sound advice—"

"Not now, Jen," Samantha cut her sister off. "I think he's here. This guy just stepped out of a limo."

"A limo? Excellent. Even better than I antici-pated. So? Tell me. What do you think?"

Samantha clutched her stomach. "I think I'm going to be sick."

As HE RODE THE ELEVATOR to the fourth floor, Nick tried to figure out how he was going to ex-plain this ridiculous situation to this Sandra, or whatever her name was. He figured the best way was to just be direct and to the point. He didn't like beating around the bush anyway. He didn't like making excuses or making up stories. Not that he imagined that Sandra, or whoever, was actually going to believe the truth when he told her. She'd probably think it was the biggest whopper of a lie she'd ever heard. She'd probably think he'd either had a change of heart or gotten himself a better date and now simply wanted to ditch her.

Well, he couldn't worry about what she thought. He'd know he was telling the truth and the rest would have to be her problem.

Still, as he reached apartment 4A, he did find himself debating whether a lie in this instance might not be more... judicious. He could say he was feeling ill and came to apologize in person and explain that—

No. No, that wasn't the answer. Direct and to the point. Maybe she'd even laugh about it. Probably too much to hope for.

He squared his shoulders and knocked on the door. No response. Maybe she wasn't home. Maybe he had the wrong address, after all. Maybe—

The door opened and Nick found himself face-to-face with one of the most beautiful creatures he'd ever set eyes on.

Samantha, wrapped in her kimono robe, her corkscrew curls falling pell-mell around her face— a sick woman wouldn't have her hair in a French twist—was so anxious about feigning being sick that she actually did feel queasy.

"I'm sorry. I'm...early," he stammered. "If you want me to wait downstairs while you get dressed..."

Samantha's heart was racing. She couldn't stop staring at him. As good as he looked from a distance, he looked even better close up. She was instantly reminded of Kevin Costner. This guy could be his double.

She tried to get a grip on herself. Just because the guy was good-looking—okay, movie-star, drop-dead good-looking—didn't mean he wasn't a jerk.

Just the opposite. In her experience, the better looking they were, the more likely they were to be jerks. Her ex-husband, Teddy, a real dreamboat, was the king of jerks.

While Samantha was struggling with her contradictory feelings about her blind date, Nick was trying to figure out why he'd said he'd wait downstairs while she got dressed. Wasn't that an awfully misleading statement? Didn't that imply that after she did get dressed he would be taking her out as planned?

As planned. That was the problem. He hadn't planned any of it, including the instantaneous attraction he was feeling for this complete stranger.

"No," she finally managed to eke out.

Nick was flustered. "No, you don't want me to wait downstairs?"

Samantha really was light-headed. "No. I mean...I'm not...feeling...very well." At least it wasn't a lie now.

"Oh," Nick muttered. This was it. His out. Being handed to him on a silver platter. She was sick. Obviously, she wouldn't be able to keep the date he hadn't made with her in the first place. And now he didn't have to explain. All he had to do was nod sympathetically, tell her he hoped she'd be feeling better soon, turn on his heel and leave. Problem solved. And he didn't even have to be the one to break the date.

He started out fine with the sympathetic nod, but then . . .

But then, he just stood there, mesmerized by her amber eyes with their sweeping sooty lashes. He'd never seen eyes quite that color before.

Samantha just stood there, too. That is, until she started to sway.

Nick caught her in his arms. "What you need, Sandra, is a nice, hot cup of tea."

"Samantha."

Nick was already guiding her across her small foyer, his arm around her waist, half supporting her. "What?"

"My name's Samantha."

Nick, flushed already by how it felt to be in such intimate physical contact with this lithe beauty, flushed even more. "Samantha. Of course."

"My friends call me Sam," she murmured woozily as he gently lowered her onto her nubby off-white cotton couch. Now why did she say that? He wasn't her friend. He was a perfect stranger. Worse, a blind date. A blind date that she'd decided she wasn't going to date.

"I'll just be a jiff, Sam," he said with a smile and a nod in the direction of the kitchen just off the cozy living room.

Samantha nodded dumbly. This wasn't going at all as she'd planned.

Chapter Three

NICK JUMPED WHEN THE kettle boiled. What was he doing? This was nuts. He could have been sitting in that dumb limo heading home this very minute. Instead, here he was in the tiny galley kitchen of a sick woman whose friends called her Sam—and he'd wasted no time jumping on that friendship bandwagon—making her a cup of tea.

Snatching the whistling kettle off the burner, he found a mug on a wall rack, but needed to do some searching in the cupboards until he dug up a small box of tea bags on a top shelf.

"How do you take it?" he called out.

Samantha, still half reclined on the sofa, her floor-length kimono hiding her drab gray pantsuit, didn't have the heart to tell him she hated tea.

"Cream and sugar." Lie upon lie. She touched her nose, thinking of Pinocchio.

Nick found a small container of light cream in the fridge. While he was at it he did a quick survey. He'd once heard that a lot could be told about a person from an inventory of what they had in their refrigerator.

A variety of lettuces in the vegetable bin, along with radishes, a cucumber, sprouts. Whole-grain bread, a tub of margarine, a carton of eggs, left-over roast chicken in a plastic container. On the top shelf, your standard-variety mustard, catsup and mayonnaise, and a few more exotic condiments—Indian chutneys, Chinese sauces, Japanese wasabi in a tube. A health-conscious woman with eclectic tastes. He approved.

"Are you having a problem?" Samantha called out after a couple of minutes had passed.

Nick hastily shut the fridge, feeling ashamed of himself for behaving like a voyeur. "No, no problem at all." If only that were true!

As he picked up the mug of steaming tea, he vowed to give it to her, tell her he hoped she'd be feeling better soon—but not too soon to follow through on this crazy date—and then beat a hasty retreat. He estimated that he could be back home in about twenty minutes.

Then he stepped into the living room, took one look at her, and all thought of leaving vanished from his mind quicker than Houdini could have said "Presto chango."

More to keep from staring at her, he took notice of the room itself. With its warm terra-cotta-colored walls, Shaker armoire painted with a yellow wash, an armchair upholstered in cerulean blue, the nubby white couch and stenciled floor, the room was delightfully whimsical.

He almost forgot about the tea until some of it spilled over onto his hand.

"Be careful," he warned as he set the mug on an oblong checkerboard-painted coffee table in front of her. "It's very hot."

She nodded. "You really didn't have to go to all this trouble—"

"It was no trouble."

She smiled up at him. The effect that smile had on him was like a physical jab. A wake-up call. *Look at what you've been missing all these years.* All of a sudden he found himself wondering what it would be like to kiss those lovely smiling lips....

"You'd better sip on that tea," he said, his face feeling flushed. "You are looking pale. Maybe you've got what Annie's got."

"Annie?" *Oh, God,* Samantha thought. *He's married. Next he'll be telling me that "for all intents and purposes" he's "separated."* That's what her last date nine months back had told her. More apt to say she'd wormed it out of him.

"My daughter."

"Your daughter?"

He nodded. "Annie. She's my daughter."

Samantha felt ridiculously elated.

"I already said that, didn't I?" Nick muttered awkwardly. He felt like a schoolboy. He looked down at his hands as though he was trying to find something for them to do. He knew what he'd like them to do. He'd like them to touch Samantha's flawless olive complexion; stroke that wild, sexy tangle of curls. He could think of a lot of things to do with his hands, all right. What he did with them, though, was stick them in his trouser pockets.

"I have a daughter, too," Samantha said, thinking that it felt good to tell one truth. Her good feeling faded fast as it quickly dawned on her that if he had a daughter, that meant there was very likely a wife.

"You do?" Nick asked with a faint frown. Should he have known that already? Had she mentioned it in her reply to *his* ad?

"Bridget."

He looked around, spotting a framed photo of a pretty, little dark-haired girl on the mantel above the make-believe fireplace. She had an enchanting smile very much like her mother's.

Samantha followed his gaze. "She was five in that picture. She just turned six. Those two shiny front teeth you see there are now missing."

Nick smiled. "I remember when Annie lost her two front teeth. She was self-conscious about it, but I thought she looked really adorable."

"Bridget looks adorable," Samantha said with motherly pride.

Nick glanced around the apartment again.

"She's with her father," Samantha said. "He has her every other weekend and one month in the summer. We're divorced. It's been two years."

"Four for me," Nick said.

They both smiled with obvious relief, only to feel embarrassed by just how obvious they were being.

Nick shifted his weight from one foot to the other as he stood there on the other side of the coffee table looking down at her. "You'd better drink your tea before it gets cold."

Obediently, she lifted the mug to her lips and took a sip. Maybe she didn't like tea, but she had to admit she liked her blind date's tender concern.

"Say, have you eaten anything this morning?" he asked.

Samantha hesitated, then shook her head. She'd been too on edge about this dumb date to eat. Only now it didn't feel so "dumb" anymore.

"I saw some eggs and bread in the fridge. To tell you the truth, I didn't eat much myself this morning," Nick said. "Ethan says I'm a whiz at omelets. Even better than Emma, and that's saying a lot."

Uh-oh. *Emma?* Divorced four years didn't necessarily mean he hadn't remarried. Was he going to tell her that Emma was a great cook, but when it came to being a wife, she just didn't understand him?

"Who are Ethan and Emma?" she asked with a forced brightness.

"Ethan's my son. He's ten. And Emma's... well, I don't know how old she is, really. She says she's in her mid-fifties, but my guess is it's closer to mid-sixties. She's our housekeeper and a complete godsend."

Samantha flashed one of those million-dollar smiles again and Nick felt as if he was glowing inside. "So what do you say?"

She looked up into his handsome face, saw that tender concern radiating from those striking emerald-green eyes and felt a rush of desire so intense she was stunned. And horrified.

Nick saw the color drain from her face. "An omelet and some toast it is, and no buts about it," he said firmly. Striding back into the kitchen, he felt inexplicably better. Maybe it was because he was taking charge of the situation. Or maybe it was simply that he'd lost his marbles....

The phone rang.

Samantha jumped up from the couch. It was probably her sister, Jen, calling to see if she'd chickened out on the date or not. There was one phone in the kitchen, another in her bedroom. She couldn't very well talk openly to her sister in the kitchen.

"I'll take it in my room," Samantha called out.

She got to the phone on the fifth ring.

"I was just about to hang up," came a faintly gruff male voice. It wasn't a voice she recognized.

"Look, if you're selling something..." Samantha started to say.

"This isn't a sales call, Samantha. I'm really sorry about this. I know it's the last minute, but first I overslept and when I woke up about twenty minutes ago, I was practically too sick to lift my head off the pillow. It must be some flu...."

Samantha listened with a baffled expression. "Who is this?"

"Who is this?" the man echoed. "How many dates are you expecting this morning, Samantha? It's Don Hartman."

It was like an ice cube shivering down her spine. "Don Hartman?" she croaked. "My...blind date?"

"Your sick date," he corrected with a laugh.

"This isn't funny," Samantha gasped.

"Hey, look, I feel as bad about this as you do. Worse. I'm the one with a fever of a hundred and two."

"No, you don't understand," she muttered, her gaze shifting nervously over to her closed bedroom door. "You're supposed to be in my kitchen right this minute making me an omelet."

"You're losing me."

"You're supposed to have two kids, an ex-wife and...and a housekeeper who lies about her age."

"I don't have any kids. I've never been married, and my housekeeper's forty-seven. I happen to know it for a fact."

"Oh, God," Samantha muttered.

"It sounds like maybe this isn't such a great day for you, either," he said slowly.

"You can say that again," she replied, dropping the receiver in the cradle as her eyes remained fixed on her closed bedroom door, afraid any moment now that the man she'd thought was Don Hartman but clearly was not Don Hartman was going to burst into her room and attack her.

Her rotten luck. The one time in ages she lets her guard down and there she was, with heaven only knew who in her house, mucking about with her pots and pans, whipping up breakfast....

What if he's some weirdo who does his victims in with poison omelets?

She shifted her anxious gaze back to the phone. Maybe she should call 911. Or at least call Jen. This was all her sister's fault in the first place. If Jen hadn't pushed this blind date on her, she never would have been expecting Don Hartman and therefore she would never have inadvertently let this nut into her house.

She slapped her hand against the side of her head. Why hadn't it dawned on her that something was off when he called her "Sandra" instead of "Samantha"? How could she have been so gullible as to think it was merely a slip of the tongue? Then again, trying not to be so hard on herself, what were the odds of a guy who wasn't her blind date showing up at her door within minutes of the time that her real blind date was due to show up, calling her by a name that was reasonably similar to her own name?

"Sam?"

She jumped at the sound of the stranger's voice from the living room, then squeezed her eyes shut. And she had to blithely tell him, *My friends call me Sam.*

"What?" she called out nervously.

"Do you like cheese in your omelet? I spied some cheddar in your cheese bin."

She clutched her stomach as she sat on the edge of her bed. She really did feel sick now. Sick with fright.

"No. No, thanks." Her eyes fixed on the door. The thing to do was to get up and go lock it, then call the police. Only she felt frozen with anxiety. Then she saw the doorknob start to turn. Her breath jammed in her throat. It felt as if her heart had stopped. Still, she couldn't move.

Kevin Costner's look-alike popped his head in. "Are you okay?"

She managed a jagged smile and a squeaky, "Fine."

He smiled back. Such a warm, engaging, tender smile. Could a burglar, a rapist, a murderer smile like that? For a giddy moment, Samantha thought that maybe she'd imagined that phone call.

"Don?" she called out tentatively as he started to shut the door.

He stopped, glancing back in at her. "Excuse me?"

"I...I was just wondering if...what...your friends...call you," she stammered.

"Nick. A couple of my old friends still call me Nickle as a joke, but I prefer Nick."

Samantha nodded numbly. "Nick." Nick not Don. The phone call hadn't been a hallucination.

"Your omelet will be ready in a couple of minutes," he said as he started to close the door again, only to pop his head in one more time. "Say, would you mind if I made a quick local call? I just want to... check on Annie."

"You want to check on Annie?" she asked suspiciously. Who did he really want to call? A member of his gang?

Nick gave her a funny look. "Annie, my daughter. Remember I told you she'd come down with a cold? I want to see if she's feeling any better."

Samantha forced a concerned smile even though she was convinced he was lying through his teeth. "Oh, right. Sure. Sure, I'd want to do the same thing if... if Bridget were sick. But she isn't. She's with her dad."

"You told me that already."

"You don't know Don Hartman by any chance?" she asked, taking a wild stab at trying to sort this mystery out.

Nick considered for a minute. He had a client by the name of Dan Hartford, but the name Don Hartman didn't ring a bell. "No, sorry. Why?"

She waved her hand up in the air. "Oh, it's not important."

"So, is it okay if I use the phone? To check on Annie?" It wasn't a total lie even though he could tell before he left the house this morning that she was on the mend. The real reason he wanted to call her was to tell her that, as things seemed to be somehow working out, he was going to be home a bit later than he'd anticipated. Or possibly more than a bit later.

"Oh, yeah. Sure," Samantha was saying. "Feel free to use the phone."

He smiled and closed the door this time. Samantha counted to ten, then darted off the bed and threw the bolt. Then she dashed back to the phone, did another ten count and very carefully, very slowly, lifted the receiver up just in time to hear Nick talking—

"Annie? Listen, I'm just calling to tell you that I've decided to stick around Samantha's place for a little while because she isn't feeling well and I felt it was only right—"

"But, Dad..."

"No wisecracks now, Annie. I'm just making Samantha some breakfast and then... Well, depending on how she feels after that—"

"But, Dad..."

"Okay, okay, you were right. She is...special."

"She can't be."

"That's a nutty thing to say, Annie. You're the one that was so hot on Samantha to begin with. You all were."

"No, dad. We were all hot on *Sandra*. We never even got a reply from a *Samantha*."

"You must have got it wrong, Annie. Doesn't she live at 11 Milburne Place, apartment 4A?"

"Close, Dad, but no cigar. Sandra lives at 17 Milborn Plaza. You got the apartment right, though. It is 4A."

"I don't believe this," Nick muttered as he stood at the kitchen entry, his dazed eyes straying across the living room to *Samantha's* closed door. It seemed he'd gotten the name right in the first place. It was the woman he'd gotten wrong!

Chapter Four

SAMANTHA WAITED UNTIL Nick hung up the phone before hanging up herself. Then she sat down on the bed and tried to sort it all through. Being a smart woman, it didn't take her long to figure out what must have happened. There was his daughter's remark about a "reply." A "reply" to what? An ad, obviously. One of those personal ads in the paper that Jen was always on her case to check out. How Nick's daughter had gotten involved was another matter, but it wasn't one that concerned Samantha at that particular moment.

What did concern her was that Nick was out there in her kitchen with those omelets bubbling on the stove, aware that he'd blundered into the wrong apartment and was cooking breakfast for the wrong date. It was Sandra he should have been making those eggs for. Sandra, who lived at 17 Milborn Plaza, apartment 4A. Sandra, who'd replied to that personal ad. Sandra, who was probably wondering this very minute what had become of her Valentine date.

And Nick, no doubt, was pacing the kitchen, trying to come up with some excuse to make to her so that he could get to his real date before Sandra gave him up for lost.

Samantha had a funny feeling in her stomach. Not like before. Not like when she was frightened that Nick might be some nut. Not even like when she first set eyes on him and felt that rush of sexual attraction. This was a new funny feeling. A feeling that something totally unexpected and yet totally special was happening.

And then she remembered something Nick had said on the phone to his daughter. He'd said, "She is special." *She*. Meaning her, Samantha. Not Sandra. Not the woman he should have been with at that very moment. Nick thought she was special.

But was she special enough to stop him from keeping his right date? Her gaze shifted to her closet. She jumped off her bed, rushed over and threw open the door. All she could do was give it her best shot.

NICK SANK DOWN ON one of the two ladder-back kitchen chairs. He felt utterly dazed. This couldn't be happening. The wrong address. The wrong woman. He dropped his head in his hands. How could he have landed in such a mess?

And yet . . .

A faint smile curved his lips. Somehow it didn't feel like the wrong address and the wrong woman. There was something about Samantha that had drawn him to her almost on sight. Oh, sure, part of it was purely physical, there was no denying that.

But there was something more. Being with her felt . . . right. So how could something that felt so right turn out to be so wrong?

He got to his feet. What if it wasn't wrong?

He sat down again. What was he going to do about this totally screwy predicament? If he could step away from his emotions for a moment, he knew what he should do. He should fess up to Samantha about the whole ridiculous mix-up and then get right out of this apartment and go explain things to Sandra who was, no doubt, wondering where the hell he was.

Only he couldn't separate himself from his feelings; which in itself was quite amazing since he'd been a pro at not letting himself experience strong emotions toward any woman ever since Beth had walked out on him. He'd made up his mind then and there that he would never put himself in a position to get his heart stomped on like that again. For four years he'd been true to his word. For four years he'd kept his heart under tight wraps. Now it was thumping against his chest like it was ready to fly right out.

He didn't want to leave Samantha. He wanted to spend the day with her.

He smelled something burning. Damn. The omelets. He jumped up from his chair and rushed over to the stove. Not too bad. Just some cheese bubbling over the frypan and hitting the burner. He turned off the flame and moved the pan to a cool burner. Well, the eggs were done. Would it be that awful to postpone telling Samantha the truth until after they'd eaten their omelets? Maybe he could tell her while they were eating.

It was while he was getting a couple of plates out of the cupboard that something struck him as odd. If this was the wrong apartment and he was supposed to be showing up, not at Samantha's door but at Sandra's door, why was it when he mistakenly showed up at Samantha's door, she didn't act surprised to see him there? If anything, she acted like she was expecting him. Like they were supposed to be going out on a date.

It was too much of a coincidence to imagine that she, too, had answered one of those personal ads, but what if it was just a regular blind date she was expecting? Obviously it was someone she'd never met before or she'd have known he was the wrong guy.

Don!

"Oh, God," he said aloud. "Don." Samantha thought he was Don. And he'd gone and told her his name was Nick. Maybe, like him, she'd thought she'd been the one who got the name wrong.

Don. Samantha had a blind date with a guy named Don. If he was right, then this Don guy was likely to be showing up any minute. And once he did, the proverbial cat would be out of the bag. Samantha would know he was an impostor. She'd probably think he was crazy. And then there was Don. He wouldn't be too thrilled, either.

Nick rubbed his hands together. Think. Think. Don would be here any minute. And then it came to him.

WHEN SAMANTHA OPENED her bedroom door she smelled something burning. Just as she stepped into the living room Nick came rushing out of the kitchen.

"Samantha, something terrible has happened."

Oh, no, she thought. *Here it comes.* What excuse would he give for making his quick getaway? What did it matter what excuse he gave? The point was, he was about to walk—make that run—out of her life. She tried to steel herself.

Well, she decided, at least she'd give him points if he told her the truth. "What is it?" she asked, unable to conceal the quaver in her voice.

Nick didn't hear what Samantha was saying. He was transfixed by the sight of her in that incredibly sexy, red jersey dress. She looked ravishing; breathtaking; like a brilliant red jewel.

"Nick?"

She'd left him speechless. He blinked several times, cleared his throat, tried to find his voice. "The eggs," he managed to say.

Samantha's throat was bone-dry. "The eggs?"

"You know...the omelets?" He couldn't pull his eyes away from her. He couldn't stop focusing on the way the bright cherry-red fabric clung to a body that was pure perfection.

Samantha smiled faintly, silently thanking her sister. The red dress was clearly having the desired effect. "Are you trying to say that the omelets are ready?" It was almost too much to hope for. He wasn't dashing out. He'd come to tell her it was time to eat. Maybe, over breakfast, he'd tell her what had happened. Maybe they'd end up laughing about it. Of course, there was still Nick's real date over there on Milborn Plaza, waiting.

"No-o-o." He had to clear his throat again. His voice was so hoarse all of a sudden. "I'm afraid...I burned them. The omelets."

"Oh," she said, crestfallen.

"While I was...on the phone. I should have been...watching more closely."

Samantha's heart plummeted to her stomach. The burned-omelet excuse. He was leaving after all. And making up a story, to boot. At least, if he'd told the truth. She told herself it was dumb to expect miracles. And yet...

And yet Nick didn't seem like other men. Maybe it was the shock of learning of his embarrassing mistake. Maybe if he had a little more time...

"You can always start over again. With another batch of eggs. It doesn't take all that long...."

Nick threw his hands up into the air. "Can't. I used up all you had in the fridge."

So much for her last shot. Samantha knew it was absolutely nuts, but she felt like crying. She'd known this guy for all of maybe a half hour and for most of that time he wasn't even the guy she thought she knew—not that she knew all that much about Don, either, but still... The point was, it made no sense whatsoever to feel devastated at the prospect of Nick's departure. She certainly had no claim on him. If anybody did, it was Sandra over on Milborn Plaza. Besides, she told herself, if Nick was going to use some lame excuse instead of being straight with her, then he was no better than her ex-husband. No better than every other lying guy she'd ever met.

Then again, she, too, was holding on to a whopper of a lie. She wasn't rushing to tell him she'd been expecting a different date who'd canceled at the last minute.

"So I thought what made the most sense," Nick was saying, "was that I should take you out for breakfast. My limo's right downstairs. I know this real nice spot...."

Samantha was sure she hadn't heard straight. "What did you say?"

Nick's heart was hammering away. And the time was ticking away. Samantha's doorbell could ring any second. Don could be stepping into the elevator right then. To be safe, he'd suggest they take the stairs.

"Would you let me take you out for breakfast?" His voice had a hint of desperation in it. Possibly more than a hint.

Not that Samantha noticed. She felt almost giddy. Nick wasn't leaving. That is, he wasn't leaving without her. Maybe while they were having breakfast, he'd get his nerve up to tell her the truth. And she'd get her nerve up to tell him.

She saw he was staring at her with great intensity and realized she hadn't actually answered him. She did so immediately. "I'd love to go out for breakfast, Nick."

He knew it was ridiculous to feel so joyful simply because this woman he hardly knew had agreed to his offer, but there it was. Joy. How long had it been since he'd experienced this particular type of joy? A lot of years.

Samantha's mind was running on an amazingly similar track. She was feeling positively gleeful; as if she was glowing from the inside out.

She smiled inwardly as she passed the mirror in the hallway beside her coatrack and caught a reflection of herself in that dynamite red dress. *Thank you, Jen.*

Chapter Five

WHEN NICK STEPPED outside into the cold morning air with Samantha, the chauffeur hurried around the car and held the door open for them. Samantha entered first. Just as Nick was about to follow her, the chauffeur handed him a closed manila envelope with his name written across the front of it. He recognized the handwriting instantly. It was Annie's.

Nick nodded awkwardly. "Thanks..."

"Don."

Nick glanced around, looking panicked. "What did you say?"

The chauffeur, a small, lean fellow with brown hair streaked with gray, wore a bewildered expression. "My name. Don. Is there something wrong?"

Nick compressed his lips and frowned. "Look, I know this might sound a little odd to you, but would you mind if we called you...something else?"

The chauffeur's brows knitted together. "You have something against the name Don?"

Nick motioned him to keep his voice down. "No, no. It's just a personal thing. You understand."

Don didn't, but he pretended he did. He'd been in this game for over twenty-five years. And he'd had plenty of stranger requests. "How about Edgar?"

"Edgar ?"

The chauffeur tipped his cap back a little. "It's my middle name. Donald Edgar Foster. If you don't like Edgar, you can..."

Nick quirked a smile. "No, no. I mean, that's fine. Edgar." He tapped the envelope. "Thanks, Edgar."

When Nick finally slid in beside her, Samantha gave him a wary glance. "Is something the matter?"

"No. No, I was just conferring with...Edgar about...where to go for breakfast." Nick felt instantly guilty. This web of lies seemed to be growing and growing.

"I thought you already had a place in mind," Samantha said.

Nick could feel the heat rise up his neck. He turned up the collar of his bomber jacket. "Oh, I did. I do. It's just...I thought I'd see if Edgar...the chauffeur...had a better idea. Sometimes they do." He gestured vaguely with his hand. "You know, they drive around so much."

Samantha smiled faintly. "Chauffeurs usually do."

"Excuse me?" Nick said nervously, glancing around as the limo pulled away from the curb and entered the traffic.

"Drive," Samantha said.

"We are," was Nick's inane reply.

She laughed. "No. I mean that chauffeurs usually do *drive*." Her laugh faded. She sounded like a babbling idiot.

"Right," Nick said, relaxing a little now that they were away from Samantha's apartment and the worries about her blind date showing up. *Too bad, Don. Your loss is my gain.*

Samantha gave the interior of the limo an appraising study, then she glanced over at Nick, pleased to see the frown lines had faded from his brow. "Can I confess something to you?"

He was instantly on the alert. "If you . . . want to." Just the word *confess* made his already guilty conscience feel even guiltier.

"I've never ridden in a limo before."

He laughed. "Neither have I." And then he realized what he'd said. This was supposedly his limo. What a blithering idiot. "I mean, I don't usually use the limo. Mostly I drive myself." If he kept this up for much longer, he'd drive himself nuts.

The glass window separating Don Edgar Foster from his two passengers rolled down.

"Excuse me, Mr. Santiago. Shall I follow the itinerary as planned from this point out?"

Nick stared at the back of the chauffeur. *The itinerary? As planned?* Then he remembered the envelope he'd tucked in his pocket. Annie had apparently seen to everything. Except for the *minor* exception of letting him in on it all.

He cleared his throat. "We...uh...want to stop for breakfast. There's a little place—"

"Chez Vladimir on Newbury?" Edgar confirmed.

Nick gave Samantha a sideways glance. "Sound okay to you?"

Samantha smiled. "It's supposed to be the 'in' spot in town for breakfast."

"It is? I mean...it is," Nick quickly corrected.

"Voted number one by a recent survey done by the *Boston Gazette*," Samantha said knowledgeably.

Nick smiled. "You're really up on...your surveys."

Samantha grinned. "No. I work for the *Gazette*. In their home-decor section."

"Well, I can see why," Nick said. "Your apartment was very...homey. And bright. Kind of like an artist's palette."

"I like colors."

His grin matched hers. "I could tell." He wasn't thinking of her apartment now, but of that bright red dress under her black wool coat.

"Actually, I'm taking classes in interior design," Samantha said. "I've always wanted to do it professionally."

It popped into Nick's mind how much fun it would be to have Samantha redecorate his place. Turn it into a bright, sunny, cheerful, whimsical home. The kids would be thrilled.

THERE WAS A RESERVATION booked for them at Chez Vladimir. A corner table right by the window. And while all of the other tables in the warm, friendly establishment had vases filled with daffodils, the vase on their table held one brilliant red rose. And a second one lay across Samantha's plate.

Samantha stared down at the rose, feeling a rush of guilt. This flower wasn't for her. It was for Sandra.

Nick was also looking at the rose and feeling guilty about Sandra. He popped up from his chair.

"Would you excuse me for a minute," he said. "I just want to . . . use the john."

Samantha was glad to have a few minutes alone to compose herself. As she watched him walk off, she vowed that when he returned she would tell him about Don. If Nick was worth his weight in salt he'd then fess up about this charade. She couldn't bring herself to tell him she knew about it already. It would mean admitting she'd listened in on his phone conversation. It would mean she was an eavesdropper. Not that she hadn't had every reason to listen in. Or at least she'd thought she had every reason. . . .

While Samantha remained at the table struggling with her conscience and her mounting attraction to Nick, Nick was at the pay phone next to the rest rooms dialing his home number again.

Annie picked up on the second ring.

"Annie. It's me. Dad. I—"

"Oh, I'm glad you called back," she interrupted. "Look, about Sandra..."

"That's why I'm calling. I can't make out her last name on the envelope. And I want to call her—"

"Oh, great. I was afraid you'd go right over there—"

"I'm still planning to go over there. To *explain*." He rolled his eyes. If he'd thought it was going to be awkward to explain the mix-up to Sandra when he'd first stormed out of his house that morning, he couldn't begin to imagine what Sandra would think when he added the extra complication of Samantha.

"Don't, Dad. Stay with Samantha— You are with Samantha, aren't you? Listen, Dad. You better hurry or you'll lose your reservation at Chez Vladimir."

"I *am* at Chez Vladimir," Nick muttered.

"Oh, great. So you read through your itinerary. It's going to be so perfect, Dad. Is Chez Vladimir great? Did you know it was voted the best—"

"Annie, will you please stop running off at the mouth. I am here at the restaurant because I— Well, I offered Samantha breakfast when I still thought she was...Sandra. Well, I knew she wasn't Sandra because she told me right off that her name was Samantha, but I—" He exhaled loudly and shook his head. "Never mind. The point is, I am going to call Sandra, and as soon as Samantha and I have finished breakfast—"

"She must really be something, Dad."

"I wouldn't know, Annie," Nick said tightly. "I haven't met her."

"No, not Sandra. Samantha. You can forget about Sandra. I hate to admit it, but she wouldn't have been right for you, Dad."

"You told me she was perfect for me," Nick reminded his daughter.

"Well, her reply to your ad was certainly convincing. I mean it wasn't just me. Emma and Deirdre...even Ethan—"

"Okay, okay, let's not rehash the vote," Nick said abruptly. "Just give me Sandra's number—"

"You don't have to call her, Dad."

"Annie, if I've taught you nothing else in life I hope I've instilled a sense of responsibility in you," he began lecturing.

"You did, Dad," Annie said earnestly. "That's why I called her."

"You called who?"

"Isn't it *whom?*"

"Annie," Nick said, at the limit of his patience.

"Sandra, Dad. I called Sandra and explained the whole thing. And guess what?"

Nick was afraid to guess. "What?"

"She lied. Her whole reply to your ad—"

"*My* ad?"

There was a brief pause on the other end of the line. "Okay, my ad. Anyway, it was a total lie—

everything she wrote. She hates horses and she's never even bungee jumped once in her life."

"I'm not exactly an equestrian, Annie. And who in their right mind would bungee jump?"

"I know, Dad." Annie hesitated. "I just wanted to find you someone who was daring and exciting. Someone who liked to live on the edge."

"Why?" Nick asked, bewildered. Not that he saw himself as the most staid of creatures, but he certainly was no daredevil.

There was another pause, this one longer. "I thought you'd want someone who was different from...Mom."

"Oh, Annie," Nick said with a sigh.

"Anyway, it's beside the point now," Annie said.

"My head is spinning." And it was only partly to do with what Annie was telling him. His head had started to spin when he first set eyes on Samantha. "Maybe you'd better spell out the point," he told his daughter.

"The point? Dad, the point is—she *lied*."

Nick was about to point out that Annie had also lied, but he realized things had moved well past that. Where they'd moved to, however, he wasn't quite sure.

"Anyway," Annie went on, "the only reason she even answered your ad—well, my ad," Annie hastily corrected this time around, "was to get her boyfriend jealous. And now they're back together again, so if you had gone to the right place it would have been the wrong place. Instead you went to the wrong place and it turned out to be the right place. So, I guess in the end it's all worked out perfectly."

It was all so crazy, Nick had to laugh.

"Does this mean you're not mad at me anymore?" Annie asked cautiously.

"No, it doesn't mean that at all," Nick said. But he was smiling as he hung up the telephone and returned to the table.

Nick slid back into his seat across from Samantha at the upscale café. With the morning rays streaming in through the window beside her, he was struck by how beautiful she looked in natural light. Then again, he couldn't imagine a light in which she wouldn't look beautiful. And in the dark...

He could envision her naked, sprawled out on cloud-white sheets, her wild auburn curls fanned out on a downy pillow. He imagined not only how she would look, but how she would feel. Soft, silky, smooth. How incredible it would be to touch her, hold her in his arms, make passionate love with her.

God, he thought with a flash of panic, *what am I thinking? I barely know this woman and already I'm imagining the two of us in bed together.*

He tried to calm down by telling himself it was purely lust. What man in his right mind wouldn't be filled with lust for a woman like Samantha?

The panic didn't subside. He knew he was lying to himself. It was more than lust. He was smitten.

"The waiter says the *crêpes avec jambon et fromage* are the *spécialité de la maison*," Samantha said, breaking into his thoughts.

Nick was still trying to cope with the realization of his feelings about Samantha. He gave her a dazed look. "Excuse me?"

"You're supposed to say, *Pardonnez-moi,*" she said with a smile. "But I'll translate for you. Crepes with ham and cheese. The waiter recommends them."

He kept staring at her. He couldn't pull his eyes away. He was enchanted by the curve of her lips, feeling an almost desperate desire to lean right across the table and kiss them. He had all he could do to control himself to stay put. He even clasped his hands tightly together.

"Is something wrong?" Samantha asked, hoping he was struggling with his conscience; hoping he was trying to find the best way to tell her the truth.

Suddenly, Nick's telling her the truth felt crucial to Samantha. She told herself that she simply was fed up with men lying to her, but she knew it was more than that. It truly mattered that Nick, especially, tell her the truth. It mattered because she hadn't felt this drawn to any man in a long, long time.

Nick cleared his throat. "No, nothing's wrong. The ham-and-cheese crepes sound fine." Actually he hated ham, but it didn't seem to matter at the moment.

While they were waiting for their food, Samantha and Nick made polite, awkward chitchat. Inwardly, Nick resolved that as soon as they'd eaten their breakfast he would *come clean.* And then he'd ask—beg, if necessary—Samantha to spend the day with him.

Then he remembered Don, Samantha's blind date. The man she'd unwittingly stood up. Thanks to him.

Nick heaved a sigh. If he told Samantha the truth, he might lose her forever. But how could he begin what he already hoped would be the start of something deeper with this lie between them? He had to tell her the truth.

They both glanced out the window at the same time, each catching sight of a distinguished-looking dark-haired man in a navy cashmere overcoat, walking by. Nick shrank back into his chair, hoping to keep out the man's line of sight. It was Jackson Vale, one of the other divorce lawyers at Nick's firm. Vale had a well-deserved reputation for being a real heavy-hitter. While they were cordial enough, Nick had made it clear on a number of occasions that he didn't like the way Vale operated. Vale, in turn, would tell Nick he went too easy on the opposition.

The opposition. That concept always saddened Nick; never more so than after his own painful divorce. How sad it was that a once-adoring and adored spouse could turn into the enemy during a divorce proceeding. Nick always made a concerted effort with his clients to work toward as amiable a parting of the ways as possible. Play it fair and be decent. Concepts that were completely alien to a man like Vale whose only goal was to get his clients everything he could and to hell with "the opposition."

Unfortunately, Vale did catch Nick's eye and smiled at him. Nick had no recourse but to acknowledge the lawyer's greeting. He nodded faintly, hoping Samantha wouldn't notice and ask any questions. Lies of omission were bad enough. Too many bald-faced lies and she was likely never to forgive him.

Nick hoped that Vale would keep on walking. If he decided to drop in to say "Hi," all would be lost. Not only wasn't Nick ready for Samantha to learn the truth, but to learn it from a total stranger—not that he was much more than that himself—would be even worse.

"Of all the nerve," Samantha snapped.

Nick shot her a look. He was stunned to see that she was fuming.

"What's wrong?" he asked nervously.

"That . . . that bastard. To have the gall to smile at me after he raked me over the coals."

Nick gestured toward Vale who was standing at the corner, his back to them as he waited for the light to turn green before crossing.

"Yes, he's the one. Didn't you see the way he smiled at me?" Samantha muttered, steaming.

"Well, actually..." Nick was about to say he thought Vale was smiling at *him*.

"Oh, I suppose Vale's no better or worse than the lot of them."

Nick felt his stomach muscles tighten. "The lot of them?"

"Divorce lawyers," Samantha said with sheer disgust. "Next to ex-husbands, I rank divorce lawyers right up there with robber barons and con artists."

Nick's heart sank. If ever the cards were stacked against him...

Chapter Six

WHEN THEY FINISHED eating and Samantha went off to powder her nose, Nick pulled out the packet from his inside jacket pocket that the limo driver had given him. Inside was Annie's itinerary for his date with *Sandra* for the entire day and evening. He was greatly relieved to see that horseback riding and bungee jumping were not included.

To give his daughter credit, she'd been exceedingly mindful of his true interests. The day was to begin with a visit to the Museum of Fine Arts where there was a special photography show. Back in his college days, he'd actually entertained the notion of becoming a professional photographer. But after his first pre-law class, he was hooked. Still, he'd never lost interest in photography even though it was now only a hobby.

Before he could continue on down the itinerary he saw Samantha returning to the table. Quickly putting the packet away, he rose as she approached.

"Ready?" he asked.

"For what?"

"Do you like photographs?" he asked.

She arched a brow. "You're not going to pull that old line on me, are you?"

Nick grinned. "Actually, I would love to show you some of my own work sometime, but I meant, would you like to see the photography show at the Museum of Fine Arts?"

Samantha let him help her on with her coat. "Is that what you do for a living?"

Nick froze. "What?"

Samantha struggled to find the right sleeve of her coat. Nick wasn't being of much assistance. "Are you a photographer?"

"Well . . . yes. I guess you could say that," he muttered. It wasn't actually a lie. She hadn't asked if he earned his living as a photographer.

As soon as Nick and Samantha exited the restaurant, the chauffeur hurried around and had their door open for them as they headed for the limo.

"Thank you, Edgar," Nick said, not quite meeting the chauffeur's eyes as he ushered Samantha inside. After he got in beside her, he told Edgar that they'd be going to the Museum of Fine Arts.

The chauffeur nodded and Nick pressed the button that rolled the partition window back up. Then he turned to Samantha.

She gave him an expectant look. Okay, this was it. He was going to tell her the truth now. She could see it in his eyes. And very nice eyes they were, too. Green as emeralds. She loved the way they sparkled; loved the crinkly laugh lines at their corners.

When it came right down to it, she loved everything about Nick Santiago's face. There was a strength and yet a sweetness there. And, yes, a touch of vulnerability.

"About what you said in there," Nick mumbled. "Back in the café."

"I said quite a few things," Samantha replied cautiously.

"About that divorce lawyer."

"Vale? What about him?"

Nick fumbled with the zipper of his bomber jacket. "I was just thinking." He paused. Samantha waited. "No divorce is ever a picnic. I mean, it's a painful experience for most of us."

"Was it painful for you, Nick?" she asked, instinctively reaching out and touching his hand. She'd meant it as a purely sympathetic gesture, but no sooner did their hands meet than it turned into something else altogether. For both of them.

Nick's fingers entwined with hers and they stared intently down at their joined hands.

"It was pretty painful," he muttered, but he was certainly feeling no pain now. Only longing. "Beth and I married right out of college. We were both too young to know what we were doing. What we wanted." Not now, though. Nick knew exactly what he wanted now. He wanted Samantha.

Their eyes met and held. Their hands were still entwined. Their grips tightened. Neither of them was altogether sure which of them made the first move, but in the next instant their mouths came together in a deep, hungry kiss.

When they pulled away they were both blushing. Samantha shut her eyes, mortified.

"That isn't...like me," she muttered, her voice sounding stilted. "I don't know what...came over me."

"Whatever it was, it was contagious," Nick murmured, watching her eyes flutter open.

She saw he was smiling. A warm, tender smile.

She smiled back. It had been a long time since a man had made her smile quite the way she was smiling now.

"Truth is, Sam, whatever it was, still...is."

She hugged her arms and glanced nervously out the window, not wanting to admit it was the same for her. "I think we're almost there. Isn't the museum right near here?" Meanwhile, she was thinking that she should just tell him about Don's call; about how he'd canceled their blind date; about how relieved she was that he had; about how much more relieved she would have been if Nick had only told her the truth.

She compressed her lips. She'd kissed a liar.

No, he hadn't lied exactly. He'd merely omitted the truth. And the day had just begun. There was plenty of time. And, she reminded herself, she was holding back, too. She could get it all over with in one fell swoop simply by telling him about Don's call and forcing his hand. But she didn't want to do that because then she'd never know if he would have told her the truth on his own.

She'd give him until after they'd finished with the museum. If he didn't tell her by then . . .

THEY WERE STANDING in front of a stark black-and-white photo of an iceberg with a jagged mountain in the background.

"Do you do mostly landscapes?" Samantha asked.

Nick hesitated. Why couldn't he just tell her he did photography as a hobby? Because then she'd ask him what he did for a living. And he'd have to tell her he was a divorce lawyer.

"No. Portraits mostly," he mumbled.

She glanced at him. "I bet they're very good."

"Why do you think so?" he asked.

She smiled faintly. "I don't know yet," she said, moving on to the next photograph, a wild seascape with one lone boat trying desperately to ride the waves.

Nick followed her over. "I feel seasick just looking at this one," he said, only half-jokingly.

"Teddy was the real sailor in our family," Samantha said. "I remember the first time he took me out I did get sick. But after a few times out, I got my sea legs. I never loved sailing, but I liked it well enough to let him talk me into spending a fortune on a boat a friend of his was selling."

"Let me guess. He got the boat in the settlement," Nick said.

Samantha's face hardened. "He got just about everything. Except Bridget, thank God. I'm sure if it weren't for Christine, he would have fought me for custody."

"Who's Christine?"

"Teddy's onetime secretary and currently his wife. So clichéd, isn't it?" she quipped, but Nick could hear the remnants of pain and anger in her voice and see it in her eyes.

Samantha stared at the seascape without really seeing it. "Teddy had a lot of secretaries."

Nick picked up on Samantha's emphasis on the word *had*. It didn't take any brilliance to understand the point she was making. Teddy had fooled around on her during their marriage. And she knew it. Nick didn't know this Teddy from Adam, but already he detested him. How could any man cheat on a woman like Samantha?

He put his arm around her and she let her weight shift so that she leaned against him, welcoming his support. "I stopped loving him a long time ago. Now I'm just waiting until I can stop hating him," she whispered.

He drew her closer, feeling the same sharp sexual desire he'd felt in the limo, but something else, as well. A desire to protect her. "Let's get out of here."

She nodded.

They were heading for the exit when Nick stopped abruptly. "We can walk for a bit. I can tell...Edgar...to wait. Unless you'll be too cold. We can ride around if you'd rather." He wondered what Annie had planned for them after the museum, but he decided to wing it for now.

"I'd like to walk. I walk a lot. Every day. For at least an hour. Three, four miles. Almost any weather. Except for a real blizzard. Last month, when we had that huge snowstorm, I—" She laughed. "I'm babbling."

"I walk every day, too. I love to walk. Except in blizzards."

"Did you walk with your wife?"

"No. Beth hated to walk. Outside, that is. She went to this fancy gym every day and used one of those treadmills. I would tell her I just didn't get it. She agreed that I didn't. And never would. She was right about that," he added dryly.

"Teddy worked out at a gym, too."

"Sounds like they might have had a lot in common."

Samantha gave him a closer look, sensing that he meant more than that their exes had both liked working out. Had Beth been unfaithful? Had she cheated on Nick just as Teddy had cheated on her?

Yes, she thought. It explained a lot. The personal ad his daughter had placed so that he'd be forced into going out on a date. That hint of sadness in his eyes. Even the hungry way he'd kissed her. Like a man who hadn't done much kissing lately. Like someone who was as afraid of getting hurt again as she was.

Beth and Teddy weren't the only pair who had a lot in common. The more time Samantha was spending with Nick, the more things she was discovering the two of them shared.

THEY WERE A BLOCK FROM the museum when Samantha remembered that she was going to give Nick until then to tell her the truth. Instead, he was telling her about a vacation in Montreal he'd taken that past summer with his two children.

"Annie loved getting to speak French to the shopkeepers," he was saying. "She was shy at first because she'd only had a couple of years of French in school, but she's not the kind of kid to stay shy about anything for very long," he added with a broad smile.

Samantha's pace slowed. "Tell me more about Annie." Maybe Nick just needed a little help in getting around to the truth.

Nick saw it as an opening, too. Saw it, but couldn't bring himself to take advantage of it. Not yet. Lawyer that he was—even though he wasn't ready to confess that yet, either—he had a strategy. What he needed to do was win Samantha's confidence, give her a chance to get to know him a little better before he sprang the truth on her.

"Nick?" Samantha prodded when he didn't answer.

He put his arm around her shoulder. "I'd rather you tell me more about you, Sam."

Foiled again, Samantha thought with regret. "What do you want to know?"

"Everything," he said, and meant it.

She glanced over at him and found herself smiling because she, too, could see that he meant it. She couldn't help thinking about the few-and-far-between dates she'd had since her divorce and how little interest any of those men ever really showed in her. They were too busy impressing her with how terrific they were. Even Teddy had never really wanted to know too much. There were so many things she'd never shared with him—feelings, longings, dreams, fears. Not that she was about to share all that with Nick just yet. Still, it did make her feel good that he wanted to know about her.

"Well, for starters I'm twenty-eight," she told him, deciding to stick to the basics.

He grinned. "You don't look a day over twenty-five."

She gave him a close scrutiny. "And you don't look a day over..." She paused, deliberating. "Thirty-five?"

"Close. Thirty-six." It was beginning to strike him as odd that Samantha knew so little about her supposed blind date. Why had she agreed to go out with a man she knew apparently nothing about?

Who had arranged it in the first place? Under the circumstances, neither were questions he could ask her.

The wind kicked up and the cold air snapped and crackled around them. Nick was about to suggest they could climb back into the limo if Samantha liked—Edgar was following at a snail's pace close to the curb—but then she nuzzled closer to him and he didn't say a word about riding.

"I grew up in Stanford, Connecticut," Samantha continued. "Me, Jen—she's my older sister— Mom, Dad, and Fundy."

Nick laughed. "Who's Fundy?"

"Our Labrador retriever. We got him right after a family trip to the Bay of Fundy up in Nova Scotia. Fundy was great. I cried like a baby when he died about seven years ago. Even though I wasn't home any more, I used to love roughhousing with him when I'd come back for a visit."

She sighed. "I'd love to get Bridget a dog one of these days. We can't have one in the apartment. Not allowed in our lease. Do you have any pets?"

"We adopted a couple of stray cats after Beth left," Nick said. "Sparkle and Spot."

"Let me guess," Samantha said. "Your ex-wife didn't like cats."

"Beth didn't like much of anything," he said sardonically.

"What about Annie and Ethan?"

"Oh, they're the exception. She adores the kids."
He hesitated. "Even though she doesn't see all that
much of them."

He caught the look of incomprehension on Samantha's face.

"She's a very successful business consultant. She
travels a good three-quarters of the year," he explained, his tone matter-of-fact, but Samantha
could detect an undertone of hurt and anger.

"All over Europe, Asia... You name it, she's
been there," he went on. "Or is planning to go
there sometime soon."

"When does she see the kids?" Samantha asked
with motherly concern.

"It's kind of catch as catch can," Nick said soberly. "She does take a month off every summer
and the kids spend that time with her. Other than
that, she pops into town when she can. A number
of times I've actually driven the kids to Logan airport so they could visit with her while she was between planes."

Samantha frowned. "Doesn't she realize how
much she's missing, not seeing them grow up? It
goes by so quickly. I still remember holding Bridget
in my arms at the hospital after the delivery. It feels
like yesterday."

Nick smiled wistfully. "Annie was an adorable
baby. So was Ethan."

"I can't imagine being away from Bridget for
weeks, months on end. I miss her even when she's

spending a weekend with her dad. Watching her learn to read, soothing her hurts, sharing in her excitement about the simplest things—'' She stopped, her face glowing with love and pride. "I love being a mother more than anything in the world. If Teddy and I hadn't split up I'd have had at least two more."

Nick looked over at her. "You still could. I mean...if you...got married again."

Samantha was completely disarmed by his remark. "Well...I guess...it's possible." What was she saying? That she would consider marrying again? She, the woman who'd vowed so often she'd lost count that she would never, ever remarry. Once was enough. Once had nearly done her in. The divorce had been the finishing touch! Two years and she was just getting back on an even keel. Would she risk that delicate balance she'd worked so hard to achieve? For another shot at love? At heartbreak?

There was an awkward silence between them.

"What about you?" Samantha asked finally.

"Me?" Nick replied uncomfortably.

"Do you think you'll give marriage a second chance?" she persisted.

Nick stopped. Since his arm was still around Samantha, she stopped, too.

He turned to her. "My folks have been married for forty-seven years. I've got an older sister in Albany, New York, who's celebrating her twentieth wedding anniversary this year. I envy them. When I married Beth I thought it was for keeps. It had nothing really to do with Beth—just that I believed that's the way it was. That it was the way it should be. You marry and you live happily ever after. Or maybe not happily ever after, but when you have problems you work them out. Because it's the most important commitment of your life. Pretty naive, huh? Especially for a—" He clammed up instantly. He'd almost said, "Especially for a divorce lawyer." This was awful. He was digging himself into a deeper and deeper hole.

Tell her, damn it. Just tell her the truth and let the chips fall where they may. But he couldn't. For some inexplicable reason it mattered desperately to him where those chips fell. Even now, some of that naiveté was clinging. The last of the romantics. Good thing he hid it so well.

Only he was having his troubles hiding it from Samantha. She was bringing out feelings in him he'd thought were long buried. Even destroyed.

"For a man?" Samantha offered.

She was looking at him, her amber eyes unwavering. Nick's expression was blank at first; he'd forgotten that he'd left off talking in the middle of a sentence. A crucial sentence. *Especially for a . . .*

He didn't correct her. He didn't say anything, feeling it would only be compounding the lies. Better to say nothing at all.

"I like that," she said softly.

"What's that?" he asked.

"I like that you believed in a fairy-tale ending. And that you shared it with me." She wanted to tell him he could share anything with her. *Tell me, damn it. Just tell me the truth and I'll* ...

Wait, she thought edgily. What would she do if he told her the truth? His lie wasn't only a barrier between them; it was also a protective wall. She wasn't ready for this. She wasn't ready for the feelings this man who'd fallen out of the blue sparked in her. If he told her the truth she'd have no excuse for keeping her wits about her. She was already feeling them slip between her fingers. And back in the limo, when he'd kissed her and she'd kissed him back, where were her wits then?

Maybe, she concluded, it was safer to tag Nick Santiago as just another one of the liars.

Chapter Seven

SAMANTHA GAVE NICK a dubious look. "A helicopter ride over Boston Harbor?"

A helicopter ride over Boston Harbor was the next item on Annie's itinerary. With a brief side note not to worry about the expense. Another school chum had a mom who had a brother who did the tours. And the mom thought it was all so romantic, she talked her brother into giving them the ride gratis.

A bead of sweat broke out on his brow. What had Annie been thinking? "Look, if you don't want to... It's not something we have to do. We definitely don't. We could do something else. A helicopter ride. It is a little crazy." "Little" was an understatement.

Samantha's lovely mouth curved into an unexpected smile. "I don't know. It sounds like fun. It's just that I never actually rode in a helicopter before."

"Then you want to do it? You're sure?" Nick asked incredulously.

"I guess riding around in helicopters is probably old hat to you," Samantha said.

"Well, actually... Not really. To be honest—" Ha! Honest. "I've never ridden in one, either." He figured every little bit of truth he could throw in might help his cause in the long run. If there was even a chance of a "long run" once he did tell all.

Samantha felt suddenly giddy and excited. She snatched hold of Nick's hand in almost the same way Bridget sometimes grabbed hers when they were going to have an adventure. As soon as their hands touched, however, the little-girl feeling was quickly replaced by feelings that were far more adult. It was like touching a match to a fast-burning fuse.

The next thing Samantha knew, her wits were flying right out of that limousine window again. Nick's went right out there with hers as they spontaneously wrapped their arms around each other.

She couldn't even muster a weak protest as his mouth moved down on hers. A second later, they began kissing wildly again. This time Nick's hands found their way inside Samantha's unbuttoned black wool coat. When he drew her against him now, he could feel her breasts press against his chest. He ran his hands down the exquisite curve at the small of her back. Through the thin jersey material of her dress he could feel her trembling. He was trembling, too. The feel and taste of her took his breath away.

"Oh, Sam, Sam," he whispered hoarsely against her hair after they stopped kissing, but still clung to each other.

The way he crooned her name made Samantha's pulse hammer. They weren't even in that helicopter yet and already she was soaring. An aching desire spread through her like a wildfire. She wanted to kiss Nick again. She wanted more than that. She wanted to curl up naked with him in a big bed with cool, white sheets and make love with him.

The fantasy shocked Samantha back to her senses. What was she thinking? She hadn't gone to bed with any man since Teddy. Sex without love had not only seemed immoral to her; it had also seemed empty and pointless. She wanted the tenderness, the feeling of being cherished, of cherishing. Feelings like that didn't happen in the blink of an eye. On Valentine's Day, no less. Feelings like that certainly didn't happen with a man who'd mistakenly shown up at the wrong apartment and was about to go flying around Boston in a helicopter with the wrong woman.

She drew back and tried to smooth down her dress, which had ridden halfway up her thighs—thighs that Nick hadn't missed noting were as lovely and silken as the rest of her. Something caught in his throat just looking at her. As for holding her and kissing her, crazy as it seemed, it was like this was his first time; that no other woman had ever existed for him; that there were only Samantha's soft, warm, inviting lips, only her svelte body, her radiant smile, her mesmerizing eyes.

The chauffeur's voice came through on the small speaker as the limousine pulled to a stop at a private airport not far from Logan. "We've arrived, Mr. Santiago." If Edgar had caught sight of their heated encounter via his rearview mirror, his voice gave no hint of it.

Still, Samantha blushed. In the heat of her passion she'd actually forgotten they hadn't been all alone in the limo. What if he'd seen them? What would he think? What did *she* think? She chided herself sharply for having been so indiscreet. If there was going to be any more kissing—

Stop that, she told herself firmly. There was absolutely not going to be any further shenanigans. Whether Nick finally told her the truth or not. She did not want to get involved in another potentially painful relationship; and as far as Samantha was concerned, any intimate relationship was fraught with potential heartache. She had her job, her daughter, her plans for her future, which included getting her credentials to do interior design and, when she made enough money, buying a little house in the suburbs for her and Bridget. Romance was most definitely not in her plans.

THERE WAS A BIG RED heart painted on the door of the helicopter.

The pilot, a jovial, heavyset young man dressed in a thick gray twill jumpsuit and flight jacket, greeted Samantha with a red rose and a broad smile.

"Happy Valentine's Day, Sandra..."

"Samantha," Nick, nonplussed, quickly corrected him.

Samantha glanced at Nick. He was beet red.

The pilot merely shrugged, no doubt thinking he'd got the name wrong. "Sorry about that. Happy Valentine's Day, Samantha. And welcome to Chip's Chopper Tours. I'm Chip. I know I got that name right," he added with a toothy grin. "Are you ready?"

Samantha once again looked over at Nick, surprised to see his complexion had gone from rose to ash in an instant. Only then did it dawn on her that he might be even more nervous about this chopper ride than she was.

"Hop aboard, folks," Chip said brightly.

Samantha leaned closer to Nick. "We really don't have to do this, you know."

"Got a bottle of champagne all ready for ya," Chip said, oblivious to their ambivalence. "You can pop the cork whenever you're ready. I had this real cute couple I took up this morning. He not only popped the cork but the big question—right when we were flying over the harbor."

"What did she...answer?" Samantha couldn't resist asking the pilot.

Chip's grin broadened. "What do you think?"

I think she's probably nuts and will live to regret that one little word one of these days, Samantha thought. She merely smiled at Chip.

Nick's normal color started to return as he thought about how romantic it would be to soar above the city with Samantha. "I'm game if you are," he said to her.

Inexplicably, so was Samantha. This really was the most romantic date she'd ever been on. Even if she wasn't the one who was supposed to be on it. As she climbed into the chopper, suddenly Sandra came to mind. She assumed Nick had phoned his real date while they were at the restaurant that morning having breakfast. What excuse had he given the poor woman? Did this web of lies even bother him?

Nick instantly picked up on her abrupt change of mood. "What's wrong?" he asked with concern as he climbed in beside her.

"What makes you think...?" she started to ask.

He took gentle hold of her hand. "You're very readable, Sam," he said softly.

Her eyes widened with surprise. "That's funny. Teddy always used to say the exact opposite. That he could never read me. That I held everything in."

Nick's expression turned bittersweet. "Beth always said that about me."

Whatever had been true for Beth and Teddy, wasn't true for them. They seemed so attuned to each other, it was astonishing to both of them. And frightening. And exhilarating.

Samantha's lips slowly parted into a shy, vulnerable smile as she lifted the rose and sniffed its wonderful scent. "Lovely."

"More than lovely," Nick murmured, but it wasn't the rose he was staring at. It was Samantha. Just looking at her made him feel giddy with excitement.

"Up, up, and away," Chip merrily shouted over the roar of the motor and the loud whirring of the spinning chopper blades.

As they headed straight up into the clear blue sky, Samantha squeezed Nick's hand tightly. But she was still smiling. Whatever the reason, her fear had vanished.

Within minutes they were flying over the harbor. Nick's eyes fell on the iced champagne bottle and for one insane moment he actually imagined popping, not the cork, but the "big question." *Samantha, will you be my valentine, not just for today but for always? Samantha, will you marry me?* And what would she answer him? *Yes.* It had to be yes. If she said no, it would break his heart.

Had he completely lost his senses? Maybe it was the sudden rise in altitude. The change in air pressure. Or maybe . . . maybe, it was love.

"Shall we?" Samantha asked.

Nick blinked rapidly. "Shall we . . . what?"

"Open the champagne."

"Oh, right. The champagne. Open the champagne. Good idea," he stammered. Or was it such a good idea? The last time he'd had champagne was last New Year's Eve when he'd let himself be talked into writing that dumb personal ad.

"Nick?"

He looked at Samantha and found himself smiling. Dumb? No way. It just may have been the smartest thing he'd ever done—in a convoluted sort of way.

He pulled his gaze away from her and snatched hold of the champagne bottle only to find his fingers were trembling so much he had a real time of it popping the cork. When he finally managed it, the champagne exploded over the lip of the bottle like Mount Vesuvius.

Samantha laughed, quickly holding out first one plastic champagne goblet, then the other.

"What shall we toast to?" she asked softly.

It was so loud in the cabin Nick couldn't actually hear her question, but he got the gist of it. He smiled. "To fate. Let's toast to fate."

They tapped glasses and sipped, their eyes meeting over the rims. The tiny, noisy cabin pulsed with electricity.

Impulsively, Nick leaned forward and kissed her lightly, then let his tongue dart out and taste the champagne on her lips. Pure elixir.

The champagne spilled over the edge of Samantha's glass. He took it from her, then clasped her hand and brought it to his mouth. He licked away the spill from her soft skin.

"Samantha."

"Yes, Nick."

"Is it just me? Or are you feeling…light-headed, too?"

Samantha shut her eyes for a moment. When she opened them again, they fell on Nick's face. "It isn't just you."

"Right down below now, you can see the ship, the *Constitution*," Chip was shouting.

They both nodded, neither of them looking, their gazes riveted on each other. They were already thoroughly enjoying the "view."

"This is the best Valentine's Day I've ever had," Samantha said.

Nick lifted up the red rose that was lying in her lap. He broke off the stem halfway down and carefully removed the thorns. Then he tucked the rose in Samantha's hair, securing the stem behind her ear.

"Perfect," he murmured.

She had to lean very close to hear him. So close that their lips grazed. A feeling that was as much panic as it was elation swept over her. *Oh, God, I really do think I'm falling in love with this man.* Her heart hammered wildly in her chest. She was well past feeling light-headed. She was spinning like a top. Spinning out of control.

"What do you think of Hancock Center?" Chip shouted.

All Samantha could think about was finding some secluded spot away from the eyes of pilots, chauffeurs, and every other living, breathing human being. She wanted to be alone with Nick. She wanted to wrap herself in Nick's arms, make wild, passionate love with him. She knew it was crazy, but everything had gone haywire from the very moment she'd laid eyes on him. All these years she'd only been deluding herself into believing she didn't need a man, that she didn't need to feel this hot, pulsating, burning desire....

Lust. Yes, she was surely feeling lust, feeling it like she'd never felt it before. Not with Teddy. Not with any man. But this was more than lust. Nick was special. He'd reached deep inside her to a place she'd told herself didn't even exist anymore.

Oh, Nick, Nick. I want you so desperately. I'm going out of my mind, I want you so much.

Her place. That was it. No one was there. No watchful eyes. Her place. Yes. Perfect.

How to get him there, though. For all her desire, she couldn't be blatant about it. She wasn't that type of woman.

That type of woman. Oh, right. Terrific. Here she was, plotting to get a man she'd known for all of half a day into her bed and she felt she should be discreet about it. What was the matter with her? Had her hormones gone completely haywire?

She was starting to get a grip on herself when Nick put his arm around her. The intensity of desire that simple contact gave her was so sharp she leaned heavily against him, drawing into his warmth, his tenderness, his utter sensuality. There was no fighting it. She closed her eyes, but all she could see were visions of Nick dancing before her eyelids. All she could feel was heat spreading through her until she was burning up. And really, it was cold as ice in that chopper.

She could feel herself being swept away by a completely uncharacteristic reckless abandon. She almost shouted at the pilot to land the chopper that instant. Then she glanced down and saw that they were still over water. Sink or swim.

Okay, then. As soon as they could safely land. Only she still hadn't figured out how to get him back to her place.

She'd make up some excuse. But what?

Nick drew a ragged breath as he took in the scent of Samantha's hair. It was a little like apples. Like walking through an apple orchard. She smelled so fresh and clean. She felt so good. He longed to kiss her again. But not here. Not with the chipper Chip right there with them. Not back in the limo with Edgar up there in the front seat.

He had to find some place to be alone with Samantha. His desire for her was so intense that it knocked all rational thought from his mind. All he knew was that he desperately wanted to be close to her, to kiss her, to embrace her, to make love with her. Was it right? Wrong? Those words held no meaning for him. It wasn't about that. It was about need and desire and a sense of connection so strong that it obliterated everything else from his mind. By a ridiculous turn of events, he'd accidentally come upon the one woman for him. It was fate.

Well, fate and his daughter, Annie.

"Coming down for a landing now, folks. Sorry to say the flight's just about over."

They both smiled tremulously. No way. The flight was just beginning.

Chapter Eight

"WOULD YOU LIKE TO GO back to your apartment now?" Edgar asked Samantha as they got to the limo.

Samantha turned scarlet. Was she so transparent that even the chauffeur knew what she had on her mind?

Nick was equally dumbfounded.

The chauffeur gave them both a perplexed look, then addressed Samantha again. "To change for the ball."

Samantha stared at him. "The...ball?"

"I wasn't sure," Edgar went on, "whether you'd prefer to dress for the ball before or after your dinner on the yacht."

Nick was growing more confused by the minute. "The...yacht?" Something told him he should have read Annie's itinerary through to the end.

"You have arranged a private dinner on your yacht, Mr. Santiago," Edgar offered, checking his watch. "It's nearly five o'clock now and you'd planned the dinner for seven. The Valentine's Day charity ball at the Ambassador Hotel begins at nine. Your tux is in the trunk, but naturally Miss—"

"Lovejoy," Samantha piped in before he mistakenly used Sandra's last name.

Edgar smiled pleasantly. "Naturally Miss Lovejoy will have to go back to her apartment to change into the proper evening attire."

Samantha swallowed hard. The proper evening attire? A ball gown? She didn't own— Wait. Yes, she did. Sort of. The gown she wore when she was a bridesmaid for her friend Nina's wedding last year. She hadn't selected it, but thank heavens, Nina had excellent taste. The gown was a simple yet elegant teal-blue taffeta design with a divine body-shaping drape down to the ankles, and even a dropped-shoulder, heart-shaped neckline. What could be more perfect for a Valentine's ball?

And to top it off, she now had her excuse—courtesy of Edgar—to get Nick back to her place!

NICK CARRIED HIS TUX over his arm as he stepped into Samantha's apartment. Was the place warmer than it had been that morning? He certainly felt warmer. He felt downright hot. And very uneasy. As much as he'd wanted—and still wanted—to be alone with Samantha, now that his wishes had been so unexpectedly and easily granted, he felt as nervous as a schoolboy. And guilty as hell.

He was here with Samantha under false pretenses. Dozens of times throughout the day, he'd silently vowed to tell her the truth. And each time he'd found some excuse to delay it. He'd deluded himself into thinking that somehow it would get easier. In truth, it was getting harder.

"Is anything the matter, Nick?"

He gritted his teeth. "Samantha."

She slipped off her wool coat. "Yes?"

Nick could feel his heart lurch. Why did she have to look so trusting? So vulnerable? Beads of sweat broke out across his brow. "Isn't it...awfully warm in here?"

"Maybe you ought to take off your jacket."

"My jacket. Good idea."

"Here, let me hang your tux up on the door for you," she offered.

"Thanks. Thanks a lot," he said, handing it over to her. "It's been a real long time since I've worn a monkey suit."

Samantha hung the tux on the hall closet door.

Nick clenched and unclenched his hands. "Last time was a couple of years ago."

Samantha turned back to him. "Oh? Another Valentine's ball?"

He smiled edgily. "No. A wedding, actually."

"Were you on assignment?"

"What?"

"Were you the photographer for the wedding?"

Nick sighed inwardly. "No. No, I was the best man," he said, dabbing at his sweaty brow with the palm of his hand. What had ever possessed him to tell Samantha he was a photographer? Oh, if only he could start this day all over again. For the life of

him, though, he couldn't figure out how he could
have altered it and still have gotten to spend all this
time with her. Had he told her the truth from the
start, she'd have sent him on his way and now it
would be Don and not him standing with her there
in her apartment. No doubt thinking just what he
was thinking. Wanting just what he was wanting...

"Would you like something cold to drink?" Samantha asked. She could use one herself. Her
throat was raw as sandpaper. Now that she had
Nick all to herself, she was nervous as hell. Would
he make the first move? Would she? This was so
awkward.

And then there was still that lie looming over
them. Could she make love with a man who was
deliberately deceiving her? If he'd lie about this,
what else would he lie about?

"I'd love one."

Samantha gave him a sharp look. "One what?"

"A cold drink," Nick said, bemused.

"Oh, right. In the kitchen. The drinks. You
know...in the fridge. Uh...juice? I think there's
orange and grape. No, I remember finishing off the
grape last night. Actually, I'm not sure about the
orange juice, either."

Samantha's obvious nervousness had the odd
effect of calming Nick. "Water will be fine, Sam,"
he said softly.

"It'll have to be tap. I ran out of bottled water."

"Tap water's great."

"Ice?"

"Sure. If you have any."

"Of course I have ice," she snapped. Now why was she suddenly so testy? Worse still, suddenly close to tears? She looked away, not budging.

Next thing she knew, Nick was steering her over to her sofa.

"Sit down, Sam. I'll get the water. A glass for each of us. Okay?"

"Okay," she said weakly.

He was back a minute later with two glasses of ice water. He handed one to Samantha and sat down beside her. She gulped the water down in long, continuous swallows. Nick followed suit, then took the two empty glasses and placed them on the coffee table.

"Samantha."

She held her breath.

"There's so much I want to say to you. So much I... need to say." He stopped and took hold of her hands. "You're trembling."

She smiled tremulously. "So are you."

Their gazes locked. There was a long silence punctuating their mix of desire and concern. It was broken, not by Nick's confession—which he'd finally steeled himself to utter—but by the shrill ring of the telephone. They both jumped at the sound.

Nick squeezed her hands. "Don't answer it." He was afraid if she left now, he'd lose his nerve.

Samantha's brows knitted together as the second ring filled the room. "I should. It could be Teddy. Maybe Bridget's sick or something."

He released his hold of her. "Right. I understand." He would have felt the same if he were in her shoes.

As the phone rang for a third time, Samantha hesitated. She'd sensed that this was the moment of truth. If only she'd thought to put her answering machine on. Then she could have played the message back to see if there was a problem right after Nick came clean.

She got to the kitchen phone on the fourth ring and said a breathless, "Yes?" into the mouthpiece.

"What are you doing there?" came a familiar voice from the other end of the line.

Samantha cursed under her breath. "Why are you calling me if you didn't think I'd be here?" she snapped at her sister.

"It didn't go well, right?" Jen mused. "You cut out early. Worse than you expected even?"

"Jen..."

"Don't give me one of your lectures, Sam."

A lecture was the last thing she wanted to give her sister at the moment.

"You have to adopt my philosophy. Win some, lose some, Sam. There are plenty of fish in the sea. Granted most of them are herrings, but every now and then you land a real catch if you just keep fishing. That's the important thing, Sam. You can't expect with one throw of the line that you're going to reel yourself in a prize salmon.''

"Please, Jen . . ."

"Okay, what was the matter with him, anyway? A total bore? A lech? A complete jerk? I honestly thought it would work out. He had so much going for him. At least so my good pal, Liz, swore to me. You know I wouldn't have fixed you up with him if I didn't trust Liz. To be honest, Sam, I'm wondering if it wasn't him at all. Maybe you were looking for faults where there weren't any. Not that I'm saying he was perfect. But who's perfect? Perfect's dull, Sam. Maybe you need to lower your expectations."

"Jen," Samantha said in a low, tight voice, "I can't talk now."

"You can't talk now?" Jen echoed. And then after a short pause, she added, "Oh. For God's sake, Sam, why didn't you say that in the first place?" She chuckled. "So you can't talk. Well, that's great. That's really great. I get it now."

"Believe me, you don't get it."

"Of course I do. I wasn't born yesterday. He's there, right?"

Samantha had to smile. "Not exactly."

"What does that mean? Sam, you sound funny. Is something wrong? He is there. Close by? Are you being coerced into getting rid of me? Oh, no, is he some kind of a nutcase? He hasn't touched you?

Oh, God, should I call the police? All you have to do is say yes, Sam. If he's listening, he won't know what we're talking about. Just a yes and the police and I will be there in a flash.''

Samantha laughed. "You watch too many crime shows on TV, Jen. I'm perfectly fine. Now, if you don't mind, I'm going to get off the phone. Nick's waiting for me in the living room.''

"Nick? Who the hell is Nick? What happened to Don? What do you mean—Nick?''

"Bye, Jen," Samantha said airily and dropped the receiver into the cradle.

WHEN SAMANTHA RETURNED to the living room it was empty. Then she saw that Nick's tux was no longer hanging on the closet door. She was flooded by a wave of panic, her heart sinking to her stomach.

Oh, no. He's gone. He lost his nerve altogether and took off.

She should have listened to him. She should never have answered her phone. This was all Jen's doing. If she hadn't called . . .

Tears spiked Samantha's eyes. She sank down on the sofa, feeling listless and forlorn. She even contemplated calling Jen back, feeling suddenly so hopelessly alone. But it wasn't Jen who could comfort her and fill this emptiness inside of her. It was Nick who, like an excavator, had discovered the pit. And he was the only one who could fill it.

She shut her eyes as the tears spilled over the rims. Then she heard a noise in her bedroom. Her eyes popped open. She leaped up from the sofa, raced across the living room and threw open the bedroom door.

A gasp of surprise and immeasurable relief escaped her lips. There he was, standing right beside her bed, his shirt off, the button of his trousers undone. He looked like one of those incredibly sexy Calvin Klein male models advertising jeans. And broad, muscled chests. Nick's chest rivaled the best of them. So much for her worrying about how she was going to maneuver them into her bedroom without appearing too forward!

Then she saw the tux lying across her bed, the starched white pleated shirt in Nick's hand. He hadn't deserted her. Nor had he taken matters of the heart—and body—into his own hands. He'd simply gone into her bedroom to change into formal attire for the evening's festivities.

Nick's expression filled with alarm as he saw the tears slipping down Samantha's cheeks—tears she'd already forgotten all about.

Instantly concluding that the phone call had brought Samantha upsetting news, he rushed to her side. "Is it Bridget? Is she hurt? Sick?"

Samantha shook her head. "No. No. She's... fine. It was... only Jen."

Nick was perplexed. "Then why are you crying?"

"I thought…I thought…you'd gone," she said breathlessly.

"Oh, Sam." He let the shirt drop from his hand and took her roughly into his arms. "I wouldn't leave you. I would never leave you. Don't you know that, Sam? Don't you know how much I want you? How much you mean to me? I know it's all happening so fast, darling, but there's no slowing it down. I'm crazy about you, Sam. I'm wild, mad, nuts about you." The words rushed out of his mouth unplanned. What had happened to all those years of being the careful, deliberate, choose-your-words-carefully legal eagle?

He panicked. He was terrified his outburst would scare Samantha off. He knew how bitter she was about her ex-husband. And that immediately brought to mind her equally bitter feelings about her ex-husband's divorce lawyer. Of all the divorce lawyers in Boston, why did Teddy have to go and pick one from his own firm, no less. And the worst one to boot.

To Nick's astonishment and joy, Samantha didn't pull away from him. She did the complete opposite and threw her arms around him.

"Oh, Nick, Nick," she cried, planting hot, moist kisses all over his handsome face, pushing aside her concerns about what he hadn't yet said; focusing now only on what he had said. He wanted her. He was crazy about her. And she felt the same way about him.

All thumbs, Nick fumbled with the back zipper of her dress.

Samantha, as eager as Nick to be rid of the garment, reached around and helped him, kicking off her pumps at the same time. He drew the dress off her shoulders. He didn't want to rush it, but he couldn't help himself. One swift tug and the dress fell with a whoosh to the persimmon carpet. She stood there in her provocative black satin-and-lace bra and matching slip, and sheer black panty hose.

She was exquisite. The sexiest creature he'd ever laid eyes on. The sight of her left Nick speechless. He couldn't even move. Instant paralysis. Except for his mind, which was consumed with yet another rush of guilt. How could he make love to her without first telling her the truth? How would she ever forgive him? How would he ever forgive himself?

But to tell her now, of all moments? Now, when she was standing there half-naked, clearly offering herself to him?

Oh, God, he wanted her so badly. He wanted to kiss her, caress her, taste her sweetness, make love with her. Only not like this. Not with this lie between them. He once again steeled his nerves. He'd tell her. He had to tell her.

Samantha mistook Nick's struggle for withdrawal. All she could see was the way his face, his whole body, shut down. They were only inches apart, but they might as well have been on opposite sides of the universe as far as she was concerned. Moments ago, she'd felt nothing but joy at standing before him half clothed, wanting nothing more than to get rid of the rest of her garments. And his. Now she felt exposed, embarrassed, ashamed of herself. And totally confused. Why had he changed his mind? Was she being too aggressive? Did he hate pushy women?

Anger started to set in. Had he just been handing her a line? What a jerk she was.

"Maybe we should change in different rooms," she said quietly, her gaze skidding away from his face.

Nick looked at her with a mix of longing and despair. Then, without a word, he knelt down, picked up his shirt, took his tux and left the bedroom.

When the door closed behind him, Samantha's eyes filled with tears again. For all she knew, this time he might really leave.

She numbly crossed to her closet and got out her bridesmaid's gown which hung in the corner, telling herself that if he wasn't out there waiting for her when she'd finished dressing, it was for the best.

"Coward," she muttered at her reflection in the mirror hanging inside her closet door.

Chapter Nine

"WHEN YOU SAID A YACHT, you really meant a *yacht*," Samantha gasped as they stepped out of the limo at the Rowes Wharf pier.

The sides of the gangplank leading up to the sleek, shiny white sloop was festooned with heart-shaped red balloons. A three-piece combo on deck began playing a romantic Gershwin medley as Nick and Samantha ascended. Two tuxedoed attendants greeted them as they got on board and led them into a large, posh, cherrywood-lined cabin replete with roaring fireplace, Chippendale couches, soft lighting, and a small dining table exquisitely set with fine English bone china, crystal goblets, and sterling-silver cutlery. The combo followed the pair into the cabin, setting up in a corner of the room, and picked up where they'd left off.

For all her earlier upset, anger, frustration and confusion, Samantha had to concede feeling bowled over by this latest extravagance. If nothing else, this was one Valentine's Day she was never going to forget.

Nick was stupefied. How in hell had Annie pulled this one off? Whose yacht was this, anyway?

Even before he spotted the photograph on one of the bookshelves lining a far wall, it came to him in a sickening flash. Jackson Vale.

Nice going, Annie. If Samantha spotted that photo of her ex-husband's divorce lawyer, Nick knew his goose was cooked.

"I don't know what to say," Samantha said, turning to him. And to the very bookshelf he was frantic for her to avoid.

Nick quickly pivoted her around toward the large picture window. "Get a gander at the view of the city." It really was a spectacular view of Boston's glittery nightlit skyline.

While she was savoring the panorama, Nick made a mad dash for the bookcase.

"What are you doing?"

Nick had just managed to stick the framed photo of the infamous Jackson Vale between two books. He spun back around to her. "Just...checking the...books."

Samantha gave him a funny look. "Aren't you pretty familiar with the books by now?"

Nick clasped his hands tightly together in front of him and fixed a very serious gaze on her. "Samantha, there's something I have to tell you."

Thank God, she thought. At last.

"This isn't—" Nick took a steadying breath.

Samantha smiled faintly. "This isn't going to be easy?" she prompted.

Nick swallowed hard. "This isn't exactly my yacht."

Samantha didn't hide her disappointment well.

Nick saw it and misinterpreted it. He thought she was disappointed that her *blind date* didn't own a yacht. Was she a fortune hunter? Had she accepted a date with a man she knew nothing about simply because he was loaded, owned a yacht, and drove around in a chauffeured limousine?

It didn't fit. That wasn't the image he had of her at all. Earlier he'd thought they were so in tune. Since the fiasco back in her apartment, there'd been this awful strain between them. She'd drawn away from him, physically as well as emotionally. And he had followed suit. He felt miserable. And yet here he was with a woman who was the personification of a real-life Cinderella enchantingly dressed for the prince's ball. One glance and she would steal the prince's heart away for ever. She already had. Only he was no prince. He was anything but.

"Whose yacht is it?" Samantha asked quietly.

Before he could decide how to answer that question, they were interrupted by one of the tuxedoed attendants announcing that dinner was ready to be served. The young, attractive blond-haired man held a chair out at the table for Samantha.

"I hope you both like goose," he said, his blue eyes twinkling.

Whatever spark had been in Nick's eyes blinked out completely.

THE DINNER WAS PURE haute cuisine—an aromatic
consommé, oysters broiled on the half shell, then
the entrée of goose in *paté en croute,* endive salad,
and finally a delicate chocolate meringue confec-
tion. Neither Nick nor Samantha could do it jus-
tice. The elegant meal, the deluxe yacht, the
glowing fire, the romantic background music—
none of it could dispel the pall that had fallen over
them.

They hardly spoke during dinner. Nick felt at a
complete loss. He'd gotten it into his head that he'd
tell her the truth after winning her trust. And now,
without understanding how it had happened, he'd
lost it. Samantha seemed guarded and distant. Not
that her change of mood in any way diminished his
feelings for her. If anything, it only served to make
him want her more. To put a smile back on her
face. To make her laugh again. To feel her warm,
giving body pressed to his...

None of it was very likely if he came clean now.
Given her present mood, that would be the coup de
grace.

Samantha, equally despairing of how they would
ever reclaim their earlier high spirits, not to mention passion, said in a flat voice, "Shouldn't we be
going?"

Nick sighed. Well, at least she was still willing to
see the date through. Maybe the festive charity
Valentine's Day ball would perk up their spirits;
revive the connection that had felt so strong be-

tween them such a short time back. At least he'd get to hold her in his arms once more, if only to dance.

THIS TIME WHEN THE LIMO pulled out, Nick and Samantha were seated as far from each other as was possible. To make the separation even more pronounced, Samantha pulled down the middle armrest. It might as well have been a mile-high steel shield.

Still, they each kept sneaking glances over at the other. Nothing could completely extinguish the spark that had ignited at first sight, then grown stronger and stronger throughout the day until they were both burning up inside. The embers were still hot; could still be rekindled. If only...

Nick was resolved. He would tell her about Sandra.

Samantha was resolved. She would tell him about Don.

"Samantha?"

"Nick?"

They both spoke at the same time.

"You first," Samantha said.

"No. No, you go ahead." Delay tactics. He was starting to lose his nerve already.

Samantha hesitated. If she told him the truth— told him she knew he wasn't her blind date—sure, it would force his hand, but it would also be admitting that not only had he lived a lie that whole day; so had she. How would Nick feel about her once he knew she'd deliberately kept up this charade all this time? How would she feel about Nick if she had to coerce him into coming clean? If he didn't tell her the truth of his own accord?

A bleak sense of hopelessness fell over her.

"Sam?" Nick prodded.

She looked over at him, studying him so intently that she was squinting as if she'd just stepped out of a dark movie theater into bright sunlight. What she was doing was memorizing his face. The crinkly smile lines at the corners of those spectacular emerald-green eyes, the way his light brown hair curled slightly at the ends, the square-cut jaw, those oh-so-sensual lips. When she'd first set eyes on him, the movie star Kevin Costner had immediately come to mind. But now she saw that Nick Santiago actually resembled no other man. He was unique. He was one of a kind. Memorizing what he looked like really wasn't necessary. She was never going to be able to get his image out of her mind even if she tried with all her might.

Nick was taken aback when Samantha abruptly turned away and lurched forward, pounding on the glass partition.

"Edgar, stop right here," she shouted.

Nick was completely bewildered. "Sam?"

She kept pounding. "Please, Edgar. Stop the car."

Nick tried to reach out to her, but she already had the door open even while the limo was pulling over to the curb.

The chauffeur, seeing what was happening, squealed to a stop to prevent a potential accident as Samantha leaped out to the street.

Nick sat there, flabbergasted. Then he turned and numbly watched Samantha fleeing down the sidewalk, disappearing around the first corner. The fairy-tale image of Cinderella racing for her coach before it turned back into a pumpkin flashed before his mind. Only his Cinderella hadn't left a glass slipper behind. All she'd left was this terrible ache in his heart.

Chapter Ten

IT HAD STARTED TO SNOW. A powdery dusting covered the sidewalk. Samantha shivered. Her light wool evening jacket wasn't much protection from the cold. All she wanted to do was go home, get out of her ridiculous bridesmaid's dress. . . .

Always a bridesmaid, never a bride. She smiled sardonically. Not true in her case. She'd gotten her shot at being a bride. Just plain dumb to have let herself think, even for a moment, that she might want a second shot at it. Dumber still to imagine it would be different with Nick. Nick with his happily-ever-after naiveté. Naive as a fox.

She searched frantically up and down the street for a taxi. Why was there never a cab around when you needed one? She stomped her feet. Her toes in her strapless teal-blue pumps were starting to go numb. She spied an open coffee shop across the street. At least she'd be able to get out of the cold, and see if they had a phone so she could call a cab. Lifting up her gown, she dashed across the street.

AFTER SAMANTHA DARTED around the corner, the chauffeur rolled down the window partition and turned back to Nick.

"Aren't you going to go after her, Mr. Santiago?"

Nick scowled.

"Look, you can tell me where to get off, but I thought the two of you had really created sparks."

Nick sighed. "Are you married, Edgar? I mean...Don?"

The chauffeur grinned. "It's okay. I've kinda gotten used to Edgar. Yeah, I'm married. Thirty-four years."

"To the same woman?"

Edgar chuckled. "You'd better believe it."

"So, it's worked out for you. That's great."

Edgar smiled sympathetically. "It's none of my business, I know, but what went wrong for you and Miss Lovejoy?"

Nick stared down at his hands. "Everything. Everything went wrong and everything went right. All at the same time. Does that make any sense?"

"Not really," Edgar confessed. "But if you want to talk about it..."

"COFFEE, PLEASE. BLACK," Samantha said dully, climbing onto a worn black-vinyl-covered stainless-steel stool at the counter. She'd called a cab company, but because it was Valentine's Day night, business was brisk. She was informed it would be a good half-hour before the dispatcher could send one over to pick her up.

Fanny Hobbs, a plump middle-aged waitress with frizzy, short red hair eyed Samantha with unabashed curiosity from the other side of the counter. The Delmont Coffee Shop wasn't exactly the type of establishment folks came to for a bite when they were dressed up in formal wear.

"Want anything to go with that?" Fanny asked as she set a white mug of steaming coffee in front of Samantha.

Unexpectedly, Samantha's eyes filled with tears. Did she want anything else? What a question. There was most definitely something else she wanted. But she wasn't going to find it at the Delmont Coffee Shop.

"How about a nice piece of apple pie?" Without waiting for a response from Samantha, Fanny cut her a large slab of the pie, slipped it on a plate, and set it next to the coffee mug.

"Go on, take a sip of your coffee," Fanny coaxed. "You look chilled to the bone."

Tears slid down Samantha's cheeks. She flashed on Nick, bringing her a cup of tea that morning, encouraging her to take a sip. He'd been so solicitous, so tender, so concerned....

"What happened? He stand you up?" Fanny surmised.

Samantha nodded, then a moment later shook her head.

"Which is it?" Fanny asked, confused.

Samantha sighed. "Well, I did get stood up by Don. My blind date," she added for edification.

The waitress rolled her eyes. "Blind dates. The pits."

"But then Nick showed up. Only I didn't know it was Nick."

"You didn't?"

"No. Naturally, I thought it was Don." Samantha paused to take a sip of the coffee. The hot drink helped a little. "I mean, who else would it be, right? Strange men don't make a habit of showing up at my door. I don't mean strange as in...weird. I mean strange as in stranger."

"Stranger as in Nick."

"Exactly," Samantha said, feeling inexplicably better to have someone to whom she could recount her tale of woe.

"LET ME GET THIS straight," Edgar said. "You thought Samantha was Sandra."

"Right," Nick said. He was now sitting in the front seat beside the chauffeur.

"Only she told you her name was Samantha."

"Right. But I thought I got the name wrong."

"And then your kid set you straight."

A frown settled on Nick's face. "Set me straight? Yeah, I suppose. And in the process set my whole world topsy-turvy."

"What I still don't get is, why didn't you tell her about the mix-up straight off the bat?"

"Believe me, I've been asking myself that same question for the past eight hours. If I had it to do over again, I would have." Nick heaved a sigh. "No. I don't know. Do we ever really learn from our own mistakes, Edgar?"

"Sure we do," the chauffeur said. "Look, I think I understand. You realized she had this other guy coming over—this blind date—and all you could think of was that if you told her the truth she'd send you on your way, and she'd be spending this magical day with some numskull named Don and you'd be off with Sandra—"

"No. Sandra was going to call off the date anyway," Nick reminded him. He'd already given him the run-through of his phone conversation with Annie. For some reason, Nick had found himself opening up to the chauffeur like he was a long-lost friend. The relief of finally telling someone his sad story helped. Unfortunately, he wasn't telling the person to whom it really mattered.

"Oh, yeah. So, you'd have been all alone."

Nick nodded. He'd been all alone for years now and it hadn't seemed to bother him particularly. Now, the thought of being alone—no, the thought of being without Samantha—made him feel totally miserable.

"You got it bad, all right," Edgar said sympathetically.

"It's crazy. Nobody really falls in love at first sight," Nick muttered.

"Who says?" Edgar countered. "I knew the minute I set eyes on my Vera that she was the woman I was gonna marry. Even told my best buddy, Hal, who was right there with me at the time. He kids me about it to this day."

"BUT HE LIED TO ME," Samantha insisted. "You can't trust a man who you absolutely know for a fact is lying to you."

Fanny took a bite of the apple pie that Samantha wasn't eating. There were only the two of them in the coffee shop. Valentine's Day wasn't a big night for customers. Plus it was late. And it was snowing pretty heavily now.

"So why didn't you call him on it, right from the get-go?" Fanny asked after swallowing the mouthful of pie.

"I . . . couldn't," Samantha answered evasively.

Fanny wagged a finger at her. "So you decided to lie, too."

"No, I didn't. It wasn't an outright lie. I just didn't tell . . . the truth."

The waitress gave Samantha a close scrutiny. "Yet, you look to me to be the kind of woman who prides herself on her honesty."

"I do. I absolutely do. Don't you understand? I feel absolutely awful about lying—about not telling Nick the truth, that is. There is a difference. Although," she conceded, "it's a gray area."

Fanny leaned forward, resting her elbows on the mottled black-and-gray Formica counter. "And don't you think that just maybe your Nick feels just as awful? Could it be that he was afraid to tell you the truth because bells went off for him?"

Samantha searched the waitress's face. "Do you really think *bells* went off?"

"From what you've told me so far, I'd say a whole carillon went off. Like the ones at my church. You should hear 'em. Mitch and I were at a wedding there last Sunday and—" Fanny stopped abruptly as she saw the tears spill down Samantha's cheeks. She plucked a napkin from the stainless-steel holder on the counter. "Here. It was 'wedding' that gotcha, right?"

Samantha sniffed and dabbed at her face. "I think I love him."

"Even if he's a no-account liar?"

"Oh, he isn't. He really isn't. All day long I felt him trying to tell me the truth. I know he wanted to. I could have helped him more. We both acted like idiots. It was going to be the best Valentine's Day of my life. And instead it's turned into the worst."

Fanny put her hand over Samantha's. "Hey, it's still Valentine's Day. There's still time to turn it back around."

"But how? I don't even know where to find him."

"Well…"

Before Fanny could give her some ideas, Samantha leaped off her stool. "Wait. I have an idea. It's a long shot. I don't know...."

"Go for it, kid," Fanny said with a bright smile.

A horn beeped outside. It was Samantha's cab. Samantha paused to lean over the counter and give Fanny a big hug.

"How can I ever thank you?"

Fanny grinned. "Whaddaya mean? Invite me to the wedding!"

THE BALLROOM OF THE Ambassador Hotel was aglow with candlelight, the heady scent of expensive perfumes, dazzling gowns of every shape, size and color, and floating, heart-shaped red balloons. On the stage, a forties-style band was playing while a svelte redhead in a glittery scarlet sequined gown that hugged her body clear down to her shoes was sexily crooning a romantic ballad into the microphone. The dance floor was crowded with couples, their arms entwined around each other, not really dancing but swaying to the music.

Romance was in the air. It stung as Nick breathed it in. If he could have, he would have held his breath. If he could have, he'd have turned right around and left.

Of course, there was nothing stopping him from leaving. Edgar/Don was parked in his limo right out in the front of the hotel. It had been the chauffeur's idea that he show up at the ball to see if, by some wild chance, Samantha had gone there. That, after searching the dark streets hoping to catch sight of his fleeing Cinderella. That, after several unanswered phone calls to her apartment.

Nick scanned the crowded room. Samantha could be anywhere. At some bar. Her sister's place. A friend's house. If he were thinking clearly, he'd know that this was probably the last place in the world she would be.

The love song ended and the singer with the sexy voice announced that the band would be taking a fifteen-minute break. There were some grumblings on the dance floor as the couples, reluctant to let go of each other, slowly made their way back to their tables.

And then, as the dance floor cleared and Nick glanced across the crowded room he saw a young woman with a head full of wild auburn curls, wearing a teal-blue taffeta gown. She, too, was searching the sea of faces there. Searching for one particular face.

She spotted him seconds after he'd spotted her. For several long moments they stood immobilized, unable to do anything but stare across the dance floor at each other. The room was so dimly lit, they couldn't make out each other's expressions. Did it matter? They were both there. They'd come for only one conceivable reason.

It was impossible to know who made the first move as they slowly started toward each other.

Halfway, they sped up until they were literally running into each other's arms, their lips meeting instantly in a deep, hungry, grateful kiss right in the middle of the empty dance floor.

They both pulled away at the same time, saying almost in unison, "There's something I've got to tell you."

Nick cleared his throat. "No. Me first." And he told her. He told her everything—about the dumb plan to place personals that he and his buddies had conceived on New Year's Eve; about Annie finding the ad he'd thrown away, rewriting it, sending it off and then selecting the "perfect date" for him. He told her about Sandra, and Samantha laughed when he got to the part about Sandra's reply having been a complete lie, made up merely to get her boyfriend jealous.

"It was all a mistake, Sam. And I have Annie, fate, my lucky stars, and you most of all, to thank for it being the best mistake any man could ever make."

"Oh, Nick," Samantha murmured, kissing him again.

"Then you're not angry?" he asked incredulously.

"I love you, Nick," she said with a tender smile, then paused.

Nick felt a flash of consternation when he saw Samantha's smile fade.

"Now it's my turn," she said anxiously.

Nick nodded, unable to imagine what secret she could possibly reveal that would cause her such worry.

"I knew you weren't my blind date."

Again, Nick was incredulous.

"That first phone call. It was Don. He canceled out on me." She told him the rest—about how she was afraid he might be some dangerous hooligan or worse; how she'd listened in on his conversation with his daughter, thinking that he might be phoning one of his accomplices.

To her astonishment, Nick started to laugh.

"But aren't you mad? I lied to you, Nick. I knew all along. All I had to do was tell you the truth and you would have had to come clean as well and we wouldn't have spent this entire day and evening feeling tortured...."

Nick pulled Samantha back into his arms, oblivious that they were all alone on the dance floor and that dozens of eyes were on them. "It wasn't all torture," he whispered against her hair. "It was also the most heavenly, magical day and evening of my life. I love you, Sam. I want to make heavenly magic with you every day and night from now on."

"Oh, Nick, so do I," Samantha said, then leaned in to kiss him again.

"Wait," Nick said.

Samantha grinned, only now realizing that they were on display. "Right. Let's go somewhere more private. Do you suppose this hotel still has any spare rooms?'' she asked, her amber eyes sparkling.

"No..."

"You think they're full?"

"No, that's not what I mean."

Samantha squinted at him. "You don't want to be alone in a hotel room with me?"

"Oh, God, Sam. There's nothing I want more." He hesitated.

Samantha arched an eyebrow. "But?"

"But...I haven't told you everything."

Samantha felt her muscles tighten. "You haven't?"

"No," he said somberly. "There's one more thing."

Samantha steeled herself. Another woman? A rare disease? Some terrible crime?

"I'm not a photographer," Nick said. "That is, I do take pictures. But...it's strictly a hobby."

"How do you earn a living?" Samantha asked, her throat suddenly dry so that her voice sounded raspy.

Nick swallowed hard, preparing for the worst. "I'm a lawyer, Sam." He swallowed again, his gaze never wavering from her face. "A divorce lawyer."

Samantha's mouth dropped open, but she didn't say a word.

"I might as well get it all out. I work at Brown, Nichols, and Carson. The same firm as...Jackson

Vale. Believe me, Sam, I don't think any better of him than you do, but we are colleagues.'' He said all this in a rush, the whole time intently watching Samantha's face in an effort to gauge her reaction.

When he saw her break into a smile he couldn't believe it. And then, to both his amazement and sheer delight, she was draping her arms around him.

''Well,'' she murmured as she pressed her cheek to his just as the band was tuning up, ''I promise I'm never going to need your services, Counselor. The next time I marry, it's for keeps.''

Nick's lips found hers and this time, freed from guilt, they kissed with all their hearts and souls.

''For keeps,'' he echoed afterward, holding her close.

She lifted her head up so that their eyes met. ''So, about that hotel room . . .''

They were both laughing as they raced arm in arm through the crowded ballroom. To their amazement, people actually started to applaud.

Postscript

Annie and Ethan Santiago are pleased
to announce the marriage of their Dad
Nicholas Santiago
to
Bridget Lovejoy's Mom
Samantha Lovejoy
on
Mother's Day

Fanny Hobbs, the waitress from the Delmont Coffee Shop, smiled and tucked the gold-embossed invitation into her apron pocket.

MR. ROMANCE

Pamela Bauer

A Note from Pamela Bauer

I love Valentine's Day. It's the perfect occasion for flowers and love letters, romantic getaways and breakfasts in bed, and all sorts of wonderful things that inspire romance writers. It's also the one day of the year I don't have to feel guilty about eating chocolate.

For twenty-three years I've been married to a man who knows the road to my heart is paved with candy wrappers. He never fails to bring home a heart-shaped box from Godiva on February 14.

He's my "Mr. Romance," although he'd never advertise for a date—not even on a dare. However, like my hero Tristan, my husband did place an ad in the personals. It happened one Valentine's Day not so long ago in a column called "Love Lines." It went something like this:

Pamela,

Roses are red
Violets are blue
You'd better be my Valentine
Or there'll be no more chocolates for you!

Love,
Gerr

It was exactly the kind of rhyme I expected from a guy who knows that chocolate may ease my craving for something sweet, but love and laughter are food for my soul. It's from him I learned that the true meaning of Valentine's Day lies not in gifts or clever verses, but in telling the ones we love how important they are to us.

So whether it be in the form of a romantic fantasy or a sentimental gesture or simply the presence of someone you love, I hope that your Valentine's Day is filled with love and laughter...and of course, a little chocolate, too.

Happy Valentine's Day!

Chapter One

HEARTS. THEY WERE everywhere. On the walls, hanging from the ceiling, lining the window ledge. Big ones, little ones, shiny ones, glittery ones.

Tristan Talbot was in a reclining position while a man in a white coat leaned over him with a drill in his hand. He was in no mood for red hearts.

"Doris did a nice job of decorating for Valentine's Day, didn't she?" Dr. Baker, or Butcher Baker as Tristan preferred to call him, remarked in an annoyingly pleasant voice.

Tristan's response was, "Oh, yeah, swell." However, with a mouth full of cotton pads and Butcher Baker's rubber-gloved fingers prying his lips apart, it sounded more like, "Oh, hell."

That was a pretty good description for his feelings at the moment. He hated even being in the vicinity of the dentist's office.

He watched Doris the dental assistant rearrange all sorts of pain-inducing tools on the instrument tray. When she handed Dr. Baker an instrument that looked like it had a fishhook at each end, he winced.

"Valentine's Day is such a fun holiday, isn't it?" she asked, not really expecting an answer.

Tristan felt like telling her he thought that this Valentine's Day was probably going to be about as much fun as sticking a bare foot in a snowbank, but there really wasn't any point. Whatever he said would be garbled.

"January is such a long, cold month, I like to brighten the place up with decorations—you know, something everyone can relate to, like hearts," Doris continued in a voice that measured right up there next to Butcher Baker's on Tristan's annoyance meter. "After all, love is what makes the world go 'round, right?"

"As a man who's been married thirty-five years, I guess I'd better agree with that," the dentist answered good-naturedly, smiling as he aimed a blast of air at one of Tristan's bicuspids.

Doris giggled. "Oh, Doctor, you can't fool me. I know you're a romantic at heart," she chided affectionately, her wire-framed glasses slipping down on her pudgy nose.

The dentist harrumphed. "I'm not so sure my wife would agree with you. Tristan, here, is the one who knows all about romance. He's the bachelor."

Tristan had become accustomed to people equating bachelorhood with having a fantastic romantic life. He wondered what Doris and old Butcher Baker would say if he told them he was going to select a Valentine from an ad he had placed in the Personals column. They probably wouldn't believe him.

Why should they, when he could hardly believe it himself? Yet last week's *Daily Tribune* held the proof. In black-and-white under the Get Acquainted headline was a personal ad he had written.

Every time he thought about it, he felt the chains of regret squeezing his insides tighter and tighter. He should never have placed the ad. He didn't want a date for Valentine's Day—especially not one from the Personals.

He should never have spent New Year's Eve with Nicholas and Alec. Every time the three of them got together, he ended up doing something out of character.

Although it really wasn't fair to blame them. It wasn't their fault he had a competitive streak that was as relentless as Butcher Baker's drill. They knew that he couldn't ignore a challenge.

And that's what this whole Valentine's Day thing had become—a challenge. It wasn't something he *wanted* to do. It was something he *had* to do. After all, he was Mr. Romance, a nickname he'd earned during his college days.

His fraternity brothers had no idea how inept he had been in the romance department in high school. They didn't know that he wasn't trying to set a record for the number of women he dated in college, but was simply making up for lost time.

The rest of the world, like Butcher Baker, thought he was in an enviable position. A bachelor. Free to come and go as he pleased, free to be where he wanted, with whomever he wanted.

When he was younger, that life had suited him well. With no commitments, he was able to pursue his love of architecture, studying abroad, taking assignments all across the country.

Recently, however, he had begun to wonder if he hadn't made a mistake not settling down in his twenties. He was tired of women who spent the entire evening trying to convince him they didn't need a man.

Were his friends right? Were there no women who shared his definition of romance? If there were, he sincerely doubted he'd find one of them through the Personals.

It didn't matter. He had no choice. Either find a date from the ad or risk losing face with his friends.

"Hey! You're closing up on me. Come on, Tristan, open wide," Butcher Baker instructed in a patronizing tone.

Tristan did as he was told, then tried to think of anything but the pain in his mouth. He wished Doris and Butcher Baker would quit going on about Valentine's Day. He closed his eyes and tried not to listen to the two of them discussing their greatest romantic moments. His mind drifted to the industrial complex he was designing. Then Doris said something that caught his attention.

"If you want this Valentine's Day to be special for you and Florence, maybe you should hire Allison Parker, the romance consultant."

Romance consultant? Tristan opened one eye.

Butcher Baker chuckled. "You think she can teach an old dog like me some new tricks?"

Doris clicked her tongue. "You're not an old dog," she rebuked the dentist, then bent closer to Tristan's head. "We have a patient who runs a professional service to help people plan romantic events. You know, special dates, weekend getaways, surprises."

Tristan tried to ask, "What does a romance consultant do?" but all that came out was jumbled jargon that sounded like his garbage disposal grinding up moldy leftovers.

Thirty years of dental assisting must have given Doris an ear for translating garbled speech, for she said, "Her company is called Special Moments and I believe it's quite popular, especially with working couples who simply don't have time to plan the details of a special evening."

"Does she still have her office over in Ridge Square?" Butcher Baker inquired absently, concentrating on packing Tristan's tooth with silver amalgam.

As a man who hired a service to clean his house, to do his laundry and to deliver his food, Tristan found it perfectly logical to hire someone to help him plan his Valentine's Day date.

After all, if this Parker woman could make a living as a romance consultant, she must know her stuff. She probably had ideas for Valentine's Day that his friends would never be able to think of. She could be the key to winning.

Half an hour later, nursing a numbed jaw, Tristan left the dentist's office with only one thought on his mind: Maybe Mr. Romance had found a way to score.

"ALLI, I'VE FOUND HIM. The perfect bachelor for you."

Allison Parker swung around in her chair and faced her office mate. "Jazz, I'm not looking for the perfect bachelor."

Jazz, a full-figured bubbly blonde, got out of her chair and came over to Allison's desk.

"I know. That's why I have to look for you."

Allison sighed. Ever since Jasmine Connors had become engaged, she had launched a Find-Allison-A-Husband campaign that was starting to rattle Allison's nerves. With Valentine's Day only a few weeks away, the tempo of the campaign had accelerated.

"He's thirty-three, has no ex-wives and no children." Jasmine plopped a three-by-five snapshot down on Allison's desk. "What a bod, eh? He's a fitness instructor at the health club over on Lexington." She looked expectantly at her friend, waiting for a reaction.

Allison picked up the photo, gave it a cursory glance, then tossed it back in Jasmine's direction. "No, thank you. Too brawny for me."

"Most women want brawn," Jazz retorted, her hands on her hips.

Allison shrugged. "I guess I'm not most women."

Jazz perched herself on the edge of Allison's desk. "If I didn't know better, I'd think you didn't want a date for Valentine's Day."

"I don't." Allison shoveled a stack of papers into a manila folder and stuffed it into a drawer.

"Why not?"

"Because Valentine's Day just isn't a big deal to me."

"I don't get it. You plan all those romantic evenings for other people, yet you don't want one for yourself?"

"One of life's little mysteries, I guess," she said nonchalantly, although there was seldom a day that went by when she didn't think how ironic it was that she created the most romantic occasions for others, yet when it came to her own life, there was nada romance.

"You want to know what I think?" Jazz didn't wait for a reply but continued on. "I think you've done this romance thing so many times for everyone else that there's nothing a guy can do to impress you."

"You're wrong." Allison continued to straighten her already tidy desk.

"Am I? You're too picky, Alli. You're waiting for a knight on a white horse to come riding through here before you'll admit to being impressed."

"That's not true," she denied. "I'm not *that* picky. It's okay with me if he leaves his white horse back at the castle stables."

Jazz folded her arms across her chest. "Alli, be serious!"

"I can't be. Not when it comes to men. The subject's too depressing."

"Look, I know you haven't exactly had the best of luck in the dating department recently—"

"The best of luck?" Allison interrupted with a screech. "I've had *no* luck!"

"The only problem you're having is one of not looking for a man. Ever since you broke up with Steve, you've been reluctant to get out there and play the field."

"And with good reason. Jazz, I'm over thirty. You know what my odds are of finding Mr. Right?"

"Oh, come on! You don't believe those statistics any more than I do."

"I don't want to, but even you have to admit that the older we get, the ones left in the game are less and less attractive."

"That's why you should come meet this guy," she said persuasively. "See if he's your type."

"Chances are that if he's old enough to date me, marriage and commitment aren't in his vocabulary," she answered cynically.

"Alli, you're starting to worry me. Whatever happened to the eternal optimist who told me that for every person walking the face of the earth there was a suitable mate roaming in search of the other one?"

"I think I've been wearing rose-colored glasses."

"You've been running into the wrong kind of guys, that's all."

"Jazz, I don't think there is a right kind."

"Of course there is! It just takes patience to find him. And you're not going to find him if you don't go out looking."

"Guess I'll just have to sit and hope my knight finds me," she said stubbornly.

"What about your image? What do you suppose your clients will say if they find out you don't have a date for Valentine's Day?"

"They'll think that I spent so many hours working to make Valentine's Day wonderful for others that I had to stay home and rest."

Jazz groaned in frustration. "You're impossible. Every time I try to fix you up with an eligible bachelor you have an excuse." She looked at her watch. "I'd better get going. I'm meeting Toby for lunch at LeeAnn Chin's. Want to join us?"

"No, thank you," she replied, grateful she had brown-bagged a peanut butter and jelly sandwich that morning. Watching Jazz and her fiancé make goo-goo eyes at each other over sweet-and-sour chicken was something she wasn't up to witnessing today.

"Will you at least think about the fitness instructor?" Jazz made one last pitch before she exited.

Reluctantly, Allison nodded. When she was alone, she picked up the photo and studied it more closely. The guy did have a good body. Not to mention a contagious smile and a sexy gleam in his eyes. But then so did Steve, the last eligible bachelor she had dated. She tossed the picture aside.

Jazz could have brawn. She wanted a man with brains. Someone who didn't feel the need to pretend to be someone else. Someone who didn't have a hard time being honest. Someone who didn't feel threatened by a successful woman.

Of course the big question was, did such a man exist?

Allison sighed. Maybe Jazz was right. She was looking for a knight.

And the chances of meeting such a man through her work were next to none. Most of her clients were married men. Besides, why on earth would her knight need to use her service? He'd know all about romance without anyone else's help.

SINCE TRISTAN'S JAW was numb and Butcher Baker had advised him not to bite on the left side of his mouth, he skipped lunch and went directly to the Ridge Square office complex.

When he arrived at the professional building, he discovered that Special Moments shared a suite with something called Just One Look. He pushed open the door and found a small, but plush office.

There were two bleached-oak desks, bookcases, cabinets and two chintz wing chairs for clients. One of the desks was vacant.

From the way Doris and Butcher Baker had talked, he had expected to find someone fiftyish wearing a navy blue suit. This woman was not anywhere near fifty. Nor was she wearing a business suit. She was young and wearing a purple sweater that clung to her quite nicely.

Tristan hoped she was the owner of Just One Look, the image-consulting service that shared the office. She had a half-eaten apple in one hand, a pencil in the other. As he moved closer to her, he could see that she was working on the cryptoquip in the morning's paper.

"Can I help you?" She looked up at him.

She had creamy white skin that was without a blemish or freckle and wide blue eyes. Her hair was striking. Coiled red tendrils refused to be confined by the scarf at the nape of her neck.

"This is Special Moments, isn't it?"

"Yes." She quickly stuffed her half-eaten apple into a brown paper sack, which in turn was shoved into a drawer. Then she looked up at him and smiled apologetically. "You caught me in the middle of my lunch."

He tried not to act like a shopper standing outside a department-store window gawking at the contents inside, but he was finding it difficult not to stare. Not just because she was attractive, but because he had this sense that they had met before and his brain was working frantically to think where.

"I'm sorry." The apology came automatically to his lips.

"It's all right. It's just that I wasn't expecting you until one o'clock," she said as she cleared away the remains of her lunch.

"Oh, I don't have an appointment."

"You're not Mr. Michaels?"

"No. I'm Tristan Talbot."

"Oh."

For just one moment, he thought she was going to ask him to leave, but then she offered him her hand, gave his a quick tug, then snatched her own back. "I'm . . . I'm Allison Parker."

"Is this a bad time?" he asked, unable to shake the feeling that she didn't want him there. "I can come back if it is."

"No, it's all right. What can I do for you, Mr. Talbot?"

Suddenly he found himself reluctant to tell her why he had come. It was one thing to hire a fiftyish Doris-type to take care of planning a date he was arranging through a newspaper ad; quite another to have this knockout of a woman know that he needed help with his love life.

"Well?" She looked at him, waiting for his answer.

He debated whether he should stay or go. Then he remembered Alec and Nicholas. Winning was more important than this woman's opinion of him.

"I'd like to hire your service."

"All right." She smiled as she sat back down and flipped open a notebook. "Why don't you have a seat and tell me what kind of special moment you have in mind. Anniversary? Birthday..." She trailed off, gazing at him expectantly.

"Valentine's Day," he answered, taking the leather chair across from her. "I need to make this the most romantic Valentine's Day a woman has ever had."

"Then you've come to the right place. I specialize in romantic events."

Her fingers were slender and white, moving gracefully as she pulled out several printed forms from the drawer. Tristan couldn't help but notice how neat everything was on her desk. Even the pencils were all leaning in the same direction in the little gray square holder.

"Are you familiar with our service?"

"Ah . . . no, I'm not."

"Here's a brochure that explains what we offer," she said, passing him a pamphlet. "And this is a list of some of the services we've provided in the past, plus comments from some of our clients."

She passed him more information, which Tristan pretended to read. Every time she looked up at him with those big blue eyes he was more than ever convinced that they had met before—although he couldn't imagine how he would forget someone who looked as good as she did.

"Why don't I get you a cup of coffee while you look those over?" She got up to go over to a small oak credenza in the corner. It was then that he saw her skirt was short and slim, with a slit up the back.

Tristan was more interested in looking at her shapely figure than in reading about her business. Her skirt barely covered her thighs and allowed a tantalizing peek at slender legs as she bent down to retrieve a cup from the lower shelf. Once again, he found himself gawking at her loveliness.

Who was she, and why did she look so familiar? It continued to gnaw away at him, the feeling that somewhere, sometime, their paths had crossed.

Just then the phone rang. She excused herself to pick up the extension on the other desk. "Just One Look. May I help you?"

There was a pause, then Tristan heard her say, "No, Jasmine's out to lunch. This is Allison. Is there anything I can do for you?"

Allison. Suddenly the red hair, the sultry voice, the big blue eyes connected to his memory bank. *Allison Parker,* the most popular girl at Kennedy High.

Everyone had said she would go places—TV, movies, Hollywood, New York. So what was she doing working as a romance consultant in St. Paul?

Worse yet, what was he doing asking her to arrange a Valentine's Day romance for him? This was the Allison who had preferred to work alone in physics lab rather than have him for a partner. This was the Allison who had broken his heart by tossing the pink carnation he had given her for Valentine's Day into the lunchroom trash can. This was the Allison who had her boyfriend give him a black eye because he had stolen one little kiss.

"Is anything wrong?" she asked as she set a cup of coffee down in front of him.

Tristan looked up at her, feeling a mixture of adolescent and adult emotions. "Did you graduate from Kennedy High?"

Her lily-white complexion turned a rosy red. "Yes. Did you?"

As if she didn't remember, Tristan thought cynically. He would bet money that she had recognized him the minute he'd walked into the room. That's why she had looked as if she didn't want him there—because she was worried that he would recognize her, too. And now that he had, she was going to play dumb and innocent. As if she had no recollection of treating him like the class nerd that he'd been.

"I was only there for my senior year. We moved from California," he reminded her.

"Tristan Talbot." She repeated his name as if she were trying to jar her memory. "Of course! Now I remember," she said, recovering smoothly and giving him a smile that was as real as a three-dollar bill. "I thought you looked familiar."

She was uneasy, as well she should be. She may have been voted a senior favorite, but she had been a snob.

Tristan leaned back in his chair. "Well, well, well." He finally had her in a position to make her squirm and he couldn't prevent himself from grinning smugly.

"Well, well, well, what?" she asked tightly.

He looked her over very thoroughly. "You've changed. I almost didn't recognize you."

She looked relieved by his remarks. Did she think he was going to remind her that she had treated him as if he were a fly at a picnic all during their senior year?

"I'm sure we've both changed. It's been a long time," she said evenly. "I didn't see you at any of the class reunions."

"I didn't go. I never really felt like part of that class."

"Everyone assumed you had moved back to California."

"I did. Right after graduation. I've only been here since last summer. I took a job with an architectural firm in St. Paul."

"Oh, you're an architect. How nice."

She was smiling and being as polite as a Minnesotan could get. Only the twisting of her pencil gave him any indication that she was not at ease. He noted that there was no ring on the fourth finger of her left hand.

"I like my work," he said smoothly. "What about you?"

"Oh, me, too," she told him, then sat back down at her desk, tugging at her skirt in the process.

"Isn't that nice," he said dryly.

"I help people plan all sorts of special occasions. Birthdays, anniversaries...even job promotions." She straightened her shoulders and folded her hands on her desk. "Which is what you came here for, right? You need help with planning a romantic evening?" Just as it had all those years ago in high school, her voice had the power to make his heart pound.

It was a bit unsettling, and reminded him of the power she'd had over him in high school. When he didn't answer right away, she asked, "Or have you changed your mind, now that you've read the brochure?"

He had the feeling she wanted him to say that he had decided against using her service. It's what he should have done. Here was the one woman he had vowed to avoid like the plague, yet he was considering paying her money to help him plan a romantic evening.

Something was stirring inside him. Something that didn't want him to make it easy for her. Something that suggested maybe it was payback time.

So instead of leaving, he gave her a wry grin and said, "I think you're exactly what I'm looking for."

Chapter Two

"YOU WANT *ME* TO PLAN a romantic evening for *you?*"

"Yes."

There was a long pause before Allison finally said, "Okay." She didn't want to look at Tristan. Ever since he had walked through her door she was having trouble connecting the tall, confident man sitting across from her to the scrawny, pesty teenager who had followed her through the halls of Kennedy High.

He had grown four inches and had a powerful build. His hair was still dark and curly, but instead of hanging moplike over his eyes, obscuring his vision, it was stylishly cut, barely grazing his forehead. He was a frog who had turned into a prince. A very handsome and self-assured prince.

"So where do we start?" he asked.

"What I like to do is fit a client's needs." She pretended he was just another client, refusing to let his piercing gaze intimidate her. "Even though I gave you the brochure so you could get an idea of what we offer, there really are no package deals."

"That's good to hear, because I think my situation is probably rather unique."

"Of course it is, and it should be." She gave him another businesslike smile. "First you need to decide how much money you want to spend."

He spread his hands. "I'll spend whatever it takes. What's important is that you arrange the most romantic Valentine's date a woman could desire."

She gave him another polite smile. "Very well. We'll do the personality profile of the woman who's going to share this romantic evening with you and take it from there. Is this for your wife?"

"I'm not married."

"Fiancée?"

He shook his head. "Not engaged, either. This is just a date."

Handsome, sexy and single. Allison's warning antennae started to hum. She shifted under his intense scrutiny. "Tell me about this woman you're dating. Does she like surprises?"

Tristan shrugged. "I have no idea."

"What about food preferences? Italian? Chinese? Thai? French?"

"I'm afraid I don't know the answer to that, either."

"Well, what about her interests? What does she like to do in her spare time?"

"Don't know."

Allison's pen poised over the form. Her antennae were buzzing at full alert. Was he another one of those good-looking men who thought of little else but their own pleasures?

"Mr. Talbot."

"Tristan," he corrected.

"Tristan, unless you tell me a little about this woman's personality, I'm not going to be able to plan an evening that she'll enjoy."

"Unfortunately, I can't do that."

"Why not?"

"Because I don't know who she is."

"Well, it's a little difficult to plan a date for someone who doesn't exist," she said in a mockingly sweet voice.

Tristan wasn't bothered by her tone. "Oh, she exists. I just haven't found her yet. That's why I want to hire you."

Allison's pen slipped from her fingers. "Are you asking me to help you find a date?"

He tapped his fingertips on the brochure she had given him. "It says here you'll do whatever it takes to make sure the special event turns out exactly as it should."

"That's true, but the service doesn't include finding men dates," she replied indignantly.

"I think you're jumping to the wrong conclusion."

"Am I?"

He nodded. "I don't want you to find me a date. I just need you to help me sort through the applicants I already have."

Jazz had warned her that the day would come when she would encounter someone who wasn't playing with a full deck of cards. Never would she have guessed it would be an old classmate from high school.

Her eyes narrowed. "You took applications for a date for Valentine's Day?"

"It's not what you think." Tristan reached inside his suitcoat. "Here. Read this." He handed her a folded-up piece of newsprint.

Allison unfolded the paper and read the small print within the red circle.

Wanted: A Warm Woman for a Cold Knight
This SWM, or knight in frozen armor, doesn't want to be stuck by himself in a Minnesota snowbank on Valentine's Day. That's why I'm looking for a SWF to melt my heart. If you're looking for a Valentine who believes that romance should be the most important part of any fantasy, write and tell me what you'd like to do on the most romantic night of the year with me, Mr. Romance.

"You're Mr. Romance?" Her words came out in a squeak.

A corner of his mouth lifted. "It's a name I picked up in college."

Allison nodded and smiled weakly. He certainly hadn't earned the name in high school. As far as she knew, she was the only girl he had tried to date.

"So you placed this ad in the paper in hopes of finding a date for Valentine's Day?" she stated calmly even though she felt anything but calm. But then she had never been able to relax around Tristan Talbot.

Ever since that first day of her senior year when he had shuffled into English class wearing clothes that looked like they came out of her father's closet, there had been a tension between them. Without asking, he had plopped himself down next to her and announced that he had already read *Romeo and Juliet* in a literature class in California.

When she asked him if he wouldn't rather sit somewhere else, he had told her he liked sitting next to a girl with hair the color of the Grand Canyon. Any sympathy she had for him being a new kid in school quickly disappeared with that crack about her hair.

She'd tried to ignore his presence, but he seemed to be everywhere she went. It hadn't helped that he was in all but one of her classes. Or that the English teacher had assigned her the part of Juliet and Tristan the part of Romeo to be read aloud in front of the class.

He had only attended Kennedy for one year of high school, yet Allison had felt as if he'd been there forever.

Now he was here in her office, requesting her services. He didn't look like the type who needed to advertise for a date. Quite the opposite. Judging by the strong curve of his shoulders and his confident air, she would have thought he'd be a magnet for women.

"I never expected I'd get so many responses," he stated honestly.

"There's been a lot?"

"Too many for me to go through. I don't have the time."

Or interest, Allison thought, judging by his attitude.

"That's why I want to hire you." He had a way of staring at her that made her want to pull out a mirror and check to made sure she didn't have apple peel stuck in her teeth. He had always looked at her like that, making her extremely self-conscious. Most boys who were interested in her in high school would have slanted her a quick glance, but he had boldly stared at her—the way he was doing now. In high school it had been annoying. Now she could see that it was a dark, intelligent gaze that conveyed intimacy. She moistened her lips.

"You want me to sort through them and choose which one I think would make a romantic date for you?" she asked.

"I think I can handle the choosing end of it," he said with a grin that sent a funny little shiver of pleasure through her. "What I need is someone to separate the legitimate replies from the bogus ones.''

"You don't think many of them are genuine?"

He shrugged. "Who knows? I mean, we are talking about an ad in a newspaper in a metropolitan area that has a population of almost three million."

She sat quietly for several moments, collecting her thoughts.

"Let me make sure I have this straight. You want me to go through your mail, pull out the ones I think might be suitable dates, give them to you, let you pick one and then plan an evening of romance for the two of you?"

"That sounds about right. So, do we have a deal?"

"No."

"No?"

She could see she had taken him by surprise.

"Special Moments is not a dating service. There's a big difference between planning a romantic evening and finding someone to spend the evening with you," she said stiffly.

"I'll double your hourly rate."

Allison almost said, "Money's not the issue," but held her tongue. If Tristan Talbot wanted to pay her double time to go through a stack of letters from women all vying for a date with him, maybe she was foolish to turn him down simply because he was somebody from her past she'd hoped never to see again.

He leaned back in his chair, folded his arms across his chest and studied her, his fingers steepled against his lips. "You surprise me, Allison."

"And why is that?"

"You're obviously creative and resourceful. Why should it matter to you whether your client's request is a little unusual? That *is* why you don't want to take the job, isn't it?"

"I admit I am a bit uncomfortable with the idea. It's not in the realm of what I consider to be professional duties."

"I have an idea. Why don't you look at a few of the letters and you can get an idea as to whether you're up to the job."

Suddenly he had switched it from whether or not she would accept the job to whether or not she could handle the job.

He was both brawny and brainy—a dangerous combination. Which would be more foolish? Turning down the money or helping him find a date?

"Should I go get them? I have them in my car." He nodded toward the door.

Allison was saved from having to make a decision when she remembered that her one o'clock appointment would be arriving any minute.

"I can't right now. I have a client coming. Why don't I think about it and let you know?" she suggested, relieved that she had found an escape from those probing eyes.

"Great." He got up to leave, automatically offering her his hand. She had no choice but to take it.

He didn't release it right away, but leaned closer to her and said in a voice that was close to a whisper. "After all the dictionaries were stolen, the librarian was at a loss for words."

She gave him a puzzled look.

"The cryptoquip in today's paper."

And with a wink he was gone.

TRISTAN DIDN'T EXPECT to hear from Allison Parker again. That was why he was taken by surprise when she called him at his office the following afternoon.

"I'll do it."

Maybe business wasn't as good as Butcher Baker and Doris thought it was.

"Great. When should I drop off the mail?" he asked.

"Anytime tomorrow will be fine. While I have you on the phone I want to ask you a few questions."

"Sure. What about?"

"The ad, for one thing. It says you don't want to be stuck in a snowbank by yourself on Valentine's Day. Does that mean you like outdoor winter activities or you dislike them?"

"I hate the cold."

"Then you'd prefer an indoor activity?"

He laughed. "I'd prefer to be in a warmer climate but since that's not possible, I'll settle for indoors with plenty of heat."

"What would you like to do for Valentine's Day?"

"Whatever it takes to make it a romantic date."

"Very well," she said in her disapproving tone that was becoming familiar.

"How long will this take you?"

"Romance requires planning, imagination and energy," she said pointedly.

Three things she obviously thinks I lack, Tristan said to himself. Aloud he said, "All good reasons to hire your services."

"If I have any other questions, I'll call. Otherwise, expect to hear from me the beginning of next week," she said in her most businesslike tone.

"I'll look forward to seeing you again," Tristan told her, but she had already hung up.

IT DIDN'T TAKE ALLISON long to realize that she would never get through all of Tristan Talbot's mail without help. That was why on Saturday morning she struck a bargain with Jazz. In exchange for her assistance in sorting through the letters, Allison would go with her to St. Paul's Winter Carnival.

She and Jazz had shared office space for the past four years and often helped each other out. Most of

Jazz's work as an image consultant took her out of the office and into the business world. While she was advising clients on what clothing to wear, Allison's work generally kept her at the office where she answered phones for both businesses.

"You know this is kind of fun," Jazz commented as she sat on the Oriental rug on the living-room floor of Allison's cozy apartment reading responses to Tristan's ad. "I never knew so many people read the Personals."

"Me, neither." Allison grimaced as she opened a box and found a dozen chocolate-chip cookies broken into crumbs. "Here's someone who thinks a way to a man's heart is through his stomach."

"So what *is* the way to this Tristan Talbot's heart?"

"That's a good question."

"I thought you said you went to school with this guy?"

"I did. That's what makes this all so awkward."

"Why? Did you used to date him or something?"

"Or something."

Jazz grabbed her forearm. "Okay, out with it. What went on?"

"Nothing. He was just this guy who had a crush on me."

"According to your sister Heidi, practically every guy in school had a crush on you."

She dismissed the comment with a grunt. "Heidi exaggerates."

"So what was so different about Tristan?"

"Here. I'll show you." She got up and went over to the cherrywood wall unit and pulled out her high school yearbook. She plopped down beside Jazz and flipped it open. "There he is." She pointed to a tiny glossy photo.

Jazz squinted. "I can't really see his face. His hair's hanging in his eyes."

"Look at what he's wearing. Straight-legged pants, a button-down-collar shirt and a tie! No one wore ties to high school."

"No, they all wore bell-bottoms and flowered shirts. Jeesh, look! Platform shoes! Fashions were really weird back then, weren't they? Tristan actually looks kind of normal."

"Yeah, normal as in captain of the chess club."

"I thought you liked chess."

"I do now, but you know what it was like in high school. Only the nerds joined chess club. And I think he was an AV guy, too."

"An AV guy?"

"Audiovisual. You know, the guys who ran the film projectors when we had to see movies in class."

"I don't think they have film projectors anymore, do they? Isn't everything on video?"

"Probably."

"So he was this nerdy guy who played chess, operated the film equipment and chased you around the school?"

"I'm hoping he doesn't remember that last part." Although from the way he had looked at her, Allison had a feeling that he remembered everything that had happened between them, including the kiss he had given her in front of the entire English class.

"So what's he like now? Is he tall? Short? Fat? Balding? What?"

Allison shrugged. "He's just an average-looking guy, I guess." That wasn't true. No woman in her right mind would call Tristan Talbot average. He was exceptional. Probably the best-looking bachelor to walk through Special Moments's door.

"Well, I need to know something about him if I'm going to help you play matchmaker."

"I'm not playing matchmaker," Allison denied. "I'm doing a job for him."

"Call it what you want," Jazz said. "I still need to know something about the guy. I mean, if he's real short I don't want to fix him up with an amazon."

"He's not short. He's probably around six feet and I don't think we need to worry about physical characteristics. He made it perfectly clear that looks weren't a criteria in choosing a date."

"Well, if that's the case, then he's an exception among men."

Which was exactly what Allison thought. She didn't understand why he would spend an unusual amount of money to select a date through the Personals—a date he didn't seem to particularly want.

"I think this woman could be put on the list of legitimate possibilities." Jazz passed Allison a photograph attached to a letter. "What do you think?"

Allison looked at the photo. "Are you kidding? Jazz, this woman looks like the most complicated piece of machinery she can operate is a zipper."

"Okay, so the picture makes her look like a bimbo, but read the letter. Her idea of a romantic Valentine's Day is having a quiet dinner for two, then strolling through the Sculpture Garden in the moonlight. That sounds like something our Mr. Romance would enjoy. You did say he's an architect."

"Are you sure this is the right picture for that letter?" Allison studied it briefly, finding it difficult to believe that someone who dressed in a leather jacket and shorts and rode a Harley would choose the Sculpture Garden for romance.

Jazz clicked her tongue. "I don't think she's a biker's dolly. Look at the shoes she's wearing."

"Is that your professional opinion?"

"I'd say she's trying to look seductive. She probably just wanted him to see what great legs she has."

"I suppose I shouldn't make a decision based on a photo."

"No, you shouldn't. If he were worried about what these women looked like, he would have required that they all send photos."

"In that case, we should probably consider this one, too. This woman looks as though she barely eats enough to keep a fairy alive. I was going to pass her up because I thought she wouldn't appreciate an expensive dinner." She handed Jazz the photo.

"She's probably one of the fortunate of this world with fast metabolism," Jazz said enviously. "I say add her to the list. Maybe Sir Tristan likes pencils."

Allison scribbled on a legal-size pad. "Okay, that's seven so far. Do you have any others that look like possibilities?"

"I kind of like this one." Jazz held up a piece of stationery. "This woman says her idea of a fantasy date is having absolutely nothing planned and doing whatever takes her fancy."

"I think Tristan wants this Valentine's Day date to be something more than doing nothing. That's why he hired me." She set the letter aside.

"Look. This one has a video with it." Jazz held up a tape. "Should we look at it?"

"Might as well." Allison took the cassette and pushed it into the VCR beneath her TV.

Jazz let out a whoop as the tape began to play. Stretched out on a heart-shaped bed was a woman wearing a tiger-print bodysuit.

"Hi. My name is Donna and I'd like to make *your* fantasy come true," the voluptuous woman onscreen said through heavily painted red lips.

Allison looked sideways at Jazz. "It says here she's a movie star."

"What do you suppose she's going to do with that whip?" Jazz asked.

"I don't think we want to know." Allison pressed the Stop button.

"I take it she's not going on the list."

"It's probably best if I give him the video and let him decide for himself," Allison replied, curious as to what Tristan's response would be.

Several hours later, they had drunk two pots of coffee, eaten four morning-glory muffins from Byerly's bakery, looked at two videotapes, listened to three audiocassettes and read dozens of letters from women from all walks of life.

There were letters from sisters writing for sisters, mothers writing for their daughters and daughters writing for their mothers. Some were even mothers writing for themselves. Some came on simple stationery, others on corporate letterhead. There were invitations to parties, recipes for love and even proposals of marriage. Some were handwritten, others typed. All were addressed to Mr. Romance.

"I never realized so many women answered personals," Allison remarked as she surveyed the mess on her rug.

Jazz picked up Tristan's ad and studied it, "I kind of wish I had."

"Jazz! You're engaged to be married."

"I know that, but I'm not sure Toby does."

"Are the two of you having problems?"

Jazz shrugged. "With Toby I never know when I should worry and when I shouldn't. You know how he is."

Allison knew all too well. She had reservations about Jazz and Toby's plans to marry. Theirs was a volatile relationship—one minute they seemed ecstatically happy, the next they were at each other's throats.

"I don't know. Maybe a little competition would do our relationship some good." Jazz stared at the Personals column pensively.

Allison grabbed it from her fingers. "I don't recommend finding the competition in the want ads."

"I suppose you're right." Jazz turned her attention to a padded mailer from which she pulled out a pair of red bikini briefs. She held them between her thumb and forefinger. "Can you believe women actually send stuff like this in the mail to men they've never met before?"

Allison shook her head in amazement.

"We've had cookies, condoms, candy and candles. They must think clever gifts will catch a man's eye."

"The question is, what kind of man do they hope to catch? Do you think this Tristan could be a knight in frozen armor?"

"Personally, I don't care whether he is or not." Allison scooped up the mail that was lying in the center of the rug and dumped it back into the large cardboard box.

"I've fulfilled part of our agreement. Now it's up to him to decide who's going to be his date for Valentine's Day."

"I say we forget about the man and go have some fun in the great frozen outdoors."

Allison groaned. "I guess this means you're not going to let me out of my promise."

"No way. Grab your mittens and let's go. Toby's game starts in an hour."

IT WAS JANUARY, the dead of winter, and Tristan felt like burrowing into a warm hole and staying there until spring arrived. On weekends he was content to sit in front of the fireplace and watch winter happen through his window. A native Californian, he had little interest in the outdoor activities that tempted Midwesterners to risk frostbite for some fun in the snow.

On this weekend, however, he couldn't hibernate. St. Paul was in the midst of its annual Winter

Carnival, an event he would have avoided had it not been for his position at Lassiter and Associates.

At the time Tristan had joined the architectural firm, he saw no reason to turn down the invitation to be a member of the employee softball team. Little did he know that he'd be playing in a softball tournament on ice in the middle of January.

But that's exactly what he was doing on Saturday afternoon. The team that last summer had played on green grass in their shirtsleeves now suited up in down-filled ski jackets to play on the frozen water of Lake Phalen.

Instead of baseball cleats, Tristan laced up big clunky rubber boots that made him feel as though he should be exploring the craters of the moon. As he sat down on the players' bench, his friend Gary Redmund handed him a roll of masking tape.

"Here. You'd better wrap some of this around your boots. It'll help keep you from slipping."

"Hey, Talbot, you're up first," Brian, his boss and team coach, announced a few minutes later as their opponents—Benny's Bar and Grill—took their positions on the ice.

Tristan looked to the pitcher's mound. There stood a man wearing a big red-and-black-checked woolen shirt with its sleeves rolled up to the elbows. A pair of thick suspenders held up blue jeans that had holes in both knees—holes that revealed bare skin, not thermal underwear. The only glove on his hand was his baseball mitt.

"What's with this guy?" Tristan asked Gary. "He looks like Paul Bunyan minus the blue ox. Doesn't he know it's winter?"

"That's Toby LaMott. Everyone says he dresses like that to intimidate the rest of us. He thinks it's a psychological edge."

Tristan could feel his competitive juices kick into high gear. He picked up his bat and took several swipes at the air, trying to ignore the awkwardness he felt, having his movement impeded by down-filled nylon. He stepped onto the batter's box—a small rectangular area marked with green paint.

"You'd better not crowd the plate," the catcher warned, as Tristan inched his boots closer to the orange cushion serving as home base. "Toby pitches inside."

"Good, cuz that's where I like 'em," Tristan boasted with more bravado than he was feeling.

"Play ball," the umpire roared, drawing Tristan's attention back to the pitcher's mound. Tristan sliced the air over the plate with the bat, indicating where he wanted the pitch.

The ball sailed toward him, fast and close—so close it swooshed the fabric of his jacket. Tristan was not intimidated. He liked to hit inside pitches and if this Paul Bunyan clone thought he could brush him back with a fast pitch, he was sadly mistaken.

A spectator didn't agree. "Way to get 'im, Toby. Pitch him inside!" came a female voice from behind home plate.

Tristan glanced over his shoulder to see who was encouraging the brute. A small crowd of spectators sat in lawn chairs, as if it were summer. One held a woman in a blue-and-white ski jacket, her blond head bare. She had her gloved hands cupped around her mouth, shouting encouragement to the man on the mound. She was obviously a Benny's Bar and Grill fan.

Tristan would have easily dismissed her had he not caught a glimpse of the woman sitting beside her. White earmuffs did little to tame the thick red curls that sprang forth from Allison Parker's head. Bundled up in a fur-trimmed parka, she sat stiffly, as if she were as cold as he was. He gave her a half smile. She didn't move a muscle.

"It's oh and one," the umpire called out, and Tristan was forced to turn his attention back to the game.

He looked at the pitcher once more and waited.

The next ball came even closer than the first one had, grazing the glove on his left hand.

"Strike two!" the umpire shouted, prompting Tristan to turn and glare at him.

"Strike? It hit me on the knuckles!"

"It's oh and two," the umpire bellowed, leaving Tristan in no doubt that his protest had fallen on deaf ears.

The catcher snickered, which only made Tristan more determined than ever to hit the ball.

"Way to go, Toby! One more and he's outta there!" the blonde screamed, obviously more into the game than Allison Parker, who sat quietly, a cup of coffee in her mittened hands.

Again Tristan looked to the man on the snowy mound who was now cranking up for the kill. Determined to get a hit, he swung with everything he had. Instead of the crack of wood meeting leather, however, he heard the swoosh of nylon and the thump of his body as it hit the ice.

"Strike three and you're outta there!" the umpire yelled with gusto.

Mortified at having swung so hard he had fallen down, Tristan could only glare at the umpire as he got back up on his feet. So much for the tape, he thought, giving his boots a nasty look as he trudged back to the bench.

He didn't want to look over at Allison Parker, but he couldn't resist a glance in her direction. As he expected, she was grinning. This time she gave him a little wave.

He was tempted to ignore her. He didn't.

"Hi. Enjoying the game?" he asked, walking around to squat beside her.

"So far."

"I struck out."

"I noticed."

"Nobody hits Toby inside, Fourteen." The blonde leaned forward, addressing him by the number that was pinned to his jacket. She didn't try to hide her smirk.

"We'll see," Tristan responded with his own smug grin. "And the name's Talbot. Tristan Talbot."

"You're Mr. Romance?" she screeched.

From the look on her face, Tristan could only guess at how Allison had described him. The nerd from high school who didn't have a clue how to behave around women.

Allison gave her friend a gentle elbow of admonition. "I thought you said he was average-looking. I beg to differ. Dynamite-looking is more like it," she said in a loud whisper.

Allison's already red cheeks turned a deeper shade. "Jazz is my office mate," she explained, making an informal introduction.

"I thought maybe she worked for Benny's Bar and Grill," he said cheerfully, winking at Jazz.

"Uh-uh. I just like to root for a winner." Jazz gave him a flirtatious grin.

"Then you're cheering for the wrong team," Tristan answered.

"You think so, Fourteen?"

"Absolutely."

"I'm surprised to see you here," Allison said. "You never played sports in high school, did you?"

"I may not have been a jock, but I played baseball as a kid."

"Have you played softball on ice before?"

"I've never even walked on ice before," Tristan admitted. "Can't you tell?"

"Lots of guys fall," Jazz assured him, eyeing him with undisguised admiration. "It isn't as easy as it looks. What position are you playing?"

"Center field."

She chuckled. "Good luck."

"You say that as if I really need it."

"You do. Benny's Bar and Grill has won this tournament three years in a row," Jazz said, then jumped to her feet to whistle and clap as Toby struck out the second batter of the inning. "I'd better see if he wants something to drink," she said before trotting over to the Benny's bench.

"Are you as big a fan of softball on ice as your friend?" Tristan asked Allison when Jazz was gone.

She laughed. "Hardly. I hate sitting outside in the cold."

"Then why are you here?"

"Jazz and I have friends on the team." Which only made Tristan wonder which men and how friendly they were with them.

Before he could find out, however, the coach waved him over. "Duty calls," he announced, and rose to leave.

"Have fun," she said with a lift of an eyebrow.

"I'm sure I will."

"Maybe you should put more tape on your boots."

He tipped the brim of his hat. "Thanks for the advice, but I think you'll see something a little different next time I'm at the plate."

It was a statement he lived to regret. Playing on ice was a lot more difficult than he had thought it would be. The places that had been plowed were too slippery to get any traction and the areas of the field that were still covered with snow were uneven and difficult to tread.

Fortunately, his teammates weren't as inexperienced. By the last inning, the score was three to two in favor of Benny's Bar and Grill. When Tristan came to the plate in the final inning, there were two outs with a man on second base.

He had already struck out three times. He was cold, tired and frustrated. If it wasn't for his competitive spirit, he would have told the coach he was finished and gone home. There was also the matter of pride. Allison Parker had witnessed him stumble and fall.

He had tried to look like a jock in front of her this afternoon. Instead, he had looked like a fool. Now he had one last chance to redeem himself.

Allison watched Tristan step up to the plate for the final time, a look of determination on his face. When he glanced in her direction, she gave him a thumbs-up sign.

To everyone's surprise, Tristan's bat connected with Toby's first pitch and sent it soaring over the second baseman's head into center field. She watched him drop his bat and start for first base, only to fall flat on his face on the ice.

Encouraged by the cheers of his teammates, Tristan quickly scrambled to his feet and ran the bases. He slid into home plate just as the catcher reached for the ball.

"Safe!" the umpire hollered.

Allison stood and clapped while Jazz squeezed her eyes shut and groaned. Toby kicked his foot in the snow, his head hung low as Tristan was carried off the ice by his joyous teammates.

"Good grief! Would you look at Toby's face!" Jazz tugged on Allison's arm as she spoke. "We've got to get out of here. I'm not going to be anywhere near him until he cools down." She slammed her folding chair shut and started for the car.

Allison debated whether or not she should try to speak to Tristan or just leave. Her decision was made for her when Jazz, close to tears, said, "Would you please hurry? I have to go to the bathroom."

Allison glanced in Tristan's direction but saw only a mob of softball players slapping high fives. When she finally caught a glimpse of Tristan, he was without his stocking cap and his curly dark hair was in disarray.

Jazz was right. He was dynamite-looking. Allison was having trouble remembering him as being anything but that.

As she left the lake, one thought played over and over in her mind. For someone who never dated in high school, he certainly had been a good kisser.

Chapter Three

ALLISON WANTED NOTHING better than to spend Saturday night with a good book, hot food and a warm bed. As soon as Jazz had dropped her off at her apartment, she had plugged in the electric blanket, taken a long hot bath and donned her footed flannel pajamas.

Then Jazz returned.

"Why do you look like my two-year-old niece at bedtime?" she asked Allison. "It's Saturday night."

"Yeah, well, not everyone has a date on Saturday night."

"No kidding!" She dropped down onto Allison's chintz sofa. "Toby's in such a bad mood I told him he could forget about doing anything tonight."

"He's not still sulking over the game, is he?"

Jazz nodded. "He's going to have to sulk alone. I'm going out. Why don't you get rid of your sleeper and come with me?"

Going back out into the subzero temperatures and blowing snow was not in Allison's game plan. Yet there was a look in Jazz's eyes that had her asking, "Where do you want to go?"

"To the Boreas Bash."

Allison groaned. "Not a street dance. It's winter! It took me two hours to warm up from sitting outside this afternoon."

"You won't get cold. It's in a tent with heat. Come on, it'll be fun," Jazz pleaded.

Allison had never been one for dances. She had two left feet, a trait she inherited from her father and one she knew better than to try to change. "You know I don't dance."

"You won't have to. We'll just listen to the different bands. Plus, there are all sorts of vendors selling food and stuff. Come on. Don't make me go alone."

"Oh, all right. I'll go to the stupid dance, but if I get cold, I leave," she warned.

To Jazz and Allison's relief, it was warm inside the tent that had been erected in the Civic Center's parking lot. The music was loud, the crowd large and the food surprisingly good. Allison was glad that she'd let Jazz talk her into going.

As Tristan elbowed his way through the crowded tent, he wished he were anywhere but at the Boreas Bash. If it hadn't been for the fact that several of his teammates considered the street dance the culmination of their softball victory, he would have beat feet home and spent the evening in front of a fire.

He was about to tell his cohorts that it was time he left when he spotted a familiar head of red curls—Allison's. She was eating something with a pair of chopsticks and appeared to be alone. Then he saw Jazz. There were several men hovering nearby and Tristan waited to see if any of them made a move on either of the women.

None of them did, so when Tristan's teammates indicated they were heading out, he stayed behind. His appearance caught Allison by surprise.

She had a mouth full of food and had to hurry up and swallow before speaking. "Hi."

He grinned. "Guess you were wrong, eh?"

"About what?"

"Benny's winning."

"Jazz was the one who made that prediction, not me."

"Are you saying you're not surprised at the outcome?"

She shrugged. "On ice, anything can happen. If Pete hadn't lost the ball in the outfield, you would have been out."

"And would that have made you happy?"

"Jazz would have been a little easier to be around. Toby's her fiancé."

"Is one of Benny's Bar and Grill players your fiancé, too?"

"No. I don't have a fiancé." She finished her Chinese food and dumped the paper container in the trash.

"Good, then you can come and dance with me." He reached for her hand, but she snatched her fingers behind her back.

"I don't think so."

"No?"

"No." There were several seconds of awkward silence, then she said, "I'm glad I ran into you, though."

"You are?" Tristan's hopes were raised.

"Yes. I didn't get a chance to tell you this afternoon, but I finished going through the box of mail you gave me and I've compiled the list you requested."

Tristan's hopes were dashed. She was all business. Nothing more. Nothing less.

"That was fast."

"We aim to please."

"Then how about a dance? That would give this client great pleasure."

"Sorry, but I don't dance with my clients," she said coolly.

"No, but I do." Jazz appeared out of nowhere and before Tristan knew what was happening, he was being pulled out toward the crowded dance area by Jazz. She did everything she could to put the make on him, but there was only one woman Tristan wanted to be dancing with and unfortunately, she stood on the sidelines looking as if she wished he would disappear.

On Monday Allison deliberately suggested that Tristan come at a time when she knew Jazz would be out of the office. It had nothing to do with jealousy—or at least she told herself it didn't. She just couldn't stand to see her friend fawn all over her client.

All the way home from the Boreas Bash on Saturday night, Jazz had talked of nothing but Tristan. She couldn't believe that he had ever been unpopular with anyone. He was charming, cute, and a dozen other adjectives Allison didn't want to hear.

It didn't help that Tristan arrived looking charming and cute, the first words out of his mouth being, "Where's Jazz?"

"Out with her fiancé," Allison responded curtly.

He took the chair across from her and plopped another stack of mail on her desk.

Allison grimaced. "What's that?"

"More responses to the ad. I picked them up on my way over here."

"I thought we were done."

"Me, too. Who would have thought one ad would generate so many replies." He shook his head in amazement.

"It would have helped if you had stated your age," she admonished him. "You've received letters from women as old as eighty-six and as young as sixteen."

"No kidding, eighty-six?"

Allison removed the rubber band from the stack of mail and sighed. "There has to be at least fifty letters here."

"And another package." He reached inside his coat pocket and produced a padded mailer.

Allison fingered the package. "Feels like clothing. You should probably open it."

She handed it to Tristan, who ripped off the end and pulled out a pair of white boxers with tiny red hearts all over them. "A gift," he said with a bemused expression.

"There's a note pinned to the front," Allison observed.

"'If you're man enough to fill these, you're man enough for me,'" he read.

"They look a little big to me," Allison couldn't resist saying.

"You think so?"

His smile was a bit lopsided, but it wasn't his smile that was causing Allison's breath to catch in her throat. It was his eyes. He was looking at her as if he were mentally undressing her.

"Speaking of gifts." She quickly made the transition, reaching for a small box. "There were lots of things, including a couple of videos. It's all in here."

"Did you look at them?"

Allison couldn't prevent the flush that colored her cheeks. "Only the beginning of one. Since they were made for you, I felt you should watch them."

She sat back down and pushed the button on her personal computer, swinging the monitor around so that they both could see. "I'll show you what we have so far." She inserted a diskette into the terminal.

"You put the information into the computer?"

She nodded. "Saves time and file space." The computer beeped and her fingers raced across the keyboard.

Tristan couldn't help but be impressed. He hadn't expected she would develop a program to catalog his prospective dates.

"Here we are. I've categorized the women according to personal interests, occupations and something I call the Q factor."

"The Q factor?"

"Quirks. I figure they can be either good or bad. Anything that might raise a red flag as to the writer's mental state. Like, for instance on this one." She pointed to the entry numbered seventy-three. Then she opened a manila folder and pulled out a photograph attached to a letter.

"This woman sent in a photo of herself sitting next to the telephone, her hands clasped in prayer, with the caption that she was waiting for you to call. Now, if you find an eager woman attractive, she's a Q plus. If you think she's a little desperate, she's a Q minus."

Tristan gave the photo a hasty glance before tossing it aside. "It's a minus."

"Okay." She clicked several more keys, then said, "Of the two hundred and fifteen letters—"

"Wait a minute," he interrupted. "You read two hundred and fifteen letters?"

"I didn't read every one. Jazz helped. And I figured we could pass over the ones with prison addresses, which amounted to..." She paused to punch several keys. "Eighteen."

Tristan listened as she rattled off percentages and statistics concerning the information contained in the replies. Although he nodded in understanding, he really heard little of what she said. He couldn't concentrate, for the knit fabric of the bodysuit she wore clung seductively to her torso. There was the faintest hint of her nipples poking through the stretchy fabric and it was driving him crazy.

"So these are the ones I thought fit the criteria you were looking for." She reached across the desk to retrieve a large brown envelope. "Why don't you take a look at them and see what you think?"

Tristan didn't want to look at any of the letters. The thought of choosing a date from responses to a Personals ad was no more appealing now than it had been last week. If anything, it was even less so.

"And if I don't find the woman I want to be my date?"

"Then I can go through that pile." She nodded toward the stack of mail he had brought with him.

He could tell by her tone that it wasn't an option she wanted to exercise. The phone rang and Allison excused herself to answer it.

Tristan eavesdropped on her conversation as he flipped through the letters from women who all wanted to be his fantasy date.

"There are still spots open then?"

Spots to what? Tristan wondered.

"Oh, good. We'll take the three-thirty. What should we bring?"

With one eye on the letters in front of him, another on Allison, he watched as she wrote on a notepad at her fingertips.

"Yes, we have Winter Carnival buttons." She paused to scribble more information. "My partner's name is Jasmine Connors."

Whatever it was that Allison planned to do, it included her office mate. Tristan continued to look at the letters but listen to her conversation.

"The World Trade Center on Saturday. We'll be there. Thanks."

As soon as she hung up, Allison apologized for the interruption.

"Okay. Any questions?"

Questions? Tristan wanted to ask her lots of things, but nothing that pertained to the work she was doing for him. He wanted to know what she was going to be doing on Valentine's Day. What she liked to do when she wasn't planning romance for other people.

She cleared her throat and he realized she was waiting for him to answer her. He had to remind himself that he was here on business, not for personal reasons. He couldn't let his attraction to her get in the way of that purpose. Because he was attracted to her—even if she did think he was only average-looking.

"I'll look these over and let you know my decision," he told her, waving the file folder in the air.

As he left her office, however, he headed straight for the drugstore where he picked up a copy of the St. Paul newspaper. He quickly flipped to the page that listed the upcoming carnival events.

There, between the antique sleigh and cutter parade being held at Como Park and golfing in the snow at Lost Spur Country Club, was the world's largest jigsaw puzzle contest at the World Trade Center. The entry fee was ten dollars per person, plus a Winter Carnival button.

Tristan smiled to himself. He would never have guessed she'd be into jigsaw puzzles. She was neat, she was PC literate and she liked jigsaws. He wondered what her romantic fantasy was.

A NATIVE OF ST. PAUL, Allison loved the atmosphere that prevailed during the Winter Carnival. As a child she had often braved the freezing temperatures and subzero windchills to watch the annual parade wind its way through downtown St. Paul.

In recent years, however, she had limited her outdoor activities to viewing the ice sculptures in Rice Park and watching the softball tournament.

Instead of volleyball in the snow and sleigh rides at the park, her carnival events now consisted of the arts-and-crafts fair at Galtier Plaza and the jigsaw-puzzle contest at the World Trade Center.

Allison loved puzzles of every size, shape and form. She especially looked forward to this year's competition because the contest puzzle was a picture of the 1992 Ice Palace, a spectacular castle that had been constructed of ice blocks on Harriet Island.

Allison and Jazz had arranged to meet at the fountain on the first level of the three-story mall. When twenty minutes had passed and Allison was still waiting, she began to worry that Jazz had forgotten about the contest. She glanced nervously at her watch and was about to use a pay phone when she heard someone call out her name. She turned around to find Tristan smiling at her.

"Isn't this a coincidence?" he said with a grin.

Allison almost said, "Are you following me?" but realized how vain that would sound. "I'm surprised to see you here."

"Are you looking for anybody in particular?" he asked, as she continued to scan the crowd.

"Jazz was supposed to meet me here fifteen minutes ago," she answered, glancing nervously at her watch.

"Are you in the puzzle contest?"

"We're supposed to be." Just then, an announcement sounded over the public address system indicating that contestants had five minutes to check in. "I'd better go to registration. Maybe she's already here."

Tristan followed her over to the table.

"I'm Allison Parker. By any chance is my partner, Jasmine Connors, here?"

"Oh! You're Allison." The gray-haired woman picked up a pink slip of paper and peered at it over her glasses. "Someone named Jasmine called to say that her battery was dead and she was waiting for a tow truck."

Allison frowned. "So what does that mean? That we're disqualified?"

The woman shrugged sympathetically. "I'm afraid rules prohibit contestants registering after the official start. But you're welcome to find a replacement for her if you wish."

"I like jigsaw puzzles," Tristan said, close to Allison's ear.

The seductive scent of his after-shave tickled her senses. "You want to be my partner?"

"I'm available if you want me." There was a double entendre in his message, causing Allison to blush. "Or do you have a rule about not working jigsaw puzzles with a client, too?"

"I wouldn't want to impose on your time," she began, only to have him cut her off with uplifted palms.

"It's no imposition."

"But you're a busy man. Isn't that why you couldn't read all the responses to the ad?"

"The mail didn't interest me. Working the jigsaw puzzle with you does."

The clerk interrupted their conversation. "You're going to have to make up your minds. We're closing registration."

Tristan actually made the decision. He plunked a twenty-dollar bill down on the table and flashed his Winter Carnival button at the woman.

"And your name, sir?" she asked with a sweet smile.

"Tristan Talbot."

"Tristan as in the knight of King Arthur's court?" This time there was a twinkle in the eyes of the older woman.

"The same. My mother is an opera buff."

"Oh, me, too," the older woman crooned. "*Tristan and Isolde* is one of my favorites. What a hero he was." She sighed, batting her eyelashes shamelessly.

She stamped both of their right hands with a blue snowflake, then said in a low voice meant only for Allison's ears, "This could be a sign. The puzzle this year is a picture of the Ice Palace and you have a knight coming to your rescue."

A knight he isn't, Allison wanted to say aloud, but instead she smiled with her teeth and said, "Aren't I lucky?"

"You're contestants number seventy-nine," the clerk said encouragingly, then directed them to a long table where the only two vacant chairs were next to a white placard with the number 79 painted in black. A strip of red tape separated their workspace from their closest neighbors, a couple of teenage boys who wore plaid flannel shirts and baggy jeans, and had baseball caps on backward.

Allison draped her coat over the back of her chair. Tristan took off his dark green suede jacket and slung it over the other chair. Dressed in a lemony yellow sweater and faded blue jeans, he looked dangerously attractive. And he smelled good, too. Allison's pulse rate quickened.

"If all the contestants would be seated, we'll begin."

The announcement caused a collective scraping of metal on tile. Tristan pushed his chair closer to Allison's.

"What are you doing?" she asked.

"Can't I sit while I work?"

"Not here. There." She pointed to a spot across the table. "We'll be bumping elbows if we both work from the bottom."

Reluctantly he slid his chair around to the other side of the table.

Allison didn't know which was worse—having him rubbing shoulders with her or having him looking at her face-to-face.

All talking ceased as the contest judge reminded everyone of the rules. At the sound of a starter pistol, hundreds of boxes overturned in unison.

Allison, who was used to taking charge with Jazz, automatically took command. "I'll turn all the pieces faceup. You start working the border."

"I'd rather do the whites. We know where the edges go," he said, sorting the pieces.

"But white's the predominant color."

"I know. If we get that portion of the puzzle done, we're home free." He gave her an engaging grin that did little to assuage her doubts.

She tried to keep her eyes on her own section of the puzzle, but she couldn't resist watching his long thin fingers at work. At one point he caught her gawking at him and she couldn't prevent the color that flushed her cheeks.

"Is anything wrong?" he asked.

She shook her head. "No, it's okay," she said, trying to ignore the effect his presence was having on her. Several times their hands had bumped as they both reached for pieces of the puzzle and each time, she felt a jolt of excitement—not only from the contact, but from the look in his eyes.

His arms were long, his hand-span wide. To Allison, he was everywhere on the puzzle. If she worked an area of the sky, he'd either find the piece she was looking for or toss her one she could use. He was good and he knew it. She could tell by the satisfied look he wore. Putting together a jigsaw puzzle was a piece of cake for him.

They worked in silence, the only communication an occasional unspoken meeting of their eyes that said, "We can do this." With only fifteen minutes to go, it looked as if they were going to finish.

Suddenly, the announcement came that someone had completed the puzzle. A collective sigh could be heard as heads turned to see who had finished. In the opposite corner of the room, two senior citizens stood and acknowledged the judge's official proclamation.

"We lost."

"Not by much. Another ten minutes and I think we could have gotten it." Allison couldn't believe the look of disappointment on his face. "Cheer up. The prize was only a hundred dollars."

"That's not the point. We didn't win."

"No, but look how beautiful this is." She fingered the picture of the ice palace lovingly.

"If you have less than twenty-five pieces remaining, please raise your hand." The announcement came over the loudspeaker system.

"Maybe we took second." Hope gleamed in Tristan's eyes. He thrust his hand up in the air.

Within minutes the runners-up were announced. They had finished fourth. The judge congratulated them and handed Allison a long white envelope.

"What's our prize?" Tristan asked.

She slipped her fingers inside and pulled out a slip of paper. "It's a gift certificate for dinner at the Heartthrob Café."

"The Heartthrob Cafe?" Tristan raised one eyebrow. "Now that seems rather appropriate for a romance consultant and her client, doesn't it?"

"You can take it," she said, setting the certificate down on his side of the table. "After all, you paid the entrance fee."

He shoved it back to her side of the table. "Not fair. We earned it together."

"That's all right. You use it. I'll take the puzzle home with me." She shoved it back to his side.

He in turn, pushed it back. "I'm not going to use this unless you're with me. It'd be a shame to see it go to waste, don't you think?"

He was staring at her again with that gleam in his eye—the one that made her wonder if he still kissed as well as he had back in high school.

"I suppose we could have lunch and discuss your Valentine's Day date," she conceded, her heart thumping.

"I was thinking more along the lines of dinner—like tonight. Or have you already made plans?"

This was her opportunity to get out of having dinner with him. The problem was, she didn't want to. "Have you made your decision as to which woman you're going to date?"

"Yes, but I don't want to discuss business, Allison. I just want to take you out to dinner."

"You mean, like on a date?"

"Yes. Is there a problem with that?"

She had to swallow before she said, "I don't date my clients."

He reached across the table and captured her hand in his. "Can't you make an exception? For a guy who wished he could have been your heart-throb at Kennedy High?"

Allison knew she should say no. She should tell him it would either be business or nothing. But she found herself saying, "Okay. For old times' sake."

Chapter Four

"AN EATIE GOURMET Burger, one I Want My Baby Back Ribs and two I Only Have Fries For You." The waiter set Allison's and Tristan's food before them, then glided away on his Rollerblades.

All of the wait staff at the Heartthrob Café wore rollerblades, gliding their way to customers to the beat of rock-and-roll oldies. Often patrons would join in the fun, singing and clapping to the music.

"You've never been here before, have you?" Allison commented as Tristan dubiously eyed a birthday celebration in progress. The guest of honor stood in the aisle, surrounded by bladers.

"No, and I think I'll avoid this place on my birthday if they're going to lob whipped cream on my nose," he said with a grimace. "With a name like Heartthrob, I thought it might be a place for a romantic dinner for two."

"It can be. I once sent a couple here who met at a malt shop when they were teenagers and wanted to celebrate their twenty-eighth wedding anniversary listening to jukebox music and sipping cherry colas."

"And was it a romantic evening for them?"

"Yes, for them it was."

His only response was a lift of his brows.

Allison took a sip of her soda, then said, "Everyone's expectations are different when it comes to what's romantic and what's not."

"And what are your expectations, Allison? Is a fifties restaurant with nostalgic music your idea of a romantic spot to have dinner?"

"It could be, depending on the circumstances."

"You mean depending on whether you're with the captain of the football team or the outstanding chess player of the year?"

He loved to make her blush. Not because he wanted to embarrass her but because she was even more beautiful when her pale complexion was tinged with color.

"Maybe in high school that was true, but I like to think I'm a little bit more discriminating as an adult," she said stiffly.

Tristan had hoped that by inviting her to dinner he would be able to shatter the illusion that had lingered from his teenage days—that Allison Parker was not the fantasy woman he had wanted her to be. So far, that wasn't happening.

"Tell me how you ended up in the romance consulting business," he prompted, wanting to put her at ease again.

He watched as she smothered her burger with catsup and mustard. "I was tired of trying to climb the corporate ladder only to hit my head on the glass ceiling."

"What part of corporate America were you tackling?"

"I was a market analyst for a local manufacturing company. That's where I met Jazz."

"You have a business degree?"

"Uh-huh." She took a bite of her hamburger, then said, "Are you surprised?"

He was. "Around the time of graduation I thought I heard you were going to some modeling school in New York."

She laughed at that. "Hardly. Starving myself so that someone can criticize my appearance never appealed to me. Besides, I'm too short and then there's my hair."

"What's wrong with your hair?"

"It's not the right shade of red."

"How can that be when it's the same color as the Grand Canyon?"

She blushed again. "Must you say that?"

"Why shouldn't I? It's a compliment. The Grand Canyon is breathtaking."

"My hair isn't."

She was self-conscious. He could sense it, but he couldn't stop himself from continuing. "You used to wear it longer."

She didn't say anything but tackled her I Only Have Fries For You, pouring a liberal dose of catsup and mustard on them.

"Do you know you're the only other person I've met who puts both catsup and mustard on fries?"

He reached for the condiments and dribbled them over his fries, smiling at her all the while.

She didn't comment, continuing to eat.

"So how did you go from doing market evaluations to running your own business?" he asked.

She dabbed at her lips with a napkin. "One day Jazz and I were commiserating about how we wished we could be our own bosses. We did some brainstorming and came up with image consulting for her and events planning for me."

"In the phone book it says you're a romance consultant."

"For a good reason. 'Events planning' sounds rather boring. Besides, most of my clients need help with planning romantic events, and from experience I've learned that if I put the word *romance* in an ad, it'll get noticed."

"And has your business gotten noticed?"

"Actually, it's surprised me. I'm doing better than I thought I would."

"Then obviously there's a great need for romance consulting." He slowly shook his head in amazement. "If someone in high school had told me that someday you'd be running your own business, I don't think I would have believed it."

"What did you think I'd be doing?"

He shrugged. "In high school you looked like you were on the track heading for the house with a white picket fence, a husband, two kids and a dog." He took a sip of his soft drink.

"I'd like a dog someday."

"But not a husband and the two kids?"

This time she was the one who shrugged. "Kids, I could get used to."

"And the husband?"

"So far, I haven't been impressed by the prospects."

He detected a hint of a challenge. The more he saw of Allison Parker, the more intrigued he became.

"You don't think there are very many romantic men out there, do you?"

"Oh, there might be one or two wandering the earth somewhere, I suppose."

He sat back and stared at her. "What I don't understand is, if you feel that way, why do you make a career out of making men look romantic?"

"I don't do it for the men. I do it for the women." She smiled sweetly, meeting his gaze.

"Is that a fact?"

"That's a fact."

Suddenly she became very businesslike. "I know you said you didn't want this to be a business dinner, but since we have this opportunity..."

She brought a briefcase from under the table. He half expected her to pull out a laptop computer from it, but out came a manila folder.

He had no doubt that everything she needed was in that folder. With her usual organized, efficient manner she presented him with a computer print-out of several romantic options and their costs.

"I wanted to give you a few ideas to think about as you consider which woman will be your date."

She gave him several minutes to look at the papers before saying, "Of course, which plan you pick will depend on which woman you choose."

Tristan couldn't find fault with any of the ideas. Included were an indoor luau at a local hotel that served Polynesian food, and dinner on an excursion train that traveled through the scenic St. Croix Valley. Everything was itemized according to cost, with another list of suggestions for flowers and candy. She had definitely done a thorough job.

"I'll make all the necessary reservations and arrangements. All you'll have to do is be there," she told him as she outlined the details.

Tristan could sense from her attitude that she suspected he didn't have a romantic idea in his head—and with good cause. He debated whether he should tell her the true reason why he had advertised for a date and hired her to plan it for him. Then he quickly squelched any such thoughts. Telling her he was only doing it to win a bet with friends wouldn't gain him any brownie points.

"Which do you think is the most romantic?" he wanted to know.

"I think you should be the judge of that."

Again he had the distinct impression that she was looking down her nose at him. It made him feel like he was seventeen again, and once again coming up short in her eyes.

"I will be the judge. I was simply curious to know which one you would have chosen." He was unable to keep the irritation from his voice.

She gave him an apologetic smile. "I'd probably choose the Hawaiian luau. I'm not exactly crazy about the cold weather."

He smiled then, an intimate little smile that reminded Allison he had a way of making her forget they were client and customer. She thought it was time to change the subject. "Do you really like jigsaw puzzles?"

"Why else would I have volunteered to be your partner?"

So much for taking charge of the conversation, Allison thought to herself. How could she have walked into that one?

"I also do the cryptoquip every morning and I don't like sitting outside in the cold, either." He lifted his glass in a toast to her. "We have more in common than the fact that we graduated from the same high school."

Again, there was that flirtatious twinkle in his eye and Allison's ego responded to it. She was warm. Very warm.

"I wonder what our classmates would say if they could see us now, eh? Nerdy Tristan Talbot, sitting across from the popular and cool Allison Parker."

"You weren't a nerd," she politely protested.

"We both know I was, Allison." He paused reflectively, then said, "That's why you were so upset when I kissed you."

"I was upset because we were supposed to be *reading* Romeo and Juliet, not acting it out. Mrs. Resch practically had a fit."

"So you do remember?"

She looked down at her plate. "Everybody in school talked about it for days," she told him, not wanting to tell him the true reason she hadn't forgotten—that he was a great kisser.

"The kiss or the fact that your hockey-player boyfriend gave me a black eye because of it?"

"He was a football player, not a hockey player."

"Same difference. He was a jock. I wasn't."

Allison knew what he was talking about without him spelling it out. He wasn't one of the "in" crowd—which had made the kiss all the more embarrassing.

"I'm sorry you ended up with a black eye. And I'm sorry I wasn't nicer to you back then, but I wasn't very nice to anyone."

"You mean I wasn't the only one you hid from?"

She reached for her jacket. "It's getting late and I think it's best for our professional relationship if I leave."

His hand reached across the table to touch her arm. "Wait. I'm sorry."

She didn't accept his apology. "Excuse me," she said, pulling her arm away from his.

She was out of the restaurant before he could get the check from the waiter. By the time he caught up with her, she was stepping into the elevator to the parking ramp.

Before the doors could slide shut, he thrust his hand between them. They bolted back open and he stepped in.

"Allison, I'm sorry. I shouldn't have brought up all that stuff from the past," he apologized, but she refused to look at him.

She stood as straight as a stick watching the numbers flash as the elevator climbed.

"It's just that ever since we ran into each other again there's been this awkwardness between us and I know it's because of what happened when we were in high school."

"Nothing happened," she said.

He smiled. "That's what I mean. I wanted something to happen. You didn't."

The elevator doors opened and she stepped out. "You were so different from any of the boys I knew," she told him as he accompanied her to her minivan.

"I wanted to be different from everyone else. I still do. Only now my individuality is expressed in my designs, not in how I dress."

"Jazz certainly is impressed by your image," she said, attempting to ease the tension between them.

"Jazz isn't the one I want to impress."

He was looking at her as if he wanted to kiss her. Ever since she had seen him, Allison had wanted that same thing—to see if she'd have the same reaction she'd had in high school.

Now that it was possible, she was afraid of what she might discover. She quickly unlocked her car and climbed inside.

"Call me when you've made your decision."

And with those parting words, she was gone.

ALL THE WAY HOME Tristan thought about how he had bungled his evening with her. Instead of putting her at ease, which is what he'd wanted to do, he had made her nervous.

And all because she hadn't responded to his flirting. Nothing had changed in the past eighteen years. She still fascinated him and made him wish that he could be with her. He was stuck on her, as Eddie Tompkins used to say to him every morning when he'd walk out of his way to follow her to her first-period class.

Stuck on her. He wanted to be with her. To get to know her better. To wind his fingers through her Grand Canyon hair. To kiss those soft lips. He wanted her to be his Valentine.

What was he thinking? He couldn't take her out on Valentine's Day. He'd never win the bet if his date wasn't someone who had responded to his ad. Valentine's Day was definitely out.

Besides, even if he did ask her, there was no guarantee she'd say yes. Probably just the opposite. After all, she thought he was average-looking and unromantic.

He'd have to prove that she was wrong.

"HE CHOSE SHANNON, the cheerleader," Allison announced to Jazz on Monday morning.

"You mean the one who was the professional dancer?" Jazz asked.

"I can't believe he chose a cheerleader!"

"Weren't you a cheerleader in high school?"

"That's a little different from a grown woman who wiggles and jiggles in front of fifty thousand screaming football fans and millions of TV viewers."

"At least she's over thirty. He could have chosen some sweet young thing."

That was of little consolation to Allison. "There were lots of women with brains on that list. Why didn't he pick one of them?"

"How do you know Shannon didn't graduate magna cum laude?" Jazz looked at her thoughtfully. "And why should you care, anyway?"

"I don't." Allison slammed her appointment book shut with a vengeance. "I'll do my job like I always do. And that's that."

Jazz wasn't so sure.

ALLISON WAS TOO BUSY the week before Valentine's Day to give much thought to anything but work. As she had agreed, she made all the arrangements for Tristan's date with Shannon, the Viking cheerleader, whose fantasy was to be far from the maddening crowd in a country setting. She planned a leisurely dinner at the Mill, a renowned country inn outside of St. Paul, followed by a sleigh ride through the moonlit countryside.

On Valentine's Day Allison rushed to fill last-minute requests for flowers and candy to be sent to loved ones, trying not to lament the fact that she had no one sending her roses or chocolates. At noon she called her mother and wished her a Happy Valentine's Day, then put on her coat and gloves to go to work at another job—this one voluntary.

For the past seven years, Allison had spent part of every Valentine's Day working at the Humane Society's orphaned animal sale. She had decided long ago that if she couldn't spend the day with someone she loved, she'd be with something she loved—animals.

The pet sale was being held in the auditorium of one of the larger department stores in downtown St. Paul. Most of the cages contained older dogs and cats who had been abandoned by their previous owners, but there were also rabbits and birds, and even a few reptiles.

Throughout the afternoon, hundreds of animals found new homes, much to Allison's relief. It was a delight to see the joy on children's faces as they left with a new pet in their arms.

As the hands on the clock approached six, Allison thought about Tristan. It wouldn't be long before the limousine would be picking up his cheerleader and taking her to the airport where he would be waiting. Together they would climb into a helicopter that would whisk them away to the Mill nestled in the northern woods. There, they'd have a quiet dinner for two. And he'd look into her eyes with that sexy stare, and kiss her....

She shook her head, trying to dismiss the image of Tristan with the lovely blond woman she had seen in the picture. They'd make a darling couple. He so dark, she so fair.

Allison was attracted to the man. There was no point in denying it. She would gladly have traded places with Shannon the cheerleader and gone off into the woods for a romantic evening for two.

Only she was here instead. In a nearly empty room with one small dog the only living creature that looked as if it wanted to spend the night with her. It was of unknown heritage. One of the Humane Society staff had said it was a mix of poodle, terrier and sheltie, but it was the color of an Irish setter. As Allison approached, the dog looked at her with the most pathetic eyes she had ever seen.

"Didn't anyone want you, either?" she crooned softly as she bent to stroke the furry head. "There must be something about Grand Canyon hair, eh?"

The dog moaned in understanding, her tiny pink tongue snaking out to lick Allison's fingers. "I wish I could take you home with me, but I can't."

"There are fifteen minutes left to complete your adoptions," a male voice announced over the speaker system.

Allison looked around, but saw no one coming toward the mutt. Her heart sank like a rock in water.

She moved the kennel closer to her work station. "There. At least you don't have to be alone while you're here."

As she sat down, she noticed a small envelope with her name written on it. A Valentine, no doubt, from the staff at the Humane Society, thanking her for volunteering to work at the orphaned pet sale.

Allison opened it to find a kiddie valentine with a picture of a dog on it, saying, "Ours is not a puppy love."

She turned it over and saw, "Be my Valentine?" It was signed: "Tristan."

A warmth spread through her and automatically she looked around the room. There, leaning against a table near the exit, was Tristan staring at her.

He wore dark denim jeans and a red sweater with a white shirt collar peeking over the neckline. In his arms he carried his green suede jacket.

"What's wrong? You look like you've seen a ghost," he said as he approached.

"What are you doing here? You're supposed to be at the airport!"

"Shannon called it off at the last minute," he told her, not looking the least bit upset that she had.

"Oh, no! And after you spent all that money!"

He shrugged. "It doesn't matter."

"I wish you had told me earlier. I might have been able to get some of it back for you."

"I tried calling your office. Jazz said you were here." He pulled his hand out from behind his back. "This is for you." He gave her a pink carnation.

"What's this for?"

"It's Valentine's Day. Don't you remember what pink carnations meant when we were in high school?"

How could she forget? Every Valentine's Day the choir had sold red, white and pink carnations that were delivered to students in their homerooms. Red meant "I love you," white signified "You're a good friend," and pink had indicated "I want to get to know you better." Allison had received three flowers in her senior year—a red one from her steady boyfriend, a white one from her best friend Gretchen and a pink one from Tristan.

"Thank you."

"I hope you're not going to trash this one."

For once she didn't blush. "No. This time I have no red one."

The dog whimpered in the kennel behind them, drawing their attention.

"His hair's the same color as yours," Tristan remarked as Allison scratched the dog's chin.

"Her," she corrected. "She's one of the few left behind." To the dog she crooned, "No one appreciates your beauty, do they?"

A wave of sentiment washed over Tristan at the sight of her nurturing the dog. "Are you thinking of taking her home?"

"I can't. It's against the landlord's rules." She looked up at Tristan. "I don't suppose you're looking for a companion?"

"I was thinking more along the lines of the two-legged kind." There was a sparkle in his eyes as he studied her shapely figure.

"A dog's less trouble. Look. She likes you," she told him when the small dog pawed the cage where Tristan stood.

Tristan couldn't resist smiling affectionately at the small animal. "You wouldn't want me. I'm not easy to live with," he said in almost a whisper.

"One of the Humane Society workers told me she was left outside the front door of a local pet hospital. She'll be obedient and loyal without much encouragement."

"I'm seldom home," he said, then made the mistake of petting the love-starved animal.

"She doesn't have any diseases."

Tristan didn't say anything. When he stopped rubbing the dog's neck, she weaseled her nose back under his hand, begging him for more attention.

"A dog this size makes a great house pet. She won't eat much and you don't have to worry about her chewing up your shoes." Allison gave him her best sales pitch. "She's not a puppy anymore."

Again, Tristan remained silent.

"She's kennel trained."

A pained expression crossed Tristan's face.

"She'll be put down if no one takes her." Allison couldn't keep the trembling from her voice.

Tristan's eyes met hers. He felt outmatched. He had not one, but two redheaded females looking at him with doe eyes. "What's her name?"

"Arizona."

He looked from Allison to the dog and back to Allison's hair, smiled, then shook his head. "You're kidding me, right?"

"See for yourself?" She held up the yellow tag hanging on the side of the metal cage. "I'm surprised no one claimed her. After all, it is Valentine's Day and she is red."

Tristan was thinking the same thing, only not about the dog. Allison was his idea of what a Valentine should be. And right now he felt as if he'd do just about anything to spend the rest of the evening with her—including buying the dog.

"I'm afraid I don't know how to care for a pet," he told her, trying not to look at either of them.

"They give you all the information you need with the adoption papers," Allison insisted.

Tristan had always lived alone and had never wanted another living thing cramping his space, yet he found himself reluctant to disappoint Allison.

"Maybe it's time I let a female into my life." He rubbed the back of his neck. "I suppose I could take her if I received the proper instructions on how to be a dog dad."

"You'll do it?" Her eyes flashed with hope.

"Only if you'll come back to my house and help me get her settled. How about it?"

Allison needed no more encouragement. She pulled a pen from her smock pocket and began filling out the adoption papers. In only a matter of minutes she announced, "You, Mr. Talbot, are now the proud owner of Arizona. Take this to the cashier and you're all set!"

Chapter Five

SHE WAS AT HIS HOUSE for the sole purpose of giving him a crash course on the care of a dog. As Allison parked her minivan behind Tristan's Lexus, she reminded herself that the only reason she was with him at all was because his real date had stood him up at the last minute.

The Valentine meant nothing. He hadn't chosen her for a romantic evening—which was obvious by his words to her when she stepped out of the car.

"I thought you said she was housebroken." Tristan stood with the door of his Lexus swung open wide, gesturing to the creature on his front seat.

"She is."

"Well, she just peed in my car."

Allison peered through the window. "Why did you let her out of her kennel?"

"She was crying."

Allison bent to find a trembling Arizona looking up at her with frightened eyes. "She's scared. Did you holler at her?" She cast an accusing glare at Tristan.

"No, I told her how proud I was that she felt so comfortable in my car she relieved herself," he drawled with heavy sarcasm.

Allison gave him one more piercing look, then gathered the tiny dog up in her arms, murmuring words of comfort. Then she attached the leash to Arizona's collar and set her down on the snowy edge of the driveway.

"It's a little late for that," Tristan said a bit churlishly.

Allison paid no attention, then gave him a smug look as the dog squatted. "Good girl, Arizona."

Tristan turned his attention to the car, removing the cumbersome kennel and the pet supplies he had purchased at Allison's suggestion. While he fumbled with the house keys, Arizona's legs appeared to weaken beneath her, one forepaw lifting pathetically.

"What's wrong with her?" Tristan asked as the dog emitted a low moan. "I thought you said she was healthy?"

"She is. She's just cold." Allison picked her up and cuddled her in her arms.

Tristan shoved the door open, the kennel clunking awkwardly against the doorjamb as he reached for the light switch.

"Can I put her down?" Allison asked as light flooded the kitchen.

Tristan slanted a wary look at her. "If she's *housebroken,* she can have the run of the place."

Allison set the dog down and watched her timidly explore her new surroundings.

"She's doing an awful lot of sniffing," Tristan said in a concerned voice.

"Relax. She's just checking out the place. Haven't you ever had a dog?"

Tristan shook his head. "My mother wouldn't allow any pets in the house—not even fish."

"And after you moved into your own place?"

"Never had the time for one. I traveled around so much with my work, I didn't think it would be fair to the animal."

"Then you really don't know what to do?"

"No, but I have a feeling I'll learn real fast," he said dryly.

And he did. Allison ran through the basics of feeding, exercising, and caring for Arizona. After only a short time in the house, the dog was as at home as Tristan. Aluminum pie tins served as water and food dishes, and an old flannel shirt became a blanket in Arizona's kennel.

"Maybe we should take her for a walk," Allison suggested when the dog ran circles through the living room, dining room, and kitchen. "She has an awful lot of energy."

"She's probably excited to be with me," Tristan said cheekily. "I have that effect on women—they run."

Allison snickered, then said, "You'd run, too, if you'd been kenneled most of the day."

Arizona's shyness had totally disappeared by the time she trotted outside. She tugged at the leash, wanting her freedom to run in the freshly fallen snow. Tristan suggested they take her to the park around the corner.

There, he and Allison sat on a bench beneath a full moon and watched the red-haired mutt romp in the snow. When she tackled a drift that held her captive, it was Tristan who rushed to her rescue.

Back at the house, they warmed themselves in front of the fire.

For Allison it was all very cozy and romantic. Unexpectedly, the day had turned out better than any Valentine fantasy she could have planned for the two of them.

"How about if I take you to dinner?" Tristan suggested as they sipped hot chocolate in front of the crackling logs. "It's the least I can do to repay you for your help with Arizona."

Repay you for your help. His words were a reality check. He was her client, not a date.

"You probably shouldn't leave Arizona alone," she told him, reaching for her jacket.

"We don't have to go out. I can make us something." He caught her wrist and gently eased her jacket away from her.

"You're offering to cook dinner for me?"

"Is there anything wrong with that?" He set her jacket aside and took both of her hands in his.

He looked as if he wanted to kiss her and the thought of his lips on hers made Allison all tingly. "Have you forgotten what day it is?" she asked.

His smile was as seductive as his gaze. "It's Valentine's Day—all the more reason why neither one of us should eat alone."

Allison extracted her hands from his and jammed them into her pockets, thinking she'd be able to think more clearly if he wasn't touching her. It didn't help. The mere thought of those hands on her skin made her weak.

When she didn't say anything, he asked, "What do you say? Can you have dinner with me or is there a knight waiting to take you on your own romantic fantasy tonight?"

She shook her head. "I quit believing in fantasies a long time ago."

"That's a shame, Allison. Every woman should have a little fantasy in her life." He reached out and traced the contour of her cheek.

Just when Allison thought she would finally feel his lips on hers, he turned her around. "You sit here in front of the fire and I'll see what I can do."

"But I was the one who was supposed to see that your Valentine's Day was special," she protested.

"It will be. Don't worry," he told her, then disappeared into the kitchen.

Arizona came to sit beside her, resting her tiny head on Allison's knee. Allison looked about the living room decorated in a Southwestern style. There were books everywhere, and she smiled to herself as she noticed a mystery that was a favorite of hers.

When Tristan returned, he carried a serving tray with two tall glasses and a pitcher filled with a red liquid. Around his wrist were two paper leis, one purple, the other orange.

"This is the closest I can get to Polynesian," he said, dropping down beside her.

A delicious warmth spread through her as Allison realized that he hadn't forgotten which of the fantasy dates she would have chosen.

He set the silver tray on the coffee table, then draped a purple lei around her neck. "Aloha. Welcome to my luau."

Allison thought he was going to kiss her on both cheeks and was unprepared for the exquisite pleasure of his lips sliding over hers. She shuddered as he eased his tongue into her mouth slowly, deliberately.

When the kiss finally ended, she whispered, "Aloha."

"There's no one who's going to give me a black eye for that, is there?" he asked.

She shook her head and smiled.

"Good." He filled the tall glasses with the red liquid and handed one to her. "Island punch."

She took a sip of the drink. "Mmm. I like this. What's in it?"

"Stuff," was all he said before disappearing into the kitchen again. He made several more trips, then dimmed the lights and put a CD on the sound system. Hawaiian music filled the air.

"Are you ready to roast the pig?" he asked as he sat down beside her.

Allison nodded.

Tristan opened the fireplace screen and poked at the burning wood. Then he speared a hot dog with one of the forks and handed it to her.

"Be careful. The fire's hot."

Arizona lay sprawled close by, oblivious to the pair of them kneeling side by side in front of the fireplace roasting wieners. The wood popped and the hot dogs hissed while Don Ho sang "Tiny Bubbles."

"Here's some bread for your pork." He passed her a bun when her hot dog was blackened. "Want a little poi?" he asked, offering her the mustard dispenser. "And of course barbecue sauce." He passed her the catsup.

Allison didn't think she could have enjoyed herself more if they had actually gone to the Polynesian room. They drank lots of Island punch, ate fruit shish kebabs consisting of fresh pineapple, maraschino cherries and marshmallows and later dipped tortilla chips in salsa, because Tristan had a craving for salsa, Hawaiian or not.

She could see that just as he had been in high school, Tristan *was* different from other men; but it was a good kind of different. He wasn't afraid of being himself, and she knew that this Valentine's Day would be one she would never forget.

After dinner he gave her three choices for entertainment. They could pretend the carpet was sand and hula in their bare feet. He could get the broom and make a limbo stick. Or they could play a video game.

Having two left feet and being about as limber as a rock, Allison opted for the video game in which knights roamed the forests surrounding a castle, slaying dragons and thieves. They played for hours, with the high point coming when Allison's knight finally reached the king's treasure ahead of Tristan's.

"I did it! I finally did it!" she boasted.

"You've played this before, haven't you?" he accused.

"No, I swear, I only use my PC for work. But now that I know how much fun this is, I'm going to get me one of these," she declared, her cheeks flushed. "This is fun."

"*You're* fun," Tristan said with a look in his dark eyes that gave Allison the crazy sensation that he was reaching out and touching her skin.

"Whew! It's warm in here, isn't it?" She fanned herself with the palm of her hand, then glanced at her watch. "O-o-oh. Look at the time. I should get going."

"Maybe I should take you. You've had enough Island punch to activate a volcano."

"And you haven't?"

He gave her a smile that was an admission of guilt. "Plan B. You could stay the night."

"I think I'd better go." She stood, then immediately dropped back down into the chair, a hand on her head. "What was in that punch?"

"I told you. Stuff."

"Stuff that's going to make it difficult for me to get around on my own." She gave him an accusing glare.

"I'm sorry."

She eyed him warily. "I'm not sure you are."

"I wouldn't lie to you, Allison."

She wanted to believe him, but she couldn't ignore the suspicion that he had hoped she'd stay the night. With him. In his bed.

"You can have my room. I'll sleep out here," he said, chinking away at her mistrust. "The sofa pulls out into a bed."

"I don't think that's a good idea," she told him. Not because she didn't trust him. But because she didn't trust herself. When he turned those searching dark eyes on her...

"I don't have a change of clothes."

"I can loan you a shirt to sleep in."

"I don't have a toothbrush, either."

"I have an extra." He gave her an endearing smile. "It's cold outside. Wouldn't you rather crash here? Arizona would feel better, I'm sure."

Allison glanced to where the dog lay sleeping. She hadn't moved since the wiener roast had ended.

She probably wouldn't move all night. The question was, Should *she* move?

"I have to be to work by nine," she told him.

"I'm up every morning at six-thirty."

"I could take a cab and come get my car tomorrow." With each protest, her voice grew weaker.

She didn't want to go and he knew it.

He took her by the hand and led her down the hallway to his room. It was decorated in gold and black. Everything looked big—the bed, the dresser, the armoire.

"Here. You can sleep in this." He handed her a Dodgers T-shirt. "The bathroom's in there." He pointed to another door.

Then he bent his head and kissed her on the lips—a very soft, gentle kind of kiss that was nothing like the kiss he had given her in front of the fire.

He was holding back, and Allison didn't like the fact that he was pulling away from her. She wanted to feel his hands in her hair, his heart beating close to hers.

As he turned to go, she stopped him. "Tristan?"

"Yes?"

"You're pretty good with the fantasy stuff."

She was staring at him with such an inviting look in her eyes, Tristan had to use all of his willpower not to throw her on the bed and show her exactly what *his* fantasy was. But the truth was, he had made the punch stronger than he'd intended.

Tonight was not the night to show her what their fantasy could be. It had been as perfect a Valentine's Day as he could have wished for. He'd discovered that what he felt for Allison was more than an infatuation. He was falling in love with her, and there was only one thing to do: be a knight and wait for his lady.

So instead of pulling her back into his arms and onto his bed, he simply smiled affectionately, then said, "Good night, Grand Canyon."

IT WASN'T AN ALARM that woke Allison the following morning. It was the sound of metal scraping against concrete.

She scrambled off the king-size bed and lifted the corner of the shade. Tristan was outside shoveling the snow that had fallen while they slept. Her car was nowhere in sight. She could see Arizona frolicking in the snow, still running circles around Tristan. He did have that effect on women, Allison mused, as she let the shade fall back into place.

The aroma of fresh coffee tickled her nose. It led her to the kitchen where she found not only coffee, but a plate of iced sweet rolls.

The temptation was too much to resist. Allison poured a cup of coffee and helped herself to a raspberry-filled bismarck. She was in the middle of devouring it when Tristan came in, bringing with him a gust of cold air.

"You're up," he commented. "Did you sleep well?"

"Yes." Suddenly self-conscious about her lack of dress, she tugged on the hem of the T-shirt.

"I see you found breakfast."

Her half-eaten bismarck sat on the table beside her cup. She nodded shyly. "You make good coffee."

"I have an appointment this morning, otherwise I'd offer to take you out for some real food," he said, shrugging out of his jacket without taking his eyes off her.

"This is fine. Actually, it's more than I usually have. Where's Arizona?"

A look of alarm crossed his face. He quickly pushed the door back open and whistled.

There was relief in Tristan's grin when the tiny dog came running inside. "She didn't want to come in, she was having so much fun." Snow splattered in every direction as Arizona shook herself vigorously.

"She's all wet! You'd better dry her off or she's going to make a mess."

Tristan disappeared, then returned with a fluffy yellow towel and began rubbing the quivering animal. As he lifted her into his arms, Allison could see that Arizona's underside was one mass of compacted snow.

"The poor little thing. She's all ice!"

"I had no idea," Tristan said apologetically, gently tugging at the ice balls.

"Look at her! She's freezing to death." Allison tried to pull the ice away, but it was a futile effort. "You know what we need? A hair dryer."

"Follow me," Tristan told her, leading her back into the master bath.

Allison plugged in the dryer and aimed a stream of warm air at the dog. With tender care, she worked the clumps of ice free while Tristan cradled Arizona in his lap. They worked together, carefully removing the snowy chunks until the mahogany red coat was dry.

Returning to her usual spunkiness, Arizona jumped off Tristan's lap and went tearing out of the bathroom.

"You made it through your first crisis," Allison observed.

"I think we'll limit our outdoor activities to necessary trips," Tristan told her.

"Or you could buy her a doggie sweater." She unplugged the dryer and put it back in the cupboard.

What had seemed like a large bathroom to Allison when she'd been in it all alone now seemed cramped. It was hot and steamy from using the blow dryer, yet she knew that the heat wasn't only a result of Arizona's mishap.

Her eyes met Tristan's in the mirror. There was a startled, sexual awareness there. She was standing in his personal bathroom with only a T-shirt covering her naked body.

"You're all wet," he said, his voice husky.

"So are you." Arizona had made a mess of Tristan's shirt and tie. "You can't go to work like that."

"Neither can you," he said with a devilish grin.

She looked down and saw what she already knew—that a wet T-shirt left little to the imagination.

She'd known all along that she and Tristan were like a chemical reaction waiting to happen. Ever since he had walked into her office, they had been two substances waiting for the right catalyst to cause spontaneous combustion. Little had she expected that a dog would be that catalyst.

Allison felt a rush of emotions. Tenderness, for the way he had handled Arizona, irritation over the way he had plied her with Island punch, forcing her to stay overnight, and now a nearly uncontrollable longing because of the way he was looking at her.

It was the way he used to look at her in high school. As if she were the most beautiful girl he had ever seen. As if he wanted to cherish her forever and ever. As if he loved her.

He couldn't love her and she wasn't going to go to bed with him. No matter how he looked at her.

"We'd better change," she said, quickly stepping out of the bathroom. Unfortunately the room she stepped into was Tristan's bedroom and he was right behind her.

And the look in his eyes said he would be perfectly willing to help her change out of her wet T-shirt. It was a look that sent a sweet arousal spiraling through her.

"I'll just pick up my things and get out of your way," she said, grabbing her clothing as fast as she could—shirt, sweater, jeans, panty hose. She flung everything over one arm and headed toward the door.

"You forgot something."

She halted, and slowly turned around. Dangling from his finger was her lacy black bra.

Tristan didn't want to tease her, but those tousled red curls and her wary blue eyes were eating holes in his willpower. Ever since she had come back into his life he hadn't been able to think of anything but making love to her.

It was no use denying it. His high school crush had become a full-blown case of head-over-heels love.

She needed a man, someone who'd cherish her and watch out for her and build a house with a picket fence for her. Someone who liked to play the same games as she did. Someone like Tristan.

That was why, when she slowly walked toward him, he said, "You don't really want to get dressed, do you?"

"We'll be late for work," she protested, but her voice was soft and seductive.

"I don't care," he answered, pressing his body against hers so that she could feel his erection.

"But you have an appointment," she said weakly.

"This is more important," he told her, then kissed her with a fierceness that told her just how important.

The moment their lips met he knew he was lost. She tasted like coffee and raspberries. When his tongue touched hers, she whimpered with wordless longing.

She dropped her clothes at his feet as her arms slid around his waist. She tilted her head back, returning his kiss with a passion that matched his—and he knew that she wanted him as much as he wanted her.

It was his fantasy come true. She was in his arms, he had his fingers in her silky red curls, and he was kissing every inch of her gorgeous face.

"I've waited eighteen years for this," he murmured against her skin.

"I hope it was worth the wait."

For an answer, he lifted her up and settled her on the rumpled covers of the bed. He liked the way she looked lying there. Soft. Vulnerable. Sexy.

She wanted him. It was there in her eyes—the same hunger that was making his blood dance. He hadn't been wrong when he thought he had seen that look last night.

His already-loosened tie went sailing over his head, his buttons nearly popped as he tugged at his shirt. She watched him undress, the desire in her blue eyes adding to the urgency of his movements.

When he joined her on the bed, there was nothing between them but the Dodgers T-shirt. She rose to her knees to take it off, but his hands stopped her.

Running his palms over her thighs and hips, he slid his hands under the shirt. Her skin was hot and smooth, her body quivering in reaction to his fingers' languorous journey. Needing to see what his mind could only imagine, he slowly eased the shirt up over her head.

He gazed at her naked flesh. "And I thought your hair was breathtaking," he murmured in awe.

He kissed her, then touched her lips with his thumb. "I knew what this would taste like, but..."

He moved his thumb to her breast, where it brushed the nipple, "This..."

She clutched his shoulders, moaning as his mouth closed over the peak of one breast. He caressed her until she was breathing as quickly as he was. Then he kissed her again, his hands moving down her sides, across her stomach, down between her legs, where his fingers found more silky red curls.

She moved restlessly, arching as his fingers explored soft, hot flesh. Tristan ached with a hunger that pulsed as strong as his heartbeat. He didn't want to rush, but she was burning away his self-control.

"There's no hurry," he whispered when her legs parted eagerly.

"Oh, yes, there is," she said desperately. "I need you."

He was quickly inside her, pushing slowly and steadily until she was moving with him in a rhythmic pulsing. There was something almost familiar about the way their bodies fit together. It felt good, it felt right, and Tristan didn't want it to ever end.

He needed to be in control, to be the one giving her pleasure, to have everything happen at his speed. Only Allison had a tempo of her own, one that caught him totally by surprise. Strong inner muscles tightened around him in spasms of pleasure.

Tristan shuddered, groaning at the effect of her caress. He gave up thinking. For once in his life, he gave in to his feelings.

Allison cried out, clinging to him as her body convulsed. There was a look of triumph in her wide eyes as Tristan swiftly followed her to ecstasy.

Overwhelmed by the pleasure he had shared with her, Tristan found himself unable to speak.

"Something happened. I've never felt so..." she said breaking the silence. How could she tell him she had felt loved when he hadn't said that he loved her?

He cradled her in his arms, nestling her head against his shoulder. "If I had known it would be like this, it wouldn't have taken me eighteen years to find you again."

With lips still swollen, she brushed her mouth across his. "I don't think I would have been ready for this eighteen years ago." She rolled over and sighed. "I'm not sure I'm ready for it now."

He propped himself up on one elbow and gazed into her eyes. "We'll take it slow, if that's the way you want it."

She smiled. "Do you think that's possible?"

His eyes gleamed devilishly. "No, but I thought it was the knightly thing to say."

Just then the phone rang.

Tristan closed his eyes as his head fell back against the pillow. "Reality check. We can't stay here all day, can we?" he asked.

Suddenly chilled, Allison pulled the sheet up over her naked body. "Aren't you going to answer it?"

Tristan groaned as his fingers inched their way toward the phone on the nightstand. Before he could reach it, however, his message machine took the call.

"Tristan, it's Ginger. Ralph wanted me to call and remind you that the meeting with Hobson Construction is at the government center, room 306. If you haven't left yet, give me a call. There's been a change in the agenda."

Tristan grabbed Allison from behind and nuzzled her neck. "See what you do to me? I would have forgotten about that meeting if my secretary hadn't called."

"I'm sorry."

He turned her around to face him, cupping her chin in his fingertips. "I'm not."

The look in his eyes sent another wave of desire crashing through her. Uncomfortable with the amount of power he had over her emotions, she eased out of his arms.

They dressed quickly, with little conversation. Tristan seemed preoccupied and doubts crept into Allison's thoughts. Had she been wrong to let this man become so important to her in such a short time?

She wished he would say something about their unexpected Valentine's Day pleasure, to tell her what it had meant to him. She wanted him to say that it had been the best Valentine's Day ever, because it had been the best for her.

Only he didn't say anything. As he backed their cars out of the garage, there was no sign of the Tristan who had carried a wet dog lovingly in his arms. Allison wondered if she had imagined that he had ever looked at her as if she were as important as the air he breathed. He was all pinstripes and business now.

He held the door for her as she climbed into her van. "I hate rushing off like this," he said, bending close to her. "Can I see you tonight?"

"If you want."

"I want," he said huskily, and for just one moment Allison saw a look in his eye that made her think she hadn't made a mistake, after all.

"YOU'RE LATE. You've had at least a dozen messages, including three from Tristan Talbot," Jazz told Allison when she arrived at the office.

Allison couldn't prevent the flush that spread across her cheeks. She flipped through the pile of pink slips Jazz handed her, avoiding her office mate's inquisitive stare.

"Where were you last night? I tried calling until after midnight and there was no answer."

"I had dinner with an old friend," Allison answered, exchanging her snow boots for a pair of black pumps. "I thought you had plans with Toby."

"So did I. But it turns out I have the most unromantic fiancé in the state of Minnesota. Do you know where he was last night? Bowling! I could have killed him."

"I thought Monday was his bowling night."

"It is, but he subs for the Tuesday-night league and someone called and asked him to fill in for him.

Can you believe it? He bowled so some other guy could spend Valentine's Day with his girlfriend."

"Couldn't you have done something after bowling?"

Jazz thrust her hands onto her hips. "I'm not going to be second best to a bowling ball, Alli. I should have listened to you. If men are single at our age, it's because they're in retarded adolescence. All it is is games, games, and more games."

Allison wanted to tell her about Tristan, but she couldn't get a word in. Jazz was talking nonstop, pacing the floor, her hands gesturing wildly.

"I should have given him back his ring. I mean, am I always going to take a back seat to his sports? I don't know why he even proposed to me. You won't need to worry about sitting home alone on Friday and Saturday nights. We'll do fun stuff together."

Allison experienced a twinge of guilt. She was grateful when the phone rang, giving her an excuse to turn to her work.

Only it wasn't a client, but Tristan on the line.

"I just called to tell you it couldn't have been a better Valentine's Day for me," he said in a voice that sent a shiver of pleasure through her.

"I'm glad you enjoyed yourself."

"Enjoyed myself is an understatement." His words made her body tingle at the memory of their lovemaking.

"That's nice to hear," she answered pleasantly, aware that Jazz could hear every word she uttered.

"You haven't changed your mind about coming over this evening, have you?"

"No. What time is good for you?"

"If you come right after work I'll take you out to dinner at a real restaurant this time."

"That sounds nice. I can be there by six-thirty."

"Great. I'll see you then."

"Who was that?" Jazz asked when Allison hung up the receiver. "Your face was red the whole time you were talking."

Allison knew there was no point in lying. "That was Tristan."

"He had so much fun with the cheerleader he wants to plan another date?"

"Actually, he didn't go out with the cheerleader. She canceled at the last minute," she replied, pretending to be searching for something in her drawer.

"Wait a minute! He's not the old friend you went out to dinner with last night, is he?" Jazz's eyes widened.

"We didn't go out."

"But you were with him."

"He came by the animal sale and bought a dog. I stopped by his place to show him what needed to be done. He's never had a dog before."

"Yeah, right."

"It's true."

"Alli, every boy's had a dog at one time or another. You don't need to make excuses about seeing him. I thought there was something different about you this morning. You had a dreamy-eyed look on your face when you came in."

Allison went over to the copy machine and made a duplicate of a paper that should have been in her trash just so Jazz wouldn't see the blush on her cheeks.

"So, Tristan turned out to be a knight, after all," her office mate mused aloud.

"For Pete's sake. We played with a dog and ate hot dogs," Allison exclaimed.

"I know you've always said you weren't going to make the mistake of falling for a good-looking man again, but I think you should make an exception with this particular man."

"I haven't fallen for him," she protested, knowing perfectly well that she was dangerously close to doing just that. "We simply have **a** lot in common."

"Oh, you mean all those high school memories."

"Leave it alone, Jazz."

"Oh, and the chess."

"Don't you have work to do?"

Jazz didn't bring up the subject of Tristan Talbot for the rest of the day. She didn't have to. Allison's thoughts were filled with him without any help at all.

Chapter Six

"YOU CAME."

The uncertainty in Tristan's eyes boosted Allison's confidence.

"Why wouldn't I?" she asked, handing him her coat.

Before he could answer, Arizona came yapping into the vestibule, jumping up and slathering Allison's legs with her wet tongue.

She had no choice but to turn her attention to the lovable dog. "I'm glad to see she's still alive." She glanced up at Tristan with a teasing smile.

"So far, so good." He hung up her coat in the front closet, then said, "I'm glad you're here."

"Me, too."

"There are so many things I want to tell you, but first..." He disappeared briefly, then returned carrying a cardboard tube.

"What's this?" she asked when he handed it to her.

"It's for you. One of the fellows at work had it hanging in his office. He had to take it down to make room for something else so I took it for you."

Allison unscrewed the top and pulled out the roll of paper inside. When she opened it, she gasped. It was a poster-size photo of the 1992 Winter Carnival Ice Palace.

"It's wonderful," she gushed. "Thank you." Automatically, she reached for him and planted a kiss on his lips. It was only meant to be a brief brushing of his mouth, but once their lips met, passion flared. Tristan kissed her so thoroughly, she felt like she was dissolving in the heat of his embrace.

"Maybe we should eat first." His voice sounded rough.

"Do you really want to?"

"Uh-uh."

Clothing fell to the floor as they stumbled their way into the bedroom. They made love with a passion Allison never knew she possessed.

When it was over, they clung to each other contentedly.

"I don't want to ever get up," Tristan said with a deep sigh.

"Me, neither." She felt like purring, she was so happy. "Unfortunately, Arizona is crying."

Tristan closed his eyes and grimaced. "I hope she's not at the back door. Maybe it'll stop."

When the whining didn't stop, he rolled over and flung his arm across his forehead. "I have to get up. I don't dare let her out alone."

"I'll keep the sheets warm," she said, rubbing against him shamelessly before he got up.

"Maybe you should get dressed," he told her as he pulled on his pants. "I'm supposed to take you out to dinner."

"Why don't you let me make something for you?"

"I'm afraid there's not much in the refrigerator."

"I'll take a look. If I think it looks like an impossible task, I'll let you take me to dinner. I'd really rather not have to go out in the cold if we don't have to."

He bent to give her a quick kiss. "Me, too. There's a silk robe in the closet. I'll be back in a couple of minutes."

Allison swung open the walk-in closet door and turned on the light. Everything smelled of his cologne. A heady sensation warmed her as she slid into the burgundy-and-navy silk robe.

She wrapped the smooth fabric around her naked body, loving the feel of silk and the scent of Tristan that enveloped her. While she was in the closet, the phone rang. She debated whether or not she should answer it. Just as she was about to pick up the receiver, Tristan's answering machine came on.

"Tris. It's Alec. Just calling to see if you scored with your Valentine's date. Call and let me know if you really were Mr. Romance."

Allison's stomach felt as if she'd been riding too long on the Tilt-A-Whirl. Tristan's interest in her had been nothing but a game. That's why he had seemed indifferent to selecting his date for Valentine's Day. He was only doing it because of a bet. And when the date had canceled out, he'd needed to find a quick substitute—*her!*

Allison stood in the middle of his bedroom disappointed, hurt and humiliated. She wanted to leave, yet she seemed incapable of moving.

Then anger took over and she threw off the silk robe. She was dressed in record time, not caring that she had misbuttoned her blouse or that her panty hose were on inside out. All she wanted was to leave and leave fast.

Fortunately, Arizona was taking her time doing her business outside, and Allison was out the door and headed for her car before Tristan noticed her.

"Allison! What are you doing? What's happened?"

"I'm going home. You've scored. That's all you needed me for, so I'm leaving." She fidgeted with her keys, dropping them in the snow twice before finally getting her door unlocked.

"Wait. What are you talking about?" he demanded, running to her side with Arizona in tow.

"You know exactly what I'm talking about. But if you insist on playing dumb, go listen to your phone message." She climbed into the car and slammed the door.

He pounded on the window, but she refused to pay any attention. She started the engine and drove away.

FIFTEEN TIMES, TRISTAN had called Special Moments, and each time Jazz had answered the phone and told him Allison was unavailable, promising to have her call him back.

She hadn't. He knew she wouldn't. So he did the only thing he could do. He went to her office.

She was there. Looking as lovely as she had the first day he'd seen her. And just as she had that day, she looked at him as if he didn't belong there.

"I'd like to talk to you," he said, aware of Jazz watching him closely.

"I have a client due any minute." Allison's tone was cold as stone.

"Then I'll make an appointment to see you."

"I'm booked."

"What about lunch?"

"No good."

"Dinner?"

"No."

He sighed. "Come on, Allison. This isn't high school. You can't run into the girls' bathroom to hide from me."

"Ah... Alli, I think I'm going to step out for a minute," Jazz announced uncomfortably, getting to her feet. "Take my calls for me, will you?" She looked warily from Tristan to Allison.

"I don't want you here, Tristan," Allison said when they were alone.

"I can explain about the Valentine's Day bet."

"Explain what? That grown men found it cute to advertise for a date to see who could 'score'?"

"It wasn't like that."

"Did you or did you not put the ad in the paper because of a bet?"

"I did, but—"

"And did you or did you not hire me to plan this romantic evening so that you could win that bet?"

"I did, but—"

Before he could finish, the door opened and an elderly gentleman entered. "You'll have to excuse me now. My client is here," Allison said to Tristan.

"I'm not leaving until I've finished," Tristan said stubbornly.

"Is this young man bothering you?" The senior citizen stepped forward in Allison's defense.

"No, Mr. Watkins. It's all right. He's leaving."

Tristan had no choice but to go or risk having some old guy beat him with his cane. However, before he left he announced in no uncertain terms: "We're not finished, Allison."

"YOU'RE LEAVING TOWN?" Jazz stared at the suitcase next to Allison's desk.

"I'm going to visit Heidi."

"Why? Because you don't want to have to face Tristan Talbot?"

"Tristan has nothing to do with it," she lied.

"And what do I tell him when he calls for you?"

"Tell him the same thing you tell my other clients. I'm out of town."

"He's going to be here when you come back, you know."

"Maybe."

"There's no maybe about it. I saw the way he looked at you when he was here. He's bonkers for you."

"Yeah, right."

"Good grief! What did the poor guy do? One minute you're all dreamy eyed over him, the next you're ready to carve his heart out and feed it to the wolves for breakfast."

"The poor guy used me to win a bet! He's no better than any of the other dirt bags I've been dating lately," Allison said, close to tears.

"What are you talking about?"

Allison briefly explained the message she had heard when Tristan had been outside with the dog. "I should have realized there was something suspicious about him from the start. He *was* too good to be true."

"Are you sure about all of this? I mean, if you haven't given him a chance to explain, maybe you have this bet thing all wrong."

"I don't. He admitted to me that he hired me to plan a romantic Valentine's Day so that he could win some contest with his friends. When his newspaper date fell through, he substituted me so that he wouldn't lose."

"Oh." Jazz grimaced.

"And why are you defending him, anyway? Just yesterday you told me you were swearing off all men, thanks to Toby's insensitivity."

"That was before he spent two hours in the cold under my car fixing my brakes. Besides, you know I can't stay mad at him."

"Well, I can stay mad at Tristan and I will," she declared emotionally. "If you want to be friendly to him, you go right ahead."

Jazz decided to take Allison at her word. As soon as her friend had driven away in her minivan, she called Tristan Talbot.

"Hi. It's Jasmine Connors. You know, Allison's friend. How would you like to have lunch with me today?"

IT WAS AWFUL. It was probably the most awful thing Tristan had to admit. His competitive streak had cost him a woman. And not just any woman, but the woman of his dreams. The one woman he hadn't been afraid to relinquish his control to. The only woman to ever beat him at a video game.

He should never have gone through with the Valentine's Day ad once he had met Allison. He should have asked her out to dinner, bought her candy, and sent her flowers—treated her like a woman instead of the girl who had scorned him in high school.

But the truth of the matter was he had been too afraid that she would treat him the same way she had all those years ago; that she would run and hide from him and he'd feel like a fool. Instead of risking her rejection, he had tried to be cool.

So he had gone ahead and let her believe that he wanted to date some fluffy cheerleader. He had even gone so far as to pay for the arrangements when he had known all along that he wasn't going to use them. Was it any wonder that Allison thought she was a stand-in for the date that never happened?

"You don't look so hot, Fourteen." Jazz plunked down across from Tristan in the coffee-shop booth.

"I struck out good, didn't I?"

"Maybe you'll get another chance to bat." She studied the luncheon menu. "Ms. Organized I've-Got-My-Life-on-a-Schedule left town without canceling her appointments."

"She's gone?"

Jazz nodded. "I've never seen her like this. I figure she must be in love."

His face brightened. "She won't talk to me."

"Not yet."

"Do you have any suggestions on how I can change that?"

"That depends."

"On what?"

"Whether you want to talk to her because she was wrong to think you used her or whether you simply want to see her again because she's a romance consultant."

"I'm in love with her, Jazz. I have been ever since I walked into English class and saw her twirling a bright red curl with her finger."

"Have you told her that?"

"There wasn't time. You saw how she was."

Jazz nodded in understanding. "And then she ran away."

Tristan chuckled. "She always did. She spent more time in the bathroom than any other girl in the senior class."

Jazz studied him carefully, then pulled a business card from her pocket. "Here's the address."

"She's in Iowa?"

"At her sister Heidi's place. She always runs to Heidi. Allison thinks she's the only one who understands her."

"Go home."

Allison looked at her slight, sandy-haired sister in stunned disbelief. How could Heidi say such a thing to her after everything she had been through?

Heidi was the one who had always understood all her man troubles. She had always empathized with her when it came to bashing the men of this world.

She was older than Allison and still single. She was a soul sister besides being her flesh and blood. How could she advise her to go home?

"Haven't you been listening to what I've been saying?" Allison cried out in frustration.

"It's because I have been listening that I'm telling you to go home."

"I can't."

"Why not?"

"Because he's there. He follows me everywhere. Looking at me with that... that look in his eye."

"Men in love behave that way at times. Some women actually like it," Heidi said dryly.

"Not us Parker women. We're strong, independent, refuse-to-be-trampled-on women."

"Which is why you're hiding out in Dubuque, Iowa."

Allison's spine stiffened. "I'm not hiding. I came because I thought you'd understand."

"What I understand is the man's spending a fortune on long-distance calls just to hear me say you won't come to the phone."

Allison twisted her red curls. "I wish he'd go back to California."

A look of dismay crossed Heidi's heart-shaped face. "You're not going to stay here until he moves, are you?"

"I've only been here two days."

Two days became three, three became four. Then two things happened that made Allison decide it was time to leave.

One was the arrival of a tall, lanky man who kissed Heidi very thoroughly and dropped his luggage in her bedroom as if it were the natural place for it to be. Geoff Sanders, Allison learned, was soon to become her brother-in-law.

The other was a cryptoquip that came in the mail, addressed to Allison. There was no letter attached, no return address, only a St. Paul postmark.

The clue said that *t* equalled *a*. Allison curled up on Heidi's sofa and worked the puzzle. The answer read: Mr. Romance was the one who canceled the date, not the cheerleader. The reason: The only way his Valentine fantasy would come true was if he dated his romance consultant.

Allison packed her bags.

TRISTAN WAS COLD and cranky. It was close to midnight, and ever since Jazz had phoned him earlier in the day to tell him that Allison was on her way home, he had been outside working.

He wouldn't be surprised if several different parts of his anatomy were frostbitten. He had tried hand warmers, toe warmers, and even a seat warmer. Nothing had kept the cold from penetrating deep into his bones.

He only hoped that Jazz was right and his efforts weren't going to be for nothing. If Allison didn't return tomorrow and the temperatures rose above freezing . . .

He didn't want to think about it. He wouldn't think about it.

He stretched out on the army cot that had served as both a bed and a desk while he had been working. He was going to have to work all night if he was to finish the ice palace by the time she returned tomorrow.

He closed his eyes, visualizing what she would say when she saw him, how she'd melt his cold heart . . . and any other cold parts that needed thawing. And then he fell asleep.

IT WAS AFTER MIDNIGHT when Allison reached the outskirts of the metropolitan area. Heidi had warned her to wait until morning before starting home, but once Allison had her mind made up to do something, she did it.

She needed to see Tristan. To talk to him calmly, honestly. To hear everything he had to say about Valentine's Day. To tell him she loved him.

As much as she wanted to deny her feelings for him, deep in her heart she couldn't. Until a week ago, she would have thought he could do nothing that would be romantic.

But that was before he created a luau out of hot dogs and paper leis. Before he gave her a pink carnation and a kiddie Valentine. Before he bought a dog he didn't want because it had hair the color of the Grand Canyon.

Before . . .

She slowed the minivan to a crawl as she headed down her street. Something loomed in the front yard of the fourplex where she lived.

It was only as she drew nearer that she could make out its shape. Allison gasped. She had just parked her minivan in front of a miniature ice palace.

It wasn't until she climbed out of the minivan that she noticed Tristan's Lexus was parked across the street.

Cautiously, Allison approached the ice structure, amazed at how close it was in shape to the ice palace she and Tristan had put together at the jigsaw-puzzle contest. Except this ice castle was dollhouse size.

And it wasn't finished. As she walked around behind, she saw that part of the back wall was missing. Peeking inside, she saw Tristan asleep on a cot.

"Mr. Romance," she said aloud, her heart swelling with love for him.

As if he heard, he stirred. When he saw her, he jumped to his feet. "You're not supposed to be here until tomorrow."

"You want me to leave?"

For an answer, he climbed out of the castle and wrapped his arms around her. "I had hoped that after Valentine's Day you'd never run away from me again."

"I'm sorry. I was afraid. Of you. Of my feelings."

"And now?"

"I love you." It came as simply as if she'd said, "It's cold out here." "Did you do this for me?" she asked, tears threatening to rob her of speech as she stared at the castle.

"It was the only way I knew to try to convince you that I can be a knight for you."

"You *are* a knight. And judging from the way you look, your armor is frozen," she whispered close to his face.

"Some parts, maybe, but not all of it." He grinned. "I love you, Allison Parker."

"Come on, Mr. Romance." She led him by the hands up the steps of the fourplex. "I'm going to melt your heart. And a few other parts."

"What about the castle?"

"We'll move the bed next to the window and look at it from inside."

Tristan brushed a kiss across her lips. "My kind of woman."

Postscript

"THERE'S A PACKAGE from Special Moments," Doris announced as she sorted through Dr. Baker's mail.

"I haven't seen Allison since her checkup in January."

"Should I open it?"

The dentist nodded, watching with interest as Doris's pudgy fingers ripped the end of the padded mailer.

"It's a box," she stated the obvious, then read the gold letters on top. "Allison and Tristan are tying the knot."

"Well, I'll be," Dr. Baker declared in amusement.

Doris opened the box and found a gold ribbon tied in a lover's knot around a piece of parchment. She slipped the parchment loose without untying the lover's knot. She read it with rapt interest. "Oh, my! Would you look at this?" Doris shoved the parchment under Dr. Baker's nose. "We're invited to a wedding."

Please join us in a celebration of romance.

WEDDING
5:00 p.m.
Saturday, July 19
St. Andrew's Church

RECEPTION
A luau at the
Excelsior Bay Yacht Club
R.S.V.P.
—Allison Parker and Tristan Talbot

SLEEPLESS IN ST. LOUIS

Tiffany White

A Note from Tiffany White

A holiday that involves my favorite things in life—pristine white tulips, rich and chewy chocolate-covered caramel-pecan candies, lace-bordered romantic mash notes and racy red teddies—is my kind of holiday. So I am thrilled to be one of the authors selected to contribute a story to *Valentine Bachelors*.

My first memory of Valentine's Day is brought back whenever I smell grade school paste. I was chosen to make the big Valentine box for our first-grade class. At six I thought more was better, and it was the gaudiest heart-bedecked wonder you can imagine. But then at six I also thought the number of Valentines one received was most important. A high body count meant I was really cool.

It was in junior high school that I discovered the more delicious thrill of the mystery Valentine. The Valentine that fantasies are spun from. Unsigned and wildly romantic, that Valentine could have come from anyone. It might have been sent by the class poet, the class jock, the class artist, the class hunk, the class brain or even the class rebel.

One can fall madly in love in junior high. It can be an unrequited, never-spoken love, or it can be like the love my heroine Elizabeth falls into—a love to last a lifetime.

Happy Valentine's Day to all my readers!

Chapter One

"A PERSONAL AD? *You!* Go on."

Gio Bonetti got up from the weight bench to let his best friend, Alec McCord, take his turn pumping iron. "You're not really going to place a personal ad in the *River City Call,* are you?"

"You bet. And guess who is going to help me write it," Alec said.

The upmarket torture chamber of chrome, mirror and the latest gym technology was crowded with men and women exercising to pulsating music. Gio's attention wandered to a curvy redhead working out on the StairMaster. And he could see every taut muscle at work, thanks to the skintight unitard she was wearing. "Doesn't sweaty skin get you hot? I swear, nothing's sexier than watching a woman in a unitard working up a sweat."

"You're supposed to be spotting me so I don't drop this two hundred pounds of dead weight across my throat," Alec reminded Gio as he wrapped his fingers around the barbell and heaved it from the rack.

"Okay, okay. Is it my fault that the gym has turned into the singles bar of the nineties? Would you look at all the gorgeous chicks. Why don't you ask one of them out, instead of placing an ad in the Personals?''

''What's wrong with placing an ad in the Personals?''

''Are you kidding? Taking a chance in the Personals is the equivalent of going out on a blind date. Haven't you ever been set up on one of those? It's a real shot in the dark. You could wind up with *anybody*. It could be a major disaster.''

Grunting, Alec finished lifting the weights over his head for the final repetition of twelve, then placed the barbell back on the rack. ''I told you— Tristan, Nicholas and I made a pact on New Year's Eve. We agreed before I returned to St. Louis from Boston that we'd advertise in the Personals for a Valentine's Day date. The three of us vowed, after winding up dateless New Year's Eve, we deserved a blowout date for Valentine's Day.''

Alec got up from the weight bench. He and Gio moved a few feet away on the bleached maple floor to finish their workout in front of a mirrored wall.

Their reflections were as different as night and day.

Dark, sexy and slight, Gio looked like the dancer he was, for his successful local bar band.

Blond and blue-eyed, Alec was taller and had one roguish dimple—two would have been overkill. His body was that of a perfectly proportioned professional athlete. A right-handed star pitcher, he'd been traded to the St. Louis Cardinals a week ago and could still throw the ball with impressive command.

"Let's see.... The perfect Valentine fantasy date..." Gio mused as the two of them selected the weights they wanted and stacked them on their respective bars. "That would have to be, say, take-out pizza, a rented video and a babe with cab fare home."

"Gio, you've been in a band too long," Alec said, shaking his head.

"Right, like baseball players don't get babes—"

"Times change. It's not like it was when I used to have a girl in every franchise city. The party's over, and frankly, I've been striking out lately. It's hard to tell what women want anymore."

"No, it's not," Gio disagreed, watching Alec jerk his barbell over his head.

Alec lowered the bar of weights to the floor and shot Gio a look.

Gio gripped his weight bar. "You're forgetting I have an advantage over you when it comes to knowing what women want."

"Because you're in a band?"

Gio tested the weight on his bar, then took several off to lighten the load. "I'm talking about the fact that I have a sister. That's my advantage. Talking with Elizabeth clues me in on women."

"Your baby sister, Elizabeth? She's a *kid*."

"My baby sister is twenty-eight years old," Gio hooted. "And according to her, every woman is looking for the 'Seattle Man.'"

"You mean that guy from the movie, *Sleepless in Seattle?*"

Gio nodded. "Yeah . . . the sensitive type."

Disgusted, Alec rolled his eyes. "Some babe dragged me to see that movie. Total fantasy. Fate, and all that garbage. Women may say they want a sensitive man, but they don't. Not really. Once they've bagged one, soon they're bored and dumping him for someone more exciting."

Alec had learned that painful truth when his own mother had left his accountant father for a race-car driver. When his father accepted a job transfer to St. Louis to get away from the memories, they had moved next door to the Bonettis. While his father had anesthetized his pain with alcohol, Alec had soaked up the warmth of the Bonetti family.

"Elizabeth says—"

"Your sister doesn't have the sense to come in out of the rain, as I recall. I was always having to rescue her. Remember that blue bicycle she used to like to ride and pretend it was her horse? One day when you were at band practice, she put on her best party dress, a long frilly number, to ride her 'horse.' She was pretending to be a princess and the skirt got tangled up in the spokes. She would have broken her fool neck, if I hadn't scooped her up before she fell."

"Elizabeth has her own travel agency now, and rides mares instead of bikes. And no guy has managed to scoop her up yet. She's way too independent, according to Mom and Dad, who are more than ready for grandchildren."

"She's stubborn, that's for sure," Alec agreed, finding himself smiling. "When she was about seven and I was teaching her to swim, she insisted she was going to marry me. She pestered me until I got her an 'engagement ring' from the gumball machine at the pool."

"I'd forgotten that," Gio said, putting his weights down with a laugh. "Though I have to admit being determined to get what she wants has paid off for her. It wasn't easy for her to build a successful travel agency by herself. We share the house we bought from Mom and Dad when they moved to Texas, but I hardly ever see her. She's always off traveling, checking out vacation spots for her clients. She left this morning to check out a new hotel in Florida."

"Maybe Elizabeth can give me some tips on St. Petersburg before I report to Spring Training on the 16th."

"The 16th? Valentine's Day is the 14th—so basically we're talking one-night stand, here," Gio surmised, keeping his eye on the redhead who'd come over to work out on the Nautilus machine.

"A *great* one-night stand." Alec wagged his eyebrows lasciviously.

"I don't think you can put that in the ad—"

"Duh. Of course, if I happened to meet Ms. Right, it could be expanded to, say, two nights— keeping in mind that I have to report on the 16th."

"Ms. Right?"

"Yeah, you know. A woman who would simplify my life, not complicate it. She'd have to be the kind of woman who'd accept my 'traditional' values."

Gio smirked at Alec's chauvinism. "Gee whiz, I think Mrs. Cleaver is already married to Ward."

"Come on, Gio. There must be a woman out there who'd like having a man who could support her. The kind of woman who'd choose not to have a career."

"Someone blond and stacked, as well," Gio teased.

"I'm more interested in someone supportive and loyal."

"Maybe you should just get a golden retriever puppy."

"I'm serious, Gio. Don't you ever get the Sunday-night blues? You know, want someone to cuddle on the sofa with a big bowl of popcorn and a movie? I sometimes think it would be a relief to have someone I could let down my guard with. I've lived alone so long, I've gotten out of the habit of conversation. I'm beginning to worry that I'm getting selfish and inflexible."

"Either you've been watching too much 'Oprah' or you've let getting stood up New Year's Eve really get to you," Gio observed wryly.

"The woman stood me up on New Year's Eve for a dog with a sore paw," Alec reminded Gio. "Any man with half a brain would have to take that as a sign."

"I'll tell you what a sign is. A sign is that woman looking that fine in a unitard," Gio said, nodding to the redhead. "Come on over to the house tonight and we'll put some burgers on the grill and work up your ad. Right now I've got to come up with the words to get Ms. Greatbody to go out with me. All this safe sex of just looking instead of touching is giving the nineties a bad buzz. Do you think she'd believe me if I told her I'd explode, if we don't have sex?"

Alec laughed out loud and shook his head.

"What?"

"Just tell her you're in a band."

"You're right. That always works."

Except this time it apparently didn't. Gio was back at Alec's side in record time.

"You're right—the nineties are starting to suck. I must be losing my touch, too," Gio complained.

"You're giving up, just like that?"

"No way am I giving up. I've only been winged, not shot down. But we're going to have to make it an early night tonight. As soon as we eat and get your ad down, I'm hitting the sheets."

"A night owl like you?"

"Word is Ms. Greatbody teaches a killer aerobics class. I'll have to be at the gym tomorrow morning before 6:00 a.m. to book it because they only reserve class-space one day in advance," Gio explained.

"Are you sure you know what you're in for?" Alec made a face.

"Hey, I'm not the one resorting to a personal ad...."

Twenty minutes later they left the gym and were confronted with one of St. Louis's sudden weather changes. Heavy, wet snow was accumulating at an amazing rate.

"It looks like someone shook one of those snow paperweights, doesn't it?" Alec said. Having played for the Los Angeles Dodgers for his entire career, he'd grown unaccustomed to seeing snow.

"Traffic is going to be one snarled mess," Gio grumbled.

IF SHE NEVER, EVER saw another snowflake, it wouldn't be too soon for her, Elizabeth muttered, stomping around her economy car and scraping the snow from the windows *again*. The flakes were as big as doilies. She was wearing pumps and her feet were stone-cold, verging on frozen. Her nose was red enough to guide Santa's reindeer and she was sore as hell from having to dig her car out of the snowdrift that some idiot—no doubt some *male* idiot—had forced her into in his haste or arrogance.

She was supposed to be in South Beach being wined and dined in style by the newest European-style luxury hotel on Ocean Drive that wanted her business. She'd been looking forward to seeing the dishy chef at Starfish on West Street that she'd been hearing so much about. Instead of his specialty—grilled lobster quesadillas with mango salsa—she was going to have to settle for whatever was in the fridge, since the blizzard had canceled her flight and her plans.

Her windows sufficiently cleared, she got in her car and maneuvered out into the traffic, which was moving at a snail's pace.

Nothing was going right.

Ever since Gio had told her Alec McCord had gotten traded to St. Louis to play for the Cardinals, she'd begun making plans. She intended to look like a knockout the first time he saw her again. When he'd gone away to college and never come back, he'd broken her heart. So what, if living in St. Louis while playing for the Dodgers would have been a tad inconvenient . . . ?

It took her until seven o'clock to get home.

Somehow it felt even longer, since she'd spent most of the day at the airport trying to get on another flight out. It hadn't helped matters, either, when halfway home, the heater in her car had conked out.

After parking her car next to several huge white lumps at the curb in front of her house, she headed up the sidewalk with her knit hat pulled down over her ears and her scarf covering her face.

She almost made it to the porch.

Only steps away, she slipped on the icy sidewalk and took a header into the snow.

"Arrrgh—!" she swore, picking herself up, not even bothering to dust off the snow. Putting her shoulder to the howling wind swirling snow everywhere, she hobbled to the porch. The heel of one of her pumps had broken in the fall.

Inserting her key in the front door, she opened it and lurched inside, slamming the door closed behind her.

Gio poked his head out of the kitchen from which the heavenly smell of carameled onions was wafting. "Elizabeth, what are you doing home? I thought you were going to Florida."

"My floot was cancel—ah, ah-choo!" she sneezed, making her way to the kitchen for sustenance and sympathy.

The door to the deck off the kitchen opened just as Elizabeth reached Gio's side.

She stopped dead in her tracks when she saw who was carrying in a plate of grilled burgers hot off the gas grill on the snow-covered deck.

"Alec..." she said, her jaw dropping in astonishment. What was he doing here, tonight of all nights when she looked like Frosty the demented snowperson?

"Elizabeth? Is that you under all that? It is, isn't it? I'd recognize those eyes of yours anywhere."

"Yespth," she sniffled, sneezing again. Why was Alec staring at her like that? And what had he meant about her eyes? Did he like them? she wondered. He was probably just teasing her like he always had, still thinking of her as Gio's kid sister instead of as a woman. Somehow she had to change that. Somehow she would make him see her as a desirable woman.

But not in her present getup.

"You'd better get out of those wet clothes and into a warm bath," Gio suggested.

Elizabeth seized on the escape Gio provided, fleeing to the safety of her bedroom.

Running a hot bath, she replayed the image of Alec standing in the kitchen. She'd followed his career, of course. But seeing him in the flesh after all this time had knocked the wind out of her. He looked as good as she remembered. No, better.

He'd not been wearing anything special—gray sweater, jeans, sneakers and a Dodgers baseball jacket. They looked excellent on him, whereas they would have looked average on any other guy. There was nothing average about Alec McCord. Or was it that she still saw him through the worshipful eyes of a young girl?

No, she saw him through a woman's eyes.

It hadn't escaped her notice how very familiar his old jeans were with the shape of him, worn white where they cupped him. She hadn't missed his sheer animal magnetism either.

And she'd looked like hell.

Elizabeth slipped into the warm, inviting bath-water. She closed her eyes, moving her legs so the water lapped at her gently. It gave her a delight-fully naughty thrill—being naked, with Alec in the next room. Through the door she could hear Alec and Gio talking. She could distinguish between their two voices, but couldn't make out their words clearly enough to know exactly what they were saying.

Was Alec thinking of her naked in her bath?

No, she was being foolish. Her Frosty-the-snowperson outfit would hardly provoke lascivi-ous thoughts.

As she lathered a soft, butter-yellow washcloth with her favorite blue hyacinth soap, hunger and curiosity warred with her need to hide. She was starved, and curious about what Alec and Gio were up to. But she didn't want Alec to see her looking a wreck.

Unless...

Inspired, she finished her bath and donned her disguise, feeling not all that different from the young girl who'd ridden her blue-bike steed dressed as a princess. Only tonight she was going to look totally unlike a princess. She was going to be a total mess. In her disguise, Alec wouldn't be able to tell anything much about the woman she'd become.

She wasn't ready for him to really see her just yet.

If she washed her hair and got all gussied up, it would be too obvious. And besides, she wasn't prepared. She needed time.

On the way out of her bedroom she glanced in the mirror and giggled. There was no danger of anyone thinking of her as desirable in her present getup. She could hide in plain sight.

When Elizabeth entered the kitchen, Gio glanced up from the yellow legal pad he was scribbling on.

"Don't you look lovely," he teased, eyeing her attire and grinning over at Alec, whose back was to her.

Elizabeth ignored him. Instead, she helped herself to the leftovers on the butcher-block snack bar, selecting an oniony burger on a sourdough bun with servings of deli potato salad and coleslaw. Setting down her plate, she took a seat at the round oak table with the two men. She felt her stomach rumble when she bit into the grilled burger. Having forgotten to eat all day, she was ravenous.

As she chewed, she looked across at Gio's scribblings while pretending not to notice the look of amusement passing back and forth between Alec and Gio.

"So, what are you two up to, now that you're back in the same town again?" she asked, unable

to read Gio's writing upside down and nervous
about seeing Alec. She *wouldn't* look at him.

"We're working on an ad," Gio replied.

"Oh, for your band? Are the karaoke contests
still cutting into your bookings?"

"It's not an ad for the band. It's sort of a personal ad for the *River City Call*."

"You're taking out an ad in the Personals!"
Elizabeth almost choked on the sip of soda she'd
just taken.

"I'm not. Alec is."

She was forced to look at Alec.

When she did, she caught him taking in her appearance. His gaze slid over her with masculine interest. Her disguise hid everything but her shape,
and Alec was taking an appreciative tour—she had
the distinct feeling he could see through her clothes.

His eyes sparkling with devilry, he suggested,
"Perhaps we ought to do one for you."

Okay, so maybe she had gone a tiny bit over-
board trying to hide from Alec until she looked her
best. It had seemed like a good idea at the time. It
hadn't worked anyhow, if the sexy glint in his
glance meant anything.

She felt a little foolish sitting across from him
swathed in her mother's ratty chenille robe, with
her own teenage fuzzy-bunny slippers on her feet,
Velcro rollers the size of juice cans in her hair, and
a gloppy green mask on her face that she could feel
hardening into stone.

If she smiled, the mask would crack into tiny lines, giving Alec a preview of what she would look like as an old woman.

Yeah. Great idea, all right.

"Don't pick on me. I've had a real bad day. I'm supposed to be in Florida dining with a dishy chef instead of stuck here in St. Louis helping you find a date through the Personals."

"See, I told you she would help us," Gio said, picking up his pen.

"I—" Elizabeth looked back and forth between the two of them and saw that they weren't going to let her weasel out. "If I help you with the ad, you two have to do the dishes."

"But we cooked!" Gio objected.

"Those are my terms," she said, lifting her chin stubbornly, wondering why Alec would want or need a personal ad. After all, Alec was a hunk and a half. A ladies' man who went through women like Madonna went through players on sports teams.

"We'll take 'em," Alec said.

"Okay, what do you have so far?" Elizabeth polished off the rest of her burger, then carried her empty plate to the sink so they could get down to work.

Gio looked at his notes. "So far we've discerned Alec is looking for someone who is a cross between Mrs. Cleaver and a puppy."

"What?"

"Don't pay any attention to Gio. I'm not that particular, really." Alec then began listing the qualities he was seeking that gave the lie to his statement. "She has to be a sports fan, of course. Of the Cardinals, not the Cubs. And it sure wouldn't hurt if she was also athletic. Someone who's morning conversation consists of more than, 'Where's the coffee?' would be nice. And since I have enough money, she wouldn't have to work. I want a woman who's willing to be under my protection."

"Under your thumb, you mean," Elizabeth said dryly. "I thought you were advertising for a date, not a wife."

Alec shrugged. "You never know. I was only being clear about my needs."

"That's where you're going wrong. No woman is going to reply to an ad like that," she informed him.

"Why not?" Gio demanded.

"Because the ad focuses on *your* wants, *your* needs. Why do you men all see things only from your perspective? That must be why women's roles in the movies are getting weaker all the time, and we still have war."

"Now that's a bit of mental gymnastics," Alec said, looking incredulous. "It's not like I said I wanted a woman who was double-jointed, or something."

Gio looked down at his notes. "Yes, you did. I have it listed right here at number five," he said, breaking the two of them up.

"So, do you two want my help with this ad, or not?" A piece of her hardened mask flicked off and landed in front of Gio, which broke the two guys up anew.

Elizabeth just glared at them as if they were misbehaving children.

"Okay, okay. Tell us what you suggest in the way of writing the ad so a woman will want to answer it. We promise to behave," Alec replied, shooting Gio a look that said to do just that.

"For starters, I suggest you begin by focusing on what will appeal to her instead of what you're looking for. Every woman wants to feel special. Show her you are a man who is sensitive to a woman's needs."

"See, I told you. The Seattle Man is what women are looking for. Heartthrobs like us have gone out of fashion when we weren't looking," Gio said.

"Come on, Elizabeth, give us a clue. I haven't the foggiest idea how to start this ad," Alec prompted.

Elizabeth couldn't believe she was in the position of giving advice-to-the-lovelorn to Alec McCord. But then, two men who'd reached the age of thirty-five without making a commitment to a woman definitely needed help. At least Alec admitted it.

"Since you have trouble with *Sleepless in Seattle,* why not focus on using a movie you can identify with," Elizabeth suggested. "For example, try selecting a baseball movie to help you write your ad."

"Great idea. We could go with *Field of Dreams.* It was a great baseball movie," Gio said. He scribbled the movie title down on the pad before him, and looked back and forth between Elizabeth and Alec eagerly. "So, what do you think?"

Elizabeth sighed. "Gio, if *Sleepless in Seattle* is a women's movie, then *Field of Dreams* is a guy movie. Pu-lease. You need a baseball movie that appeals to both men and women."

Gio looked at his sister. "You aren't going to suggest that Madonna flick are you?"

"You mean, *A League of Her Own?* No."

"How about *Bull Durham?*" Alec interjected.

"That'll work," Elizabeth agreed. "Women liked that movie. I liked that movie."

"But how do we use it?" Alec asked.

"Well, let's think about it. What did the guy who got the girl do in the movie?"

Alec grinned wickedly. "He was the pitcher."

"The pitcher didn't get the girl in the end," Elizabeth reminded him.

"Yeah, but he had some great one-night stands," Gio muttered, winking at Alec.

"Wait a minute," Elizabeth said, her eyes narrowing with suspicion. She had to know why. "You haven't said why you're putting an ad in the Personals...." She looked back and forth between her brother and Alec, waiting.

"Tristan and Nicholas, Alec's college buddies, put him up to it. The three of them made a pact," Gio answered for Alec.

"Oh, no, I'm not going to be a party to some frat guys' contest to pick up women," Elizabeth objected, getting up. "You two can count me out of this stunt. You'll have to write your ad on your own." She used Gio's remark to make good her escape to the bedroom to wash off the facial mask she could feel hardening to the point of no return.

"But Elizabeth—"

Gio's pleas fell on deaf ears.

Behind the bedroom door, Elizabeth went to rinse away the green goop in the adjoining bath. Her disguise had been so good, she doubted the police detective she'd just broken up with would have recognized her.

Relieved of the hardened mask, her face felt a little tingly. She glanced at her reflection in the mirror and mouthed the word, *Coward*.

Not only had she fled the kitchen because she wanted to remove the facial mask, she'd also fled because she'd begun to realize she wanted Alec to choose her for his fantasy Valentine's Day date.

She'd been afraid he'd see the truth in her eyes— the only unveiled part of her body; the only thing about herself she'd been unable to disguise.

Seeing Alec again had brought memories flooding back to her. It had also shed light on why none of the men she'd dated measured up. She'd been comparing them to Alec subconsciously, and finding them lacking.

It was clear to her now that she couldn't go forward with her romantic life until she'd worked through her feelings for Alec.

He'd been very kind to her when she was growing up. He'd teased away her scraped knees, made her feel better about her braces, listened patiently to her problems. Because of that, she'd bestowed him with mythic proportions. How could she expect any man to measure up to that?

With her career successfully established, she was ready to concentrate on her personal life; ready to marry and begin a family. She wanted to recreate the warm, happy family her own parents had provided. But now she knew that she couldn't do that until she had put her feelings about Alec to bed.

She felt herself blush.

To bed.

There was only one way for her to find out how deep her feelings for Alec ran. She had to get him to choose her for his fantasy Valentine date.

But how was she going to do that?

And there was Gio to consider.

Gio would have a stroke if he learned his womanizing best friend was dating his baby sister.

ALEC WALKED AROUND the baseball diamond at Busch Memorial Stadium the following day.

It certainly looked different, covered with snow.

He remembered coming to baseball games with Gio at the stadium. It was at Busch Stadium that he'd gotten the fever to lace up his first pair of cleats. The applause from the fans had been music to his ears over the years. Not many people got that kind of show of approval for a job well-done.

Baseball had brought him a lot.

Women. Lots of women.

But not women like Elizabeth. He'd forgotten how good he felt around her.

There was—always had been—something special about her. Even when she was just a kid, she'd made him feel like he belonged. Like he was part of the Bonetti family.

But he wasn't.

He wasn't part of any family.

He was a loner. And lonely.

The women he'd dated had taught him not to trust women. The women he'd dated had always been more interested in dating a professional athlete than in Alec McCord.

Baseball was a game of agility, concentration and skill. But more important to the women he'd dated, it paid big bucks. The kind of serious money that could finance a very comfortable life-style.

He had this little test he used on the women he dated. When he felt a relationship getting serious, he'd mention his dream to coach high-school baseball.

It worked like a charm. It made women disappear.

Somehow he didn't think it would make Elizabeth disappear.

And then he laughed, his breath visible in the frigid air.

Gio would kill him if he knew Alec was thinking about his baby sister.

Chapter Two

"MOVE IT OR LOSE IT, you old fart," Elizabeth muttered at the bald, fat cat chomping on a cigar in the old Cadillac driving at least thirty miles under the speed limit in the middle of two lanes. Finally she passed him but continued to be downright cranky as she navigated through the clogged rush-hour traffic on Highway 270. Overcome by impatience, she got off one exit early and crossed over Manchester to Lindbergh on her way to pick up the take-out dinner order she'd faxed ahead for.

The coffee machine had broken down first thing when she'd arrived at her Creve Coeur office, and then her assistant had called in sick. Her day had gone downhill from there. A hotel strike had stranded one of her tour groups and she'd spent the entire day unsnarling that mess, only to have her computer go down moments later.

Taking it as a sign, she'd closed the office a half-hour early—little good that it had done her. By the time she pulled into Fuddrucker's restaurant it was six o'clock. The only good thing about her terrible, rotten bad day was seeing the fresh stack of the Thursday weekly edition of the *River City Call* in the stand next to the restaurant entrance. On the way out of Fuddrucker's, she picked up a copy.

Alec's ad would be in the Personals.

It was the first thing she checked when she got home, nibbling on limp, cold french fries. She flipped past the front-page headlines on the latest police-board squabbles with the mayor, past the article on yet another legal thriller, past the entertainment section and on to the back of the newspaper to the regular advertising section.

Shoving the bowl of chili and paper sleeve of fries into the microwave, she pushed the timer for one minute and began scanning down the rows of personal ads.

She knew she wouldn't have any trouble trying to decipher which ad was Alec's. Sneaky, bratty little sister that she was, she'd snuck out to the kitchen the night of the blizzard after Alec had left and Gio had gone to bed, and found their rough draft for the ad.

Even she had had to admit it wasn't bad.

"Aha!" she said out loud when she spied it.

Reading it, she smiled. . . .

Personal

Want your feet rubbed?

Want a bedtime story?

Want your libido stroked?

Be my fantasy Valentine date.

Sleepless in St. Louis

Gio and Alec were shameless, ripping off the

movie's title and signature line. She knew it would work like a charm, though. Alec was going to have more responses to his ad than he would know what to do with.

And somehow she had to figure out a way that he would pick her reply out of all the others that came in answer to his ad.

The microwave pinged, announcing her food was ready. As she took it out, she wondered just when she'd reached her decision to go after Alec. Had it been when she'd first seen him standing in the kitchen doorway with a plate of grilled burgers in his hand and a happy-to-see-her look on his face? Or when he hadn't laughed when she'd joined them at the kitchen table wearing the green goop on her face, only teasing her gently as he'd done all her life? Or was it just that she had to know...?

She loved Thursday nights.

Gio wouldn't be home until after midnight because he would be playing a standing club date with his band. She had the whole house to herself.

And the television.

Vegging out on Thursday nights was a ritual for her. A respite from the sometimes-high-pressure travel industry. She called the block of half-hour sitcoms from seven to nine o'clock her "mental-health break." Nothing was allowed to interfere. When the sitcoms were over tonight, she'd grind a handful of fresh coffee beans, then put on a pot of coffee to get her through working up her response to Alec's ad.

She'd known Alec forever. Surely she would be able to come up with the perfect response, or at least the one he was looking for. Even if she had to pump her brother a little for information.

Discreetly, of course. Gio couldn't know what she was up to.

FRIDAY MORNING DAWNED sunny and bright.

And so did Elizabeth's mood.

After a quick shower, she pulled her hair back from her face and fastened it at the nape of her neck. She was quiet in the kitchen, careful not to wake Gio, certain he hadn't come in until the wee hours. Breakfast was a quick toasted English muffin with jam and a glass of milk.

Gathering her stuff for the trip to her office, she glanced over the final draft of her response to Alec's ad it had taken her till midnight to come up with....

Dear Sleepless in St. Louis,

I can stand on my own two feet.
I want a man who will tell me the truth.
However, I've lost my libido....
Reward to finder.

Satisfied with what she'd written, Elizabeth scrawled a signature beneath her typed reply. Instead of "Elizabeth," she'd signed "Libby," a derivative of her name that she had never used.

She folded the note and placed it in a plain business envelope. Copying the address for the *River City Call* onto the envelope from the newspaper, she used the number of a post-office box she'd just rented for the return address. That way, neither Alec nor Gio would know who "Libby" was until it was too late for either of them to object.

On her way to work she drove through the post-office parking lot and deposited her reply to Alec's ad in one of the blue mailboxes lined up out front.

She took a deep breath as she pulled out into traffic and headed for her office.

Now it was up to fate.

ON MONDAY ELIZABETH decided to give fate a helping hand.

She'd dressed carefully in a conservative navy pantsuit, with no jewelry and her hair was pulled back in a neat chignon For a half hour before she left the house she had practiced her speech in the mirror.

Could she pull it off? she wondered, her palms sweaty, her mouth dry as she drove into the parking garage across from the *River City Call* in the downtown business district.

Sne was about to find out.

The parking-garage elevator took her up to a walkway that led to the newspaper's offices, where a receptionist directed her to the advertising department down the hall. It was deserted except for an older woman typing at one of the desks.

"Excuse me . . ." Elizabeth said, and the woman looked up.

"Can I help you?" the woman asked, turning away from her typing.

"Yes. Yes, I'm Detective Pat Brackman." She held up her ex-boyfriend's business card briefly to establish her credibility, then slipped it into her pocket.

"What can I do for you, Detective?" the woman asked, only slightly more interested in her than in the typing she'd had to abandon. "Everyone is in a meeting right now and I'm holding down the fort."

"This will only take a minute," Elizabeth assured her with what she hoped was a note of authority in her voice. "What I need is to see any responses you've received for this particular personal ad." Elizabeth handed the woman the Personals section with Alec's ad circled in red.

"Is there some problem, Detective?" The woman was now definitely more interested in Elizabeth than her typing. "Perhaps I should get someone—"

"No. No, that won't be necessary. All I need is to see the mail you've received. I won't have to take it with me."

"Well...I guess that would be all right. Wait right here and I'll check on it for you." The woman took the newspaper with her.

Elizabeth shifted her weight from one foot to the other while she waited nervously for the woman to return. It seemed to be taking a long time.

She turned at the sound of footsteps in the hall behind her. "Where's Tilly?" a young man pushing a mail cart asked.

"Tilly?" Elizabeth repeated, puzzled.

The young man nodded.

"Oh, *Tilly*. She, ah, had to check on something. Said she'd be right back. If you'd like I can take that for her for you."

"Thanks," the young man said, anxious to complete his rounds. "I'm running late today." He handed Elizabeth a stack of mail with a thick rubber band around it.

Elizabeth nodded as he pushed off, then sorted through the stack of mail he'd given her.

To her chagrin, most of it was in response to Alec's ad. There were lots of business envelopes like the one she'd sent. Several pastel envelopes held greeting cards, she was sure. One or two of the envelopes were perfumed. And the remaining two were made of a ritzy bond, the kind used in expensive personalized stationery sets.

Her envelope wasn't among them.

She prayed it had already arrived. Otherwise, her scheme wasn't going to work.

"Sorry it took me so long, Detective. There was quite a response to that ad already," Tilly said, winding her way down the aisle between the empty desks while dragging a gray mail sack behind her on the tile floor. The sack was bulky and nearly full, from all appearances.

"All of that is for one ad?" Elizabeth asked. "Are you sure?"

"I'm afraid so."

"Oh, this is your mail," Elizabeth said, handing Tilly the pile in her hand and taking the mailbag.

Elizabeth opened the bag, sorting through it while Tilly scanned the stack of mail, handing over the responses to Alec's ad.

"Here we go," Elizabeth said, pulling her envelope from the others. "Now, here's what I want you to do. I want you to keep all the responses together except this one. When the person requests the replies to his ad, I want you to tell him there was only one and then give this one to him."

"But what will we do with all these others?" Tilly asked, slipping the new responses into the mailbag.

"Hold them for a few days before turning them over to the man who placed the ad. Just give him the one, for now."

"Is there something wrong?" Tilly asked, peering over her glasses.

"We're investigating this man," Elizabeth answered, hoping her face wasn't turning beet red from the lie. "This reply is from a policewoman. We sent it through the mail so he wouldn't become suspicious."

"You're investigating him. Oh, my," Tilly said, her eyes wide. "I don't suppose you can tell me why?"

Elizabeth shook her head no. "Let's just say he's been taking advantage of women and I— I mean, the police department plans to put a stop to it."

"I see."

Elizabeth tried to stem the tide of guilt she felt at the lurid thoughts her claim had triggered in Tilly's mind, if the woman's expression was any indication. "You'll make certain that he is to only receive this response, then...."

The woman nodded, all serious business. "Of course, Detective. I'll personally take care of it myself."

Elizabeth nodded. "Good. The department appreciates the newspaper's cooperation."

Her mission accomplished, Elizabeth turned to leave, forcing herself to walk normally when she felt like fleeing before she got caught impersonating a police officer.

She spent the rest of the afternoon putting together a tour package for a Toronto Blue Jays home game that included the high spots of a city that was now setting trends of its own in design and the arts. Of course, working with a baseball team kept her thoughts on Alec—and Tilly, who was probably spinning some suppositions about him to the staff of the *River City Call*. Some *wild* suppositions.

Somehow she had a feeling she'd set something irreversible in motion. She hoped that it was something good.

Something that didn't involve jail time.

"YOU'VE GOT TO COME with me," Alec insisted.

"Having second thoughts, are you?" Gio teased, sitting down to join Alec while the rest of the band packed up from their gig at the Broadway Oyster Bar. The New Orleans-style bar was funky, right down to the band's name, Knickerbox, chalked on a large blackboard under the heading, Appearing Tonight.

"I'm not having second thoughts. Here, have some of these," Alec said, sliding a still half-full plate of shrimp toward Gio, then taking the fresh round of Dixie beer the waitress brought over at his signal. "All I want you to do is come along with me for moral support when I go to the *River City Call* in the morning to pick up my responses to my ad, okay?"

"You know you'd have better luck finding a date for Valentine's Day standing in line for the john," Gio said. "The bathrooms here are so tiny, you could get engaged while waiting your turn." He popped a shrimp into his mouth and chewed slowly, purposely being obstinate. After taking his time swallowing, he asked, "If I go, what's in it for me?"

"What's in it for you?"

Gio grinned, full of late-night mischief. "Yeah. Like, do I get to pick through the letters you discard?"

"You mean for a date? What happened to Ms. Greatbody? I thought you were in love."

"I am, but she doesn't believe I'll explode if I don't have sex with her."

"Smart woman."

"Look, you didn't say you were a baseball player in the ad. The woman I select will never know I'm not the guy who wrote the ad in the first place, you know. Where's the harm?"

Alec rubbed his chin. "I suppose you're right," he agreed, after thinking it over. "All right, once I select the one I want for my fantasy date, you can go through the stack and pick one for yourself. Heck, pick two—whatever."

"Stack?" Gio repeated, reaching for another shrimp. "Aren't we a bit cocky?"

Alec shrugged. "You helped me write the ad. What woman could resist the two of us?"

"You're right." Gio clinked his beer against Alec's in a toast, following the shrimp with a chug. "I'd feel better about this, though, if Elizabeth had helped us write the ad," he said, setting his beer back down on the table.

"Where is Elizabeth tonight? Doesn't she come watch you sing with the band anymore like she used to?"

"Sometimes. But like I said, we hardly get a chance to see each other, we're both so busy. She works overtime a lot and I work late hours at the clubs with the band. She headed for South Beach over the weekend to make up the trip that the snow canceled out."

"Maybe we can all have dinner before I leave for Spring Training. She can tell me about St. Petersburg. Heck, I'm going to be living back in St. Louis now, so it'll be like old times."

"Elizabeth would like that."

"So tell me, do you ever allow Elizabeth to date? I bet you make her bring all her beaux home first for you to check out and approve, don't you?" Alec teased.

Gio laughed. "Hardly. Elizabeth makes her own choices. She usually does come around to my way of thinking though, when I really object to someone. But she's pretty stubborn about getting her own way."

"And pretty good at it, too, as I recall," Alec said.

Gio nodded. "Yeah."

"NOW REMEMBER, NO WISE remarks," Alec prompted Gio the following morning as the two friends entered the building housing the *River City*

Call. "You're only along to lend me moral support."

"Not too moral, I hope. I'm counting on some of those letters being really hot."

"You'll be lucky if you don't get someone who wants to see your SAT scores and make sure you're housebroken," Alec said, shushing Gio as they approached the receptionist.

The receptionist sent them along down the hall to the advertising department. When they got there the phones were ringing off the hook. The first person free to talk to them was an older woman in glasses. She looked over her glasses at Alec and Gio.

"I'm with him," Gio said quickly, pointing to Alec.

The woman looked at Alec expectantly.

Alec felt like he had the first time he'd bought condoms at the pharmacy—guilty, a little excited and a lot embarrassed.

Finally he found his voice. "I'm... I'm here to pick up my mail."

The woman just continued to stare at him as if he were a specimen under a microscope—one that had just crawled out from beneath a rock. He wondered if she didn't approve of the personal ads the newspaper ran or if she just didn't approve of him. Probably both.

"Mail?" the woman repeated at last.

"Right. My mail for the personal ad I had you run on Thursday. Here's a copy of the ad and my code number," he said, taking both from his wallet.

"We usually just mail the responses to the advertiser," the woman explained, not the least bit forthcoming.

"Uh...but I'm going to be out of town," Alec explained. "I wanted to pick up my responses before I left."

"I see." The woman's eyes narrowed as she checked out the two of them. She looked down at the ad and at Alec's code number, and suddenly became more agreeable. "I can give you your responses if you have some form of identification."

"Identification!" Gio hooted. "Do you watch baseball at all, ma'am? Don't you know who this is?"

Alec shot Gio a silencing look.

"This is my friend, Gio Bonetti," Alec explained, handing the woman his driver's license. "I brought him along in case you needed someone who could identify and vouch for me in order to give me my mail."

"The driver's license will do," the woman answered, looking it over carefully. She handed the license back to Alec. "I'll get your mail. Stay right here."

"Sure you don't want us to help?" Gio asked eagerly.

"I can manage," the woman assured him.

"Don't forget, I get your leftovers," Gio said, nudging Alec as the woman went to the back of the office, stopping to whisper something to a few people who were manning the phones. Every person she spoke to looked over at Gio and Alec.

Alec and Gio exchanged a quizzical glance at the covert stares they were attracting.

"What's the deal?" Alec whispered.

Gio shrugged. "Maybe your ad broke a record for the most answers—"

"Here we are, Mr. McCord."

"That's all?" Alec asked, taking the single envelope the woman had returned with.

"You're joking, right?" Gio said.

"I assure you there's no joke," the woman replied without humor. "There was only one response to your ad, Mr. McCord."

"Is that normal? Don't you usually get a lot more responses?" Gio demanded.

"Let's go, Gio."

"But Alec, there has to be some mistake. Are you sure you've got the right name, ma'am—Alec McCord?" Gio persisted.

The woman looked from Gio to Alec. "I'm sorry, Mr. McCord, if you're used to getting a better response from your ads, but I can assure you this is the only reply we've had to your ad so far. Perhaps more will come in and you can check back with us after you return from your trip."

"This is the first time I've placed a personal ad—" Alec explained. "I've never..."

"Uh-huh." The woman nodded, clearly trying to placate him, but the censure in her eyes said she believed otherwise. For some reason this woman didn't like him, and Gio's persistence was only making things worse.

"Thank you, ah..."

"Tilly," the woman supplied.

"Yes, well, we're leaving now," Alec said, doing everything but grabbing Gio's arm to drag him off.

When they were on the elevator going down to the parking garage, Gio took up where he'd left off. "There's some mistake, Alec. There has to be more mail."

Alec laughed, surprising Gio.

"You aren't disappointed?" Gio asked.

"You're the one who's disappointed. You were planning on taking the extras."

"Yeah, but only one response!"

"Maybe it's fate," Alec said. "Maybe this is the woman who'll be the love of my life."

"Yeah, more likely it's that disaster I warned you about," Gio grumbled.

ON HER WAY HOME a week after she'd gone to the *River City Call* offices, Elizabeth stopped at Carolyn's gourmet French deli. She placed an order for Carolyn's famous chicken salad and a couple of

French rolls, then lingered over the selection of confections. Making a choice at Carolyn's was always difficult. She offered five different kinds of chicken salad, including the one that bore her name that she'd practically built her business on. Elizabeth had followed Carolyn when she'd moved from her first shop to the larger, airier store on Clayton Road.

The food on display was always beautifully prepared and mouthwateringly delicious. She felt like a kid with her nose pressed up against the candy counter as she tried to decide which piece of cake she wanted most.

Finally she opted for a slice of banana-split cake.

She planed to eat it in celebration.

Her next stop was the post office on Gravois to check her post-office box for Alec's reply to her response to his ad. Somehow she'd had a feeling all day long that it was lying there waiting for her.

On her drive from Carolyn's to the post office, she slipped in a tape of Cajun music she'd bought in New Orleans. She'd acquired a taste for it after a trip to New Orleans inspired by the Dennis Quaid and Ellen Barkin movie, *The Big Easy*. While she hadn't run into Dennis Quaid there as she'd fantasized, she had fallen in love with the ambience of the laid-back city and its Cajun music.

She was at the post office in twenty minutes. The parking lot was crowded with secretaries dropping off the office mail, but she managed to find a parking spot after a short wait. Inside she took a deep breath and closed her eyes to send a silent wish before inserting her lock-box key in the lock.

Opening her eyes, she let out a squeal of delight, then looked around, embarrassed. No one had paid her any notice. They were all rushing to get home to dinner, intent on their own lives. Reaching inside, Elizabeth took out the letter.

She recognized Alec's bold handwriting even though there was no return address on the envelope. While she was sorely tempted to rip open the letter right then and there, she restrained herself. Locking her post-office box, she carried the letter back with her to her car and set it on top of some travel brochures she'd brought home to study.

She was an adult. She could wait until she was home to read her mail, just as she'd willed herself not to dip into the white take-out sack from Carolyn's that sat on the floor on the passenger side of her car.

The only thing that could disrupt her plan to read Alec's letter with her mail was Gio being home.

When she arrived there a few minutes later, she was relieved to find she had the house to herself.

She set the travel brochures and Alec's letter down on the table and shrugged out of her coat, then went to unpack the sack from Carolyn's. Dividing the double order of chicken salad, she left half in the container for Gio. She put it in the refrigerator and took out an open bottle of Stone Hill wine.

Minutes later, she had her meal assembled and was sipping her glass of wine as she opened Alec's letter and read.

Dear Libby:
Meet me at 7:00 p.m. on Valentine's Day at the bronze horse sculptures in the Adam's Mark lobby. I'll be wearing a red rose in my lapel. Truthfully, I'm certain that together we can find your lost libido—although I may have to sweep you off your feet. But it will be rewarding. That, I promise you.

Sleepless, but Hopeful
in St. Louis

Elizabeth set down Alec's letter. She could feel the earsplitting grin on her face as she reached with excited anticipation for the celebratory slice of banana-split cake.

Oh, yes. She was going to have her cake and eat it, too.

"I TOLD YOU, you should have mentioned you were a professional baseball player in the ad," Gio said as the two of them planned Alec's fantasy date later that night. They were sitting at the kitchen table at Gio's place. Elizabeth had gone to bed hours ago.

"No, that was the whole idea. I wanted to see what kind of women would respond if they didn't know I was who I am."

"You mean what kind of *woman*. There was only *one* response."

"Don't remind me," Alec said, staring at the lone envelope.

"Do you think there could be some mistake?" Gio suggested. "Tilly didn't exactly look like she approved of you. Maybe she destroyed all the others." There was a mischievous twinkle in Gio's eye. "Maybe that letter is from Tilly!"

Alec glared at him as he took a bite of his Chinese chicken salad.

"It was a joke!" Gio dodged the fortune cookie Alec threw at him.

"Not a funny one," Alec advised him. "Come on, we've got to get this date down. And it's got to work on the first try. Remember, I've only got the one response to my ad to work with. There's no backup date."

"Okay, okay." Gio tore into his swordfish. "What have we got so far?"

"The limo. A bouquet of long-stem red roses in the front seat waiting for the right moment. Dinner on the *Robert E. Lee*—"

"No, that won't fly."

"What won't fly?"

"The *Robert E. Lee*. It's closed down. They're working on it and it won't be open for months."

Alec made a bold scratch through the *Robert E. Lee* on his list. "This is your town, what do you suggest?"

"Tony's," Gio said without hesitation. "Tony's is the best restaurant in St. Louis, hands down. It's got five stars or something."

Alec scrawled Tony's on his list.

"What else?" Gio asked, taking a drink of wine.

"That's all I've got, so far. I thought maybe a box of chocolates back at the apartment since it's Valentine's Day."

"No, too traditional. Choose some other sweet. I know—brownies. Elizabeth loves brownies."

Alec added brownies to the list.

"Where are you planning to go after Tony's—straight to your apartment?"

"I thought a ride up in the Arch would be romantic...seeing the city at night."

"Really? I've never been up in the Arch. But then I live here, so that figures. You only see the tourist attractions when you're out of town."

"You really should go up in the Arch—it's magnificent, especially at night."

"Well, if Ms. Greatbody ever comes around..."

"Still striking out with her, eh?"

"I'll wear her down," Gio said with conviction "Now, back to you. You've got the staples, I assume. Champagne, music, protection.."

"Of course. I think that covers everything,' Alec said, folding his list

"Almost." Gio's dark eyes twinkled again. "What are you going to do if the woman who answered your ad is a dud?"

"I'm going to be polite—and end the date with the trip up in the Arch to see the twinkling lights of the city... and then give her your phone number."

Chapter Three

ALEC GLANCED DOWN AT his watch as he stood next to the bronze horse sculptures in the lobby. The sculptures were nine feet tall and imposing. He hoped he looked as powerful and sexy. It was ten till seven. He'd gotten there early to make sure he didn't miss Libby. He didn't want any screwups on his fantasy Valentine's date.

He'd no sooner thought about it than a screwup appeared. Another guy wearing a red rose in his lapel was standing off to one side of the horses. Great. There was no way he could tell the guy to scram. But what if Libby thought the guy was him?

Alec didn't know why, but he'd come to like the idea of there being just one response to his ad. It sort of took the responsibility away from him. It wasn't as if he'd made a lot of good choices when it came to women.

Who was he kidding? It wasn't as if he'd made any choices at all. He'd taken what had come so easily to him.

Taken women for granted.

He'd never put himself on the line by pursuing any woman. That way he'd avoided looking like a fool. No woman was ever going to make a fool of him the way his mother had his father. Still, he knew women dated him because he was famous.

As he stood there trying to will the other guy to leave, Alec wondered what Libby looked like. Gio had said not asking for a photograph had been just plain dumb.

"LIBBY" STOOD ACROSS the lobby by the bank of elevators on Alec's left.

She had arrived early and slipped in through a side entrance. She'd gone to the gift shop and bought a magazine. As she stood observing Alec, she hid her face behind its pages. But the time set for their meeting was approaching and she was both scared and excited about revealing her identity.

What would Alec say when he found out "Libby" was Elizabeth Bonetti, girl next door? But not tonight, if she could help it. Her plan was to knock Alec's socks off. To make him think of her as a woman—a desirable woman—instead of Gio's kid sister. To produce that sexy gleam in his eye.

Alec's black tuxedo was a perfect complement for her dress. She'd chosen red in honor of Valentine's Day.

She'd checked her coat as Alec had, wanting him to get the full effect of the dress that had cost two weeks' salary. She knew that initially, he was bound to object because she was Gio's sister. Gio was the typical overprotective older brother and most certainly wouldn't want a ladykiller like Alec dating her. No, Gio would probably prefer her to take her vows and join a convent.

It was seven o'clock.

Elizabeth ducked into the ladies' room and checked her appearance one last time. The bodice and narrow long sleeves of her dress were black velvet, which set off her complexion. The red silk sheath skirt that fell to the floor from an Empire waist had a slit up the front to midthigh, showing off her legs.

She smoothed her hands down the skirt, then added a final touchup to her Stoplight Red lipstick. Bending from the waist, she shook her hair and then straightened to let it settle in a dark cloud of curls around her face. She adjusted the costume-jewelry pendant that hung on a velvet ribbon from her neck. It rested just at her cleavage, meant to draw Alec's attention to what she considered one of her best features. She was going for broke tonight. It was her one chance to find out just what there was between her and Alec.

It hadn't escaped Elizabeth's notice that another man lounging by the bronze horse sculptures was also wearing a red rose in his lapel. She supposed that wasn't that unusual, given it was Valentine's Day. The opportunity to walk past the stranger before approaching Alec was too good to pass up. Would Alec be disappointed when he assumed she was the other guy's date?

Would he even recognize her?

And what would he do when he did?

She was truly nervous now that the time to pull off her scheme had arrived. A fluttering swarm of butterflies had taken up residence in her tummy, and her palms were damp.

Gathering her courage and silencing her qualms, she made her approach. Alec really did look smashing in his tuxedo. She only hoped he liked how she looked half as well. Alec was looking down at his watch checking the time. It was a few minutes after seven, she knew.

"Barbara?" the other man asked as she drew near, a hopeful look on his face that boosted her confidence.

She shook her head no. "Sorry."

Alec had turned at the sound of conversation and watched her approach, an appreciative look on his face—a look that grew incredulous when he recognized her.

"Waiting for someone?" she asked, trying to remain calm and cool when she reached his side.

"Elizabeth?" he said, surprise in his voice.

"No... Libby."

"You! No, it can't be. How in the world did— *You?*"

"Me," she said, smiling at his astonishment.

"No, I don't think so," Alec said, shaking his head and backing away from her like he was Superman and she was kryptonite. "How in the world— Why? What were you thinking?"

"Why not?" she demanded. She hadn't gone to all this trouble to have the date blow up in her face. She'd expected him to object. But she also expected to wear him down as she always had in the past. Alec had never been able to say no to her when she decided she really wanted something, and she was counting on the past holding true to form.

"For openers, Gio would kill me. I'd have to be crazy to go out with Gio Bonetti's baby sister, no matter how sexy she looks. I'm way too young to die."

He'd said she looked sexy! She had him up against the ropes. "But you have to," she insisted, her eyes wide, her lips pouty.

"Oh, no, you don't. Don't try wheedling your way with me, Elizabeth. You're not getting your way this time," Alec vowed, more to himself, it seemed, than to her.

"But Gio won't have to know—" she began.

"No, Elizabeth."

"But—"

"*No.*"

It was time to pull out all the stops. Time for waterworks. If there was one thing Alec McCord had never been able to withstand, it was her tears.

"What will I tell my friends?" she sniffed, bringing out the tears. "I can't tell them my blind date got one look at me and bolted. Please. Pu-leez, Alec," she begged, wiping at the damp tears on her cheek.

They were attracting attention from the other guy with the red rose in his lapel. Even passersby were glancing in their direction.

"Oh, for heaven's sake, Elizabeth." Alec handed her his handkerchief.

"Does that mean you'll go through with the date?" she sniffled, dabbing at her nose.

"One date," he said, resigned. "But only this once. And you've got to promise me that your brother, Gio, will never know."

"I promise," she agreed quickly, handing back his handkerchief, smiling sweetly while he tried to hastily rearrange his plans for the evening into something that wouldn't get him killed.

"We could go bowling," he suggested.

"Like this?" Elizabeth looked down at her dress. "No, I don't think so. I want the date I heard you and Gio planning. I told all my friends that—"

"Okay, okay. I never have been able to say no to you and you're taking advantage of it. But dinner on the *Robert E. Lee* riverboat is off." So was dinner at Tony's five-star restaurant.

"Why?"

"Because they're making repairs to it and it isn't open. It won't be open until May."

"But I had my heart set on a romantic dinner on a riverboat," Elizabeth said, doing her best to make her bottom lip quiver. She knew she ought to be ashamed of herself, but it was Valentine's Day and she was with Alec McCord. She wanted romance, damn it.

"A romantic dinner, eh? How does any man say no to a woman in a dress like that? When did you get so grown-up, and why didn't I notice?"

"You've been out of town."

"Yeah, but I'm back. What am I saying?" Alec covered his face with his hands. "Gio would kill me if he knew what— Let's get our coats. I've got an idea."

"You're not taking me home," Elizabeth warned. "No tricks... You promised me a date."

"One date," Alec reminded her.

With any luck that was all she'd need, Elizabeth thought.

"One date," she agreed.

THIS COULDN'T BE happening to him.

He'd just met the most beautiful woman he'd ever seen and it was his best friend's kid sister. When had she grown out of pigtails and braces? He supposed he deserved this odd twist of fate. Deserved to be tortured this way.

Outside the Adam's Mark, he placed Elizabeth's arm in the crook of his, guiding her down to the curb where he had a limo waiting. Once they were seated comfortably in the limo, he instructed the driver to take them to Wharf Street on the Mississippi riverfront.

The limo headed down Chestnut to Wharf Street where the riverbank was paved with cobblestone. When the limo turned onto Wharf and had gone a short way, he told the limo driver to pull over and stop.

"You're kidding, right?" Elizabeth said, glancing out the window.

Alec ignored her. The limo driver came around but Alec was already out. Alec extended his hand to Elizabeth, "Come on, brat. Don't pout."

Elizabeth sighed and glared at him, but she gave him her hand and let him assist her out of the limo.

"I can't believe you're taking me here," she grumbled, staring at the restaurant he'd substituted for a romantic dinner on the *Robert E. Lee.*

"You said you wanted to eat on a riverboat—"

"But, McDonald's!"

"McDonald's *Riverboat* Restaurant. I think it's perfect."

"You would. Would you mind telling me what's so perfect about it?" she demanded to know as he guided her aboard the restaurant, careful that she didn't snag her heels and tumble on the cobblestone.

"Where else would you take a kid, but to McDonald's?"

"I'm not a kid."

Of course, she was right. She wasn't a kid. It was just that he was having trouble dealing with her being a woman. A beautiful, desirable woman.

He settled her at a table by the window overlooking the flowing Mississippi River and went to place their order at the counter.

"You can't complain about the service," he quipped when he returned minutes later with cheeseburgers, fries and soft drinks.

"People are staring at us," she said as he set the fast food down on the table. "I don't think many people come here in tuxedos and evening dress."

"Good, we can start our own trend . . . Libby."

His calling her that brought them back to the situation at hand.

"Whatever possessed you to answer my ad, Elizabeth? Was it some crazy dare you made with your friends or something? Are you trying to annoy Gio? Or is it what it's always been with you? You just enjoy seeing me—"

"That's it," Elizabeth said. "I just enjoy seeing you." She unwrapped her cheeseburger and bit into it.

Why did he have the feeling she was filling her mouth to keep herself from saying more, Alec wondered. What exactly was Elizabeth up to now? He'd gotten used to her schemes over the years— he'd never been able to deter her from them—so he supposed he ought to just hang on for the ride.

Whatever Elizabeth had in mind couldn't be so bad.

As long as he kept his eyes off the twinkling pendant she wore; and more important, the generous cleavage it accentuated.

He jabbed several fries in catsup and then nearly choked after he put them in his mouth when he remembered Elizabeth's reply to the ad he'd placed.

He was all for her standing on her own two feet.

All for her demanding a truthful suitor.

It was the part about the lost libido that had him choking. Surely she didn't think that he...

Gio would kill him.

Sure, Elizabeth's brother was all for a one-night stand—but not with his baby sister.

Elizabeth had been kidding, he decided. This was a lark to her. A way to perturb him. She might look like a grown-up woman... only she wasn't fooling him. This was the nervy kid who got into scrapes and then came running to him to save her. Apparently she'd decided it would be even more fun to involve Alec in the mischief she was so fond of making.

His eyes skirted her cleavage despite his best intentions. It surely was too bad that Elizabeth was Gio's kid sister. If she weren't, he'd take her up on her dare

Take her to bed, and see about claiming that reward.

"Are you okay?" Elizabeth asked, concern in her voice as he reached for his soda when he'd stopped choking.

No, he wasn't okay. And he knew he wouldn't be until this date was over and he'd taken Elizabeth home, where she'd be safe and sound—or rather, *he* would be.

"I'm fine," he lied.

"You know, this is kinda fun," Elizabeth said, looking out the window at the river churning past them below. "It must have been something when riverboats used to line the riverfront leaving off cargo and picking up passengers for New Orleans."

"Yeah, I can see you traveling by riverboat," Alec said. "First thing you'd do is hook up with a riverboat gambler who'd— "

"What do you mean, 'hook up with'?" Elizabeth interrupted. "I'd *be* the riverboat gambler."

Alec shook his head. "Women weren't allowed to be riverboat gamblers back in the 1800s."

"We'd just see about that."

"Yeah, you probably would," Alec said indulgently. "It's good to see you've channeled all your drive into a successful travel agency, instead of getting married."

"What's that supposed to mean?" Elizabeth demanded, pouting.

"It means being married to you would probably be like living in 'I Love Lucy' episodes."

"Alec McCord, you take that back."

"Why? It's true. The only thing more dangerous to me than a designated hitter is you with time on your hands."

"I could be happily married, I'll have you know."

"So why aren't you?"

"Because I've been busy building my business."

Having polished off his cheeseburger, Alec wadded up the tissue it had been wrapped in. "So you haven't dated much—"

"For goodness' sake, I've dated all kinds of men in my travels. I'm twenty-eight, after all. And it's the nineties, not the fifties, you know. Women can go about without a chaperone—or their older brother and his friend's permission."

"What sorts of men?" Alec found himself asking, his tone that of a chaperon.

Elizabeth trailed her french fry in his catsup. "What kinds of men?" she asked, pausing to think a moment before continuing. "All kinds. There was a count in Italy, a race-car driver in France, a soccer player in Canada and an actor in New York."

"And none of them stole your heart?"

She shook her head no. "The count was too stuffy, the race-car driver was crazy, the soccer player too macho and the actor too in love with himself."

"Sounds like you might be a bit difficult to please. Have you ever thought of that?"

"Let's go outside on the deck."

"Sure you won't be too chilly?" He cleared the trash from their table and helped her with her coat when she said no.

"How come you never married?" she surprised him by asking when they stood against the railing and listened to the lapping water while staring up at the starry sky.

"No one ever asked me," he offered, making light of her question. "And I guess, like you, I'm difficult to please." He found himself sliding his hand around her shoulder.

"I want what my parents have," Elizabeth said on a sigh, leaning into him.

"Who doesn't?" Unfortunately, happy marriages like Elizabeth's parents' weren't the norm. It was something Alec was afraid to hope for. He didn't want to give a woman the power to hurt him, to leave him—as his mother had.

"It's all your fault, you know, that I'm not married."

"What?"

"I keep comparing all the men I date to you and they keep coming up short. You were my hero and no one can measure up to you. You always took care of me, cared about me, protected me."

"What are you saying?"

"What I'm trying to tell you is that the reason I answered the ad was to get you out of my system. I need to get past you so I can get on with my life. Now that I have my travel agency established, I'm ready to have a real relationship with a man. Something that involves commitment.''

"So, is it working?''

"Well, your idea of a gourmet dinner hasn't exactly swept me off my feet.'' She giggled, dispelling some of the tension between them, making him smile and relax. The *girl* he remembered was playing peekaboo from inside the grown woman. Elizabeth's bright red lipstick was only a provocative memory, having disappeared with dinner. Her bare pink lips looked even more inviting. He wouldn't think about it. Down that path lay...who knew what? But whatever, it was complicated and meant trouble.

"Good, I'll see what else I can do to disappoint you,'' he said, trying to inject the atmosphere with a note of humor as he reached to push away a loose strand of hair the wind had blown across her face.

Instinctively she reached to do the same, and their hands collided. The sexual tension that had been dispelled returned tenfold.

Alec brought her hand to his lips and bestowed a soft, lingering kiss to her palm.

"I...I shouldn't have done that—any more than I should do this...." He pulled her into his arms, his mouth descending to the delicate curve of her lips.

And stopping.

He shook his head as if to clear it, then set her away from him.

"We should go on to the next step of the date," he said, trying to ignore the flashes of passion in her dark eyes.

"I thought we were," Elizabeth said, looking at him with puzzlement. "Aren't you going to kiss me?"

"No. The plan was for the date to go from the dinner on the riverboat to a ride to the top of the Arch."

"But I live in St. Louis. I've lived here all my life. I've been there, done that."

"At night?"

"Well, no."

"I have. I took a ride up to the top of the Arch one night when the team was in town and the second game of a two-game series was rained out. Trust me, a view of the city at night is romantic."

"Why aren't you going to kiss me?" She stepped back into his arms. "Are you afraid of me?"

"Yes."

"Are you sure it's not Gio you're afraid of?"

"I'm afraid of you... and Gio... and myself." The last was said beneath his breath. He took her hand and tugged. "Let's go."

"Kiss me first," she insisted, closing her eyes and lifting her face expectantly.

Rather than argue, he buzzed a quick kiss to her lips.

"Now let's go—"

"That wasn't a real kiss."

"Elizabeth—"

"I'm not going. Not until I get a real kiss."

She meant it, too. He knew. It didn't matter that they were no longer alone out on the deck. Other diners had come out to enjoy the balmy night that still had a hint of winter.

"Aw, hell, Elizabeth," he swore in frustration at her show of stubbornness. He knew that look in her eye only too well. The man who took her on was going to be led a very merry dance.

Her smile of victory was short-lived when he swept her up into the crooks of his arms, denying her the kiss she wanted.

"Alec, what are you doing? Put me down this minute," she hissed through clenched teeth. "People are starting to stare."

He blithely ignored her plea. Instead he carried her off the fast-food riverboat, all the while counting his blessings that Elizabeth wasn't shrieking or kicking. When they reached the top of the cobblestone bank, he put her down and helped her into the limo as the driver held the door.

"Where are we going?" she demanded to know.

He told the limo driver to deliver them to the Arch.

Alec sat in his corner of the limo looking at her like she might bite. He watched her warily as she inched closer and closer on the short drive to the Arch. When she was dangerously close, he knocked on the window to get the driver's attention.

The driver lowered the window. "Sir?"

"The box . . ." Alec commanded.

"Yes, sir." The driver handed back a white florist's box.

Alec placed it on the seat between them.

"Are those for me?" Elizabeth asked.

"They're for Libby, yes," Alec answered as they pulled up to the parking area near the Arch.

As the driver got out to hold the door, Elizabeth untied the bright red ribbon from the long white box and squealed with delight at the dozen long-stem red roses inside.

She insisted on carrying the bouquet as they walked to the Arch.

Alec held her arm as they went and she kept smelling the roses and jabbering on and on about how romantic he was. The limo, the *Robert E. Lee* restaurant—if it had been open—the roses . . .

"Damn, it's closed," he said when they reached the Arch entrance.

"That's okay," Elizabeth assured him.

"But it says it closes at six. I know I went up in the tram car at nine o'clock at night when I was here pitching against the Cardinals."

"And when was that?"

"In July."

"The Arch doesn't stay open after six until May. I should have remembered that."

"Now what?"

"Well, what did you have planned for after the Arch?"

"I thought a leisurely romantic dinner and a trip to the top of the Arch would pretty much take care of the evening. I wasn't planning on a fast-food dinner and the Arch being closed." He wasn't planning on telling her what he'd had planned for "Libby" after the Arch. That kind of encouragement she didn't need. He had to come up with Plan B—the one where he lived if Gio found out about their date.

When they returned to the limo, he told the driver to give them the scenic tour while they decided exactly where they wanted to go.

"I want dessert," Elizabeth announced as the limo pulled onto Wharf Street.

"Dessert?"

She nodded. "Dessert."

Dessert was good, he thought. Much better than dancing. She could have insisted on slow dancing. That way led to certain disaster. But dessert in a public place was something he could handle.

"Okay," he agreed. "How about the Crown Candy Kitchen? We can have a World's Fair sundae or one of their famous chocolate-banana malts."

"No, I don't want to go there."

"Then how about going to Tippin's for coffee and pie? Something, say, in a French apple with a crumb topping or a Boston cream—"

"No. I don't want to go to Tippin's for pie."

"Is it dessert you want, or to give me a hard time, Elizabeth?" he asked in frustration.

"Both," she answered with a smile.

He grumbled, but ruminated for a dessert she couldn't say no to. Finally he recalled something Gio had said about one of Elizabeth's favorite haunts. "I've got it. We can go to Café Zoë for *tiramisu.*"

"Uh-uh."

"Dark chocolate mousse, then?"

"No."

"Maybe you could give me a hint, here—"

"I want a brownie with a scoop of French vanilla ice cream, topped with hot fudge. Any suggestions on where we could score that, Alec?"

Yeah, he knew exactly where.

His apartment.

But how did she know?

"Cyrano's..." Alec offered hopefully.

"I was thinking more along the line of your apartment," Elizabeth said, as he was afraid she might. "I heard all the plans you made for this date when you and Gio were in the kitchen."

"Then you know—"

"That dessert was meant to be foreplay...? Yes, I know. And I'm planning on holding you to it."

Chapter Four

ELIZABETH HAD NEVER seen anyone take so long to eat a hot fudge brownie sundae in her entire life. While she'd practically wolfed her dessert down, Alec had dawdled over his.

It was enough to give a woman a complex.

She looked across the butcher block at him. He looked very handsome, if uncomfortable, perched on a stool in his tuxedo. Alec had the qualities she found most attractive in a man—charm, confidence, kindness and humor. Though he was like Gio in that having such a lot of choice when it came to women, he was spoiled.

Trouble was, she was also spoiled in her own way.

And it was all Alec McCord's fault. He was the one who'd always indulged her—the one who'd given her a taste for a sensitive man. One dressed in wolf's clothing, to be sure, but a sensitive man nonetheless.

She knew perfectly well that Alec would rail at being called sensitive. It was a side of himself she knew he was afraid of; a side of himself he'd managed to keep well hidden from everyone except her. He hadn't worried about her because she was a kid.

It was time for him to worry, she decided, watching him leisurely lick the last of the hot fudge from the back of his spoon.

"You know what I feel like doing?" she asked, when he looked up at her.

"Going home?" he suggested, ever hopeful.

She shook her head no. "I feel like dancing."

"You do?"

"Uh-huh. *Slow dancing.*"

Had she actually seen him swallow with trepidation? In any other situation, she knew Alec would be only too happy to accommodate a woman bent on seducing him. It was just her bad luck—and his—that she was Gio Bonetti's baby sister.

Well, what Gio didn't know wouldn't hurt anyone.

She got up from her stool and went in search of some music. She was sure Alec had some at the ready. The candles he'd set out hadn't escaped her notice any more than the fact that he hadn't lit them.

"It's late," Alec hinted broadly.

She turned around and gave him a look. "It's not even ten o'clock."

"I have to get my rest. I've got to report to St. Petersburg for Spring Training."

"On the 16th. This is Valentine's Day—the 14th. You'll have twenty-four hours to rest up after tonight before you have to report to training camp.

Besides, if I stay the night, it'll be easier on your pitching arm...."

"Elizabeth!"

"Oh, don't 'Elizabeth' me," she said, upon spying the compact disk he'd already slotted to play.

"Harry Connick, Jr., Alec? Did you already unpack your music or did you purchase this disk special for tonight?" She pressed the Play button on his rack stereo system and the strains of "My Funny Valentine" filled the room.

"It'd be a shame to waste all this atmosphere, Alec. Come on dance with me...one little ol' dance. What could it hurt?" she coaxed, reaching up to loosen his tuxedo tie, undoing the formal bow.

He swore and unbuttoned his top button himself without any urging from her.

"One dance," he agreed. "And no more."

"One dance," she conceded, melting into his strong arms, resting her head on his broad shoulder.

He was a good dancer. His lead was confident yet his embrace was loose. He held her away from him, kept his distance.

"You don't have to be so scared, you know. I only asked you to dance. It's not like I asked you to marry me."

"Marry you?"

She definitely had his attention.

She nodded, and he gazed down at her. "I can just imagine what marriage would be like with you, Elizabeth."

"You can? What would it be like?"

"Permanent. You'd never let me go."

"You're right. I seldom make the same mistake twice."

"You're the sort of woman who's a full-time number-one priority."

"What's wrong with that?" she demanded to know.

"Nothing. It just means you need a man who's ready to settle down."

"And you're not— What? Were you planning on waiting until you were fifty-five?"

He didn't answer her.

She rested her head on his shoulder again. She knew Alec was afraid of marriage. Afraid of losing like his father had. But she also knew the celebrity-athlete image wasn't going to continue to serve him as his career as a baseball pitcher was winding down.

It was no secret to her that Alec craved a home and family like the one she and Gio had been raised in. With her travel agency on its feet, she was ready for the same turn in her life-style. The difference lay in the fact that she was willing to take the chance on finding love and true happiness, and Alec was hesitant to give a woman that much power to hurt him—the power to leave him, as his own mother had.

She had to convince Alec that not only was she a woman, but she was the woman for him.

And she had to do it tonight.

The song ended and Alec punctuated it by tipping her backward into a spontaneous romantic dip. The movement was so unexpected, she lost her balance and they both fell onto the carpet.

Alec grinned up at her. "Well, that does it. The dance is definitely over. Time for you to go on home." He clearly was still determined to avoid her plans for a full-out seduction. But hadn't she seen just the tiniest bit of weakening in that sexy grin of his?

"I think not," she vowed, holding her advantageous position. When they'd collapsed together on the carpet, she'd landed on top. "What is it with this determination of yours to have me go home early? Do you turn into a werewolf at midnight or something?"

"You keep up wriggling around on top of me like that and you'll be finding out shortly what kind of wolf I turn into," he warned. "This is grown-up stuff, Elizabeth. You're not a kid anymore."

"Finally we agree," Elizabeth said, watching as he did his best to avoid noticing that her cleavage was threatening to spill out of her dress at any moment. "Tell you what, Alec. I'll make you a deal."

"What kind of deal?" he asked warily.

"One kiss," she answered. "One kiss and I'll leave without any argument."

Alec looked at her, the disbelief in his eyes easy to read.

"I promise."

"You promise...?" Alec's tone was skeptical at best.

"I kept my word about just one dance, didn't I?" she persisted. Leaning forward, she began raiding his lips with little baby kisses until she elicited the response she wanted.

Alec sealed her lips with his, taking her up on her open invitation. His tongue coaxed and teased until she was limp atop him from the sexy insinuation. The desire in his eyes made her weak. This wasn't working out at all the way she'd planned.

He was supposed to be putty in her hands instead of the reverse. In a heartbeat she'd lost control of the situation. She was still on top, but Alec was still leading. And the dance was as old as time.

The kiss ended with him tracing his thumb along her lips with a look of wonder on his face. Just maybe she'd lost the battle, but had a chance to win the war.

"Let's do it again," she begged.

"I thought you said only one kiss, that you'd leave without argument after one kiss."

"Do you want me to leave?"

"No, but I think it would be for the best."

"Let me stay...please."

"I'm not doing this, Elizabeth."

"Fine, then lean back and enjoy. I'll do it."

"For heaven's sake, what kind of men have you been dating? Does Gio know you're...you're—" He broke off, exasperated.

"Good in bed...?" she supplied nonchalantly.

"Elizabeth!"

"That's Libby to you, remember," she corrected, grinning down at him. "And to answer your question seriously, I've been dating shallow men. You know the sort—the kind of men who are interested in only one thing."

"You're saying men like me."

"No, I've been dating men who want me. You don't want me."

"Oh, I want you, all right. I'd say there's plenty of physical evidence to back that up, if there was any doubt about it."

"Then let me make love to you, Alec."

"Just once," he hedged, weakening.

"I promise," she agreed.

He considered her offer, clearly sorely tempted, then shook his head no with obvious reluctance. "No, I don't think it's a good idea."

"But why not?" she demanded.

"Because it won't work. I'm like a potato chip. Once a woman makes love to me..."

"I'll take my chances," she insisted, ambushing his comic bragging, which she instinctively knew wasn't bragging at all.

"Well, you can't say I didn't warn you," he said, his lips tilting and his eyes shining with wicked delight as he thrust his hands into her mass of dark curls.

She felt his breath, chocolate scented on her lips as he pulled her mouth to his, tasting, and then abandoning all play for the real thing.

Irresistible.

He was utterly irresistible.

He could bring her to the brink with his drugging kisses.

And he knew it.

It was time for her to wipe that smug look off his face. She eased herself up until she was sitting astride him, the slit in her skirt just allowing it. As he watched, she trailed her red manicured nails across her cleavage, the act and the look in her eye pure provocation.

He didn't comment, just swallowed dryly... waiting.

With just a bit of a tug on the velvet bodice, she let her breasts tumble free.

"I was wondering—" he began.

"If they were real?"

"Oh, no. I could tell they were real. I was wondering what it would be like if they came out to play." When he reached up to close his hands over them in a gentle caress, she uttered a soft cry, and moved her hips evocatively against his straining fly.

The passion his eyes had been hinting at flared to a raging blaze. He tugged, bringing a nipple to his mouth and licking, watching her the whole while.

She felt herself flush at the sensation of being watched while her body reacted wantonly to his caresses. When he turned from licking to sucking, her soft cries became moans of pleasure. She wanted to feel him, to release the hardness pressing urgently and insistently against her.

Sliding her hand between them, she began easing down the zipper of his tuxedo pants with great care until she held him firmly in her hand. Then they petted like teenagers out of control in the back seat of the limo on prom night.

"This is ridiculous," Alec said when he finally drew breath.

"Sublime," she countered.

"But, Elizabeth, I have a perfectly comfortable bed—"

"I don't want to wait. Do me now, please," she begged, reaching behind her to slide down the zipper on her dress. Her mission accomplished, she pulled the dress over her head in a flash of black velvet and red silk and tossed it aside on the floor.

Alec was still almost fully dressed in his tuxedo while she sat astride him in nothing more than a whisper of black silk stockings, lacy garter belt and panties. The contrast of black against her pale skin when she looked down made her feel wicked and sophisticated.

"When you put it like that, how can I refuse?" Alec said, deliberate in his scrutiny as he lingered to admire the view. Lazily he curled up to tickle her belly button with his furled tongue.

"Stop that," she said, slapping him away on a chain of girlish giggles.

"Ah, an uppity woman. I have ways of making you do my bidding," he teased, levering her beneath him.

"Rumor has it..." Elizabeth commented. "I'm waiting—"

"Good things come to those who wait."

"I'm not looking for merely good," she teased, watching him shrug out of his tuxedo jacket and toss it to join her dress on the floor in a telling tableau.

He reached down and tweaked an impudent nipple. "What are you trying to do you, little minx, give me performance anxiety?"

"You who've pitched before thousands, gets nervous before performing for one? I find that difficult to believe."

He pulled off his shirt, tossing it to join the growing pile of discarded clothing. "We're not talking about baseball. And I'm trying to perform for someone who wants me to fail. Isn't that right?"

She nodded, reluctantly agreeing to the truth of his statement. She did want him to fail. Wanted him not to be as great, wanted *them* not to be as great as she knew in her heart they would be together.

"Well, get ready to be disappointed," he said, kicking out of his tuxedo pants after toeing off his shoes and socks.

That was going to take a small miracle, she thought, her gaze caressing every delicious inch of him.

Dressed, Alec was handsome as hell.

Naked, he was spectacular.

"And not disappointed in the way you want. I mean, prepare to be disappointed that I'm going to be the best potato chip you've ever tasted."

There was a swagger in his walk as he went to the stereo system where he rummaged through some tapes until he found what he wanted. He returned to stand over her, reaching out his hand to her as the singer on the stereo asked, "May I have this dance for the rest of your life?"

She accepted his hand and let him pull her up into his arms to dance to the romantic ballad. If she'd thought slow dancing was erotic before, it was nothing compared to slow dancing with Alec naked.

He nibbled her neck, his hands on her buttocks as he pushed her ever so suggestively against him. She was going to melt into a puddle of desire, if he didn't stop his delicious torment. She felt like climbing all over him. She was hot—hotter than she'd ever been before. She wanted Alec more than she'd ever come close to wanting any other man.

He was dangerous, exciting, a dream lover.

And she felt safe in his arms.

Safe. Safe in a way that belonging made you feel safe. Safe in the way of knowing that the other person wants the best for you.

Safe enough to be reckless.

As he slid sexy openmouthed kisses along her neck, she found herself nibbling his ear while making breathy moaning noises that seemed to stir him on.

His response was instantaneous. He began kneading her buttocks, the heat of his agile hands actually dampening the silk of her lacy panties.

"We're never going to make it through this song," she whispered hoarsely.

"Song? Is there music playing?" he asked, slipping his hand between them to unsnap the garters holding up her silk stockings. She held her breath as he raised his head from her neck to her mouth, thrusting his tongue inside at the same instant he pushed down her panties and slipped fingers that knew their way around a fast ball inside her yielding body.

Neither of them heard the music any longer as he backed her up against the wall and replaced his all-too-talented fingers with his penis. Thrusting with sure, confident strokes as she wrapped her legs around his hips, he brought both of them to climax in quick succession.

The two of them slid down the wall slowly, limp and momentarily sated. Their foreheads were braced against each other, while both tried to regain their breath. They were hot, sweaty, and grinning like fools.

"Why are you grinning?" she demanded to know.

"Because I...I...ah, I—"

"Yeah, I know," she said. "I guess I've always known. I just didn't want to admit it to myself because I was so disappointed when you went off to L.A."

"You were barely seventeen when I signed on with the Dodgers. Just a kid..."

"But not anymore—"

He pulled her onto his lap and his mouth settled over hers in a sensual, leisurely kiss. Breaking away finally, he smiled. "No, not anymore," he agreed.

"So, how did the fantasy Valentine date rate?" she asked, on a playful note.

"You mean dinner at a fast-food restaurant and making love standing up?"

She nodded.

"Well, I have to admit it wasn't what I had in mind."

"It wasn't?" She tried unsuccessfully to keep the note of disappointment from her voice.

"No, it was better," he answered, making her heart sing.

"Really?"

"Yeah, 'Libby.' I think we got us a problem here. What do you think?"

She nuzzled against him, happily. "Could be."

"Why don't we talk about it in bed?" he suggested, standing and carrying her across the room toward the bedroom.

For once in her life she gave him no argument.

They made love again. A lazy, Sunday-afternoon kind of love, and afterward they fell into a deep sleep.

The morning sunlight woke Elizabeth. She stretched and yawned, then smiled.

Mission accomplished. Alec McCord lay asleep beside her, and he wasn't going to Spring Training until they talked.

About last night.

About their future.

Far from having gotten him out of her system, she'd only made him more firmly entrenched. Alec belonged to her future as well as her past. She felt certain she could make him see that they belonged together. A man couldn't hide the way he felt during intimacy. He'd given himself away to her, whether he realized it or not.

But for now she was hungry. There would be plenty of time to talk. Talk was always better on a full stomach, anyway. She pushed back the covers, finding her black stockings tangled at her feet. Picking them up, she rolled them into a ball and set them aside.

Getting up gently so as not to wake Alec, she walked to his closet to find something to wear. She found a pair of jeans she rolled the cuffs on and fastened the too-big waist with a belt for a paper-bag effect. She added a white undershirt that she knotted just beneath her breasts.

Dressed, she padded barefoot to the kitchen to see what she could find to eat.

Plain toast or cold cereal wouldn't do. She felt like a celebratory breakfast.

Rustling around in the cabinets and refrigerator, she came up with the barest of ingredients to make French toast. Cinnamon and vanilla, she knew, would have been too much to ask of most bache-lors' kitchens. So she'd make do with eggs, milk and some stale Italian bread she cut into one-inch-thick slices.

She made use of the bananas she found. She sliced them and stuffed the French toast. She used the oranges to make fresh juice.

Adding a pot of coffee to the mix only enhanced the aroma of simmering butter and citrusy juice filling the kitchen.

There was no syrup, so she slathered peanut but-ter and jelly on top of the French toast when it was golden. Then she went to wake Alec for breakfast.

And their little talk.

When she entered the bedroom, she saw that Alec had burrowed underneath the covers.

Well, it was time for him to come out of hiding.

She pulled the covers back and kissed the nape of his neck.

He moaned.

She tickled his ribs. "Come on, wake up, sleepyhead. Time to get up."

"What are you doing up in the middle of the night?" Alec asked, opening one eye.

"It's not the middle of the night. It's almost noon."

"Is it?" He yawned and sat up. His eyes blinked at the bright sunlight flooding the bedroom "So it is."

"Come here, you." He reached for Elizabeth, pulling her to the bed. "Tell me I'm not dreaming, tell me that you're really here."

"I'm here," she said, as he wrapped her in the warmth of his embrace.

"Hmm...that's some cute outfit you've got on." He began working at the knotted undershirt, trying to untie it.

"I made breakfast for us. French toast, fresh juice and hot coffee. It's going to get cold."

"Then we'll warm it up—"

Flustered, she looked away. She was not yet comfortable with him. Getting exactly what you wanted, she was finding, sometimes took some getting used to.

Especially when she didn't know exactly what Alec wanted. Oh, she knew what he wanted at that instant; the same thing she did—to feel that incredible oneness with another person.

He caught her chin and made her look back up at him. "You aren't sorry about last night, are you? I couldn't bear it, if you were sorry."

"No. I'm not sorry. Last night was—"

"Let me remind you what last night was," he said, pulling the undershirt he'd unknotted over her head. "Don't be shy with me, now," he coaxed, his thumb tracing the outline of one pink nipple. "Nothing's changed just 'cause it's morning. You're so pretty."

The awe in his voice touched her, broke through the reserve that had come with the dawn.

"You still want me, don't you, Elizabeth?"

"Very much."

He raked his hand through her hair, cupping the back of her head and bringing her mouth to his lips. He kissed her so long and so well, she couldn't have told him her name if he'd asked.

His kisses were drugging; they made her dizzy with want. She kissed him back, her kiss all acquiescence and encouragement.

Her kiss set his skilled hands in motion until her breathing was ragged, her whispers, erotic suggestions.

She felt her curves mesh with the lithe hard lines of his broad chest as he stretched her out across the bed.

He started to laugh as he began helping her out of his jeans.

"What?" she asked.

"It's novel unzipping my own jeans—when they aren't on my body, is all."

The idea of it brought a smile to her own lips as she lifted her hips for him to slide the jeans off.

"Ah, I see you wear my jeans the same way I do."

When she looked puzzled, he explained, "Without any underwear."

He was in a playful mood and began drawing something on her belly, asking her to identify what he was drawing.

His moving fingers tickled and aroused her.

"This is a very detailed drawing," Elizabeth said, trying to concentrate and finding it absolutely impossible with the sensations he was causing her body to feel. She began squirming.

"I am a great artiste, but even I cannot draw on a moving canvas. You must remain very still or my work will be ruined," he said with exaggerated affront. "You're not guessing what I am doing, *madame*. Shall I give you some hint?"

"Oh, I know what you're doing," Elizabeth replied, giggling as the drawing began to take up more and more space on the canvas of her flushed skin, as his fingers trailed ever lower on her belly and then moved to the insides of her thighs.

"It's an octopus," she guessed.

"See, I am a great artiste. You have guessed correctly, *madame,* on your very first try."

"I have?"

Alec nodded, and to her chagrin he stopped his delicious drawing when she would have had him make it even more detailed. He lay back across the bed.

"Now it is your turn, *madame.* We shall see if you are also a very talented artiste," he challenged with a flourish, waving his hand before his body in invitation.

She took his challenge.

"I work in a different medium, sir. But I think you will find that I am equally as talented as you," Elizabeth said saucily, caught up in his fanciful game. And quite delighted by it because he was allowing her to see a vulnerable side of him; letting himself be completely free with her.

"I see you work in watercolor," Alec growled when she began using her lips where he'd used his fingers.

"Are you objecting to the medium I'm working in, sir? Because if you are—"

"Oh, no. No, it is quite satisfactory. Please do continue."

Her tongue licked his flat brown nipples and then her teeth tugged, raking them.

She felt him groan.

As she moved downward, kissing and nipping her way to his belly, she heard him catch his breath when she introduced her hand as well as her mouth into her artistry. "What was that?" she asked, commenting on the sounds he was making.

"I, ah, was just saying that perhaps, *madame,* you are a prodigy."

She laughed, then closed her mouth over him, showing him that indeed she was.

She could hear him drawing in slow, deliberate breaths as he arched up from the bed. And then he was on a roller-coaster ride he couldn't stop.

She was the one pulling the switches, controlling the ride. When it was over his eyes were closed, his body limp with a slight sheen of perspiration. It made his golden skin glow.

"Thank you," he said, when his eyes finally blinked open and he saw her beside him. He hugged her to him and rained tiny kisses on her face.

"You know what?" he asked, pushing himself up on his elbow and smiling down at her.

"What?"

"I'm famished. Let's shower and go warm up that breakfast of yours."

"Okay, do you want to go first?"

"Together," he suggested.

"Together?"

"Right. I'm not a selfish lover, Elizabeth."

"Oh. Then by all means together," she agreed.

In the shower they took up their drawing game
again. She lathered his back and then began drawing in the soapsuds with her finger.

"Who's the romantic now?" he asked, when he
guessed correctly that she'd drawn a big heart with
their initials inside.

"Alec, will you tell me something?" she asked
pensively.

"I'm at your mercy."

"This is serious."

"What is it?"

"Did last night—did it . . . Did it live up to your
expectations of a perfect Valentine fantasy date?"

"No."

"Oh . . ."

He turned and pulled her into his arms. "Last
night exceeded my expectations of a perfect Valentine fantasy date."

"You wouldn't lie to me, now, would you?"

His grin was sexy as he teased. "Of course not,
Libby."

Fifteen minutes later Alec was in the kitchen
warming up breakfast in his robe while she pulled
on his jeans and undershirt again.

Alec poked his head into the bedroom a few
minutes later to announce breakfast was ready.

Elizabeth looked up from where she sat on the
bed staring at the sack of mail from the *River City
Call* that she'd found stashed in the corner of Alec's
bedroom.

"What were you planning on doing with these?" she asked, holding up handfuls of letters responding to his ad.

"Nothing."

"Nothing?"

"Well, to be honest, Gio has dibs on them."

Elizabeth relaxed, shaking her head. "He would."

Elizabeth left the sack of mail and joined Alec in the kitchen for breakfast. They were sitting at the table playing footsies beneath it with their bare feet, licking sticky jelly from each other's fingers as they fed each other breakfast, enjoying the afterglow of new lovers when the door to Alec's apartment swung open.

"Alec, I've come to collect the mailbag. How many chicks wrote— Elizabeth!"

"Gio!" both Alec and Elizabeth said in stunned surprise.

Chapter Five

GIO HAD STOPPED DEAD in his tracks, his face red with fury.

Elizabeth watched the scene unfold in slow motion as the two men she loved most in the world confronted each other. It was the worst possible way for Gio to find out about the two of them. She'd wanted time to prepare him for the idea of his best friend and his baby sister being together. She'd wanted to— Why hadn't she thought about the possibility of this happening? They should have gone somewhere else. It was all her fault.

"What in the hell is going on here, Alec?" Gio demanded, marching toward him. Gio's body was rigid with anger and his hands were balled into fists at his sides.

"Now, I can explain, Gio. Wait until you hear me out. Don't do something rash—"

Elizabeth knew Gio wouldn't listen. She recognized the stubborn look on his face.

"Gio, don't!" she cried, trying desperately to stop her brother from doing something he'd only come to regret later.

"Shut up, Elizabeth. This is between Alec and me. You stay out of it."

"But you don't understand, Gio. This...this was all my idea," she tried to explain, hoping to distract him until he'd cooled down and she could reason with him. He had the hot temper that went with a passionate nature.

"I seriously doubt that. His nickname hasn't been 'Slick' since the seventh grade for nothing. Alec can talk the bark off a tree."

"They call you that—really?" Elizabeth asked, wondering why this was the first she'd heard of it.

Alec shrugged at the questioning look in her dark eyes.

"Yes," Gio answered for Alec. "And this time he's been too slick for his own good. I'm going to pound you until you're so ugly you get a new nickname. One you're not going to like half as much."

"Gio, listen to your sister. She's telling you the truth. You're jumping to the wrong conclusions, here," Alec warned, rising from his chair and putting his hands up in front of him, palms outward in a conciliatory gesture. He wanted more than anything to stave off the fight he knew Gio was itching to start.

Gio stopped and looked from Elizabeth to him and back again.

"That isn't the dress you were wearing when you left last night," Gio accused.

She glanced guiltily at the tangle of clothing still in a pile on the living-room floor. Gio followed her glance to the red-and-black velvet-and-silk dress mingled with Alec's tuxedo. She knew if he'd had any doubt about what exactly had gone on last night, the discarded clothing confirmed his worst suspicions. Alec had taken advantage of his little sister. Elizabeth saw his conclusion in his eyes.

Gio turned back to Alec with blood in his eye.

"Don't be a fool, Gio," Alec pleaded. "I'm bigger than you are."

"Yeah, a bigger jerk. I can't believe you'd use Elizabeth like this. How could you?"

"It's not—it wasn't..." Alec continued trying to explain, but his words were falling on deaf ears.

"You're not good enough for her, don't you get it?" Gio challenged, just before his fist connected with Alec's jaw, sending the taller man sprawling.

Alec hadn't tried to protect himself. He'd taken the punch Gio threw full on.

"Get dressed, we're going," Gio instructed Elizabeth, nodding toward the door. "And you stay away from my sister. You hear me, Alec?"

Alec didn't say anything. He didn't get back on his feet. He didn't try to fight for Elizabeth. He just remained braced with his back against the wall, rubbing his red and swollen jaw.

"I'm not leaving," Elizabeth said adamantly.

"Oh, yes, you are," Gio retorted. "You're leaving if I have to carry you out of here."

She looked to Alec to encourage her position. Looked at him to ask her to stay.

He didn't say a word.

Crushed by his dismissal, she gathered up all her things, left the room to dress, and allowed Gio to usher her out of Alec's apartment as he wanted.

But not because she didn't want to stay.

And not because Gio didn't want her to stay.

But because Alec didn't want her to stay.

ONE WEEK TURNED INTO two as she and Gio barely spoke to each other, neither of them wanting to discuss what had happened. Both of them were embarrassed, angry and hurt.

With themselves, with each other and most of all with Alec.

Once again Alec had gone off and left her, this time for St. Petersburg instead of Los Angeles. A different coast, but the pain was still the same, the distance still as great.

Each time he'd left without goodbye.

Or a promise to return.

The dumbest thing she'd ever done was answer his ad, "Sleepless in St. Louis."

She hoped with all her heart he was now "Sleepless in St. Petersburg."

It was probably too much to wish for, what with all the fans who traveled to Florida to watch the Cardinals in Spring Training. There would be wall-to-wall women to help him forget her—if he needed any help at all.

ALEC WAS PITCHING like an amateur.

Or worse—a has-been.

He was a wreck, a walking zombie. Had been ever since he'd arrived in St. Petersburg two weeks ago. He couldn't seem to eat much of anything, and sleep was an impossibility.

All he could think of was Elizabeth.

He should have stopped Gio from taking her. But at the time he'd thought maybe Gio was right. That he wasn't good enough for her.

His career as a baseball player was coming to an end. He didn't know what the future held for him.

The trouble was, he didn't want a future that didn't include Elizabeth.

GIO HATED SEEING his sister so miserable.

Hated being responsible in part for her pain.

He didn't like them being estranged, even if he did believe he'd done the right thing.

Maybe there was a way to make everything come out all right.

ELIZABETH SAT UP LATE into the night.

It was Thursday night but her usual sitcom block hadn't made her laugh. It wasn't their fault. Making her laugh had become a pretty hard ticket.

She'd already worked her way through Letterman and now she was on Kinnear. Both were funny men, but neither was doing the trick. Nothing could take her mind off Alec.

ALEC LOOKED AT THE WALL calendar in the locker room.

March 11th.

In one month the team would be back in St. Louis for the home opener.

Back in St. Louis.

Back where Elizabeth was.

Of course, he could go see her now. Just get on a plane and try to explain why he hadn't fought for her, why he hadn't asked her to stay.

He knew he hadn't looked like much of a hero in her eyes, but at the time he'd done what he thought was the right thing. At the time, he'd believed Gio might be right when he'd said Alec wasn't good enough for his sister. But he knew now that Gio had been wrong.

He wanted the best for Elizabeth. No one would ever love her more than he did. No one would take better care of her than he would.

But he would wait to see her.

Because he finally had a plan.

ELIZABETH LOOKED AT the calendar on her desk.

April 11th.

Tonight was the Cardinals' opening game of the baseball season. Alec would be back in St. Louis.

She tried to put it from her mind by working on a new idea of hers for her travel agency—minivacations, from one to three nights long. To get the best values she had sought out small hotels and bed-and-breakfasts.

Discounts for the weekend were often as high as thirty percent. So far, she had packaged a small hotel in Dallas that had loads of charm, an ocean-side inn in Newport Beach that offered everything from windsurfing to gourmet dining, and several renovated cottages in the French Quarter of New Orleans circling a spectacular courtyard.

All three cities were popular business destinations, so her clients could tack the minivacation onto the end of a business trip if they so desired. She was working on including other business centers like Boston, New York and Miami in her package grouping.

She recalled the European-style hotel she'd visited in Miami recently and put in a call to it. She was sure the antique furnishings and nearby boutiques would appeal to some of her clients, the more adventuresome of whom could go rollerblading in the Art Deco district of South Beach.

When she next glanced down at her watch, it was past five.

The game started at seven-thirty.

The game she wouldn't think about.

That gave her two-and-a-half hours to get home, get changed and get to the stadium.

She opened her purse and took out the ticket Gio had bought her for the season opener as a peace offering. It was taped together. She'd torn it up on first sight.

But when Gio had gone so far as to admit that maybe he'd been wrong about Alec, she'd considered that maybe she had, too.

Gio had apologized for letting his temper get the better of him, and suggested that they both give Alec a second chance.

She had reluctantly admitted that Gio had had cause to be upset. And they'd made up. They were back on speaking terms, and stealing-each-other's-food-from-the-refrigerator terms.

But she wasn't certain that going to the game was such a hot idea. Sure, she'd be able to see Alec pitch. When it came to Alec, she knew she had about as much willpower as a teenager with a credit card.

She and Alec had never gotten around to talking before Gio had barged in to rescue her.

But hadn't he really just rescued Alec?

After all, she'd practically insisted Alec make love to her.

Actually, there was no "practically" about it. She had insisted.

And worn him down until he had granted what she was so determined to have. She had thought they'd found something special together.

But what if he hadn't felt the same way?

She had to know.

That was the bottom line. Embarrassing as it might be, she had to know. And she had to take a chance that Alec had felt the same powerful connection she had when they'd made love. Had to take a chance that he was too proud or too afraid to come to her.

Just as making love had told her what she needed to know about her feelings for Alec, seeing him again would settle how things stood between them.

She didn't want the possibilities she'd glimpsed to be sacrificed to misunderstanding and pride.

Her decision made, she put the ticket back into her purse and snapped the purse shut.

She should go to the game.

She would go to Alec one last time.

HER SEAT—when she found it in the crowded stadium—was practically on the field. Gio must have paid a small fortune for her ticket.

She had a front-row seat for all the pageantry of the baseball season's opening game. It was hard not to be affected by the majestic Clydesdale horses pulling a beer wagon in their annual trot around the field.

"Peanuts, get your peanuts here!" a vendor singsonged from the aisle. There was a flurry of activity as money was passed down to the vendor and bags of peanuts were tossed back with the accuracy of a twenty-game-win hurler.

As Elizabeth put her change away in her wallet, her gaze fell on the tattered baseball card she kept in it. Alec's picture grinned up at her from the face of the card. She'd been carrying the card around in her wallet for years, just as she'd been carrying around her crush on him.

The crowd began clapping after the opening speeches were over and the Cardinals took to the playing field. They were playing their archrivals, the Chicago Cubs. Her attention was riveted to one specific player: the starting pitcher.

Alec took the pitcher's mound and began warming up his arm. Elizabeth wished she'd given in to her urge to bring binoculars to the game.

The leadoff hitter for the Cubs stepped up to the plate and swung his bat to loosen his shoulders. As she watched, Elizabeth felt herself grow tense. She wanted Alec to do well.

And he did, striking out the lineup for the Cubs—one, two, three. She was on her feet cheering with the rest of the crowded stadium when the inning was over. Could he feel her staring at him? she wondered. If he did, he didn't glance her way to acknowledge it. He looked down at the Astro-Turf as he jogged off the field.

The first hitter for the Cardinals got on base with a grounder, the second hit a pop fly for an out and Royer hit a triple that brought the run on first base home. A strikeout retired the side and the Cardinals took the field again.

The home stadium was abuzz with how well Alec was pitching after he struck out the next three batters the Cubs had to offer. Elizabeth felt herself start to relax a little. Alec's velocity and control were good. Clearly, his game wasn't going to be the problem tonight, so she could return her concern to the reason she was at the game.

Now that she was there, she wasn't certain how she was going to gain Alec's attention. However, it would have to wait until the game was over unless he noticed her first. She was hard to miss in a bright red cotton sweater and white slacks. Team spirit hadn't been her only motive for dressing in red.

But Alec failed to notice her.

As each inning passed he left the field with his attention on the AstroTurf and not on the crowd. As each inning passed the crowd grew quieter.

By the end of the seventh inning, the lighted electronic scoreboard told the story. Cubs 0, Cardinals 1. Alec was in the midst of pitching a nohitter. The crack of the bat meeting the horsehair ball was the sound missing from the festivities.

The seventh-inning stretch brought most of the stadium to their feet. Elizabeth needed sustenance and headed for a hot dog and soda, climbing the concrete steps toward the concession stands. It felt good to stretch her legs and ease the tension from her body.

The line for the ladies' room was its usual nightmare, so that by the time she made it back to her seat most of the crowd had already returned to theirs. The players hadn't yet taken the field, but there seemed to be a murmuring in the crowd. She hadn't noticed it at first because she'd been distracted by something that had happened while she'd been buying her hot dog and soda.

She thought she'd seen Gio.

It had only been out of the corner of her eye. And when she'd turned after making her purchase, he was gone. If he'd been there at all. Surely he would have told her if he was planning to go to the game, unless after springing for her expensive seat, he'd elected to be a bleacher bum high in the clouds for just a few bucks.

The restlessness of the crowd around her grew and she turned to where everyone seemed to be looking as the Cardinals took the field to start the eighth inning.

She read the message printed in bright lights and nearly fainted.

With joy.

With her hand over her mouth to cover her surprise and tears streaming down her face, she looked to the pitcher's mound.

Alec was staring straight at her.

Afraid to believe what she'd read, she looked at the electronic scoreboard again and read the message lighting up the night and her heart.

Elizabeth Bonetti

Don't you think twenty-one years is a long enough engagement? Please say you'll marry me in front of all these witnesses. Promise, then, you'll make me "Sleepless in St. Lucia."

Love,
Alec McCord

She looked from the electronic scoreboard back to the pitcher's mound.

Alec was there. On bended knee.

Waiting.

Staring straight at her.

And so was everyone else.

She was crying, she was sure her face was as red as her sweater and she started nodding her head, yes.

The crowd went wild with enthusiastic applause.

And Alec stood grinning, flashing a happy thumbs-up sign to signal he'd gotten her answer.

Elizabeth knew then that she had seen Gio. That Gio had been in on this special night.

She could barely see Alec on the pitcher's mound as the game resumed and she wiped her damp face. From the aisle she heard someone call her name and looked over to see Cupid, in the human form of her brother Gio. He motioned for her to join him.

The two of them slipped out as the crowd's attention returned to two outs and a 3-2 pitch. Unfortunately, the sound they heard as they made their way to the dugout was the crowd's groan as a bat cracked, connecting with the strike Alec had thrown.

The ball sailed out of the stadium, ending Alec's chances of a shutout game.

"Oh, no, Alec's no-hitter is over," Elizabeth said when she heard the sound.

Gio squeezed her hand. "It doesn't matter. I'm sure Alec got what he wanted most tonight."

And that started her crying all over again.

"Wait," she said as they passed by the ladies' room. "I want to go in here and splash some cold water on my face, okay?"

Gio nodded, and waited, flirting with a waitress at a nearby concession stand. By the time Elizabeth had repaired her makeup and returned, Gio had a date for Saturday night.

"How long have you known about this? And don't try telling me you haven't been in on it from the start—I know you too well."

Gio gave up his try at feigned innocence. "I couldn't stand seeing you so unhappy."

A look of horror crossed her face as a sudden thought occurred to her. "Gio, you didn't—"

"No. Marrying you was all his idea. All I did was help him facilitate the proposal he made tonight. The whole thing was what he wanted to do."

"Are you sure?"

"Why don't you ask him yourself?" Gio said, seeing Alec waiting as they climbed down into the dugout.

Alec was grinning and slapping hands with the other players on the team. Apparently Gio was right.

Her yes was more important to Alec than the loss of a shutout game.

She heard the coach tell Alec he was pulling him out and sending in a new pitcher for the last inning and Alec didn't give the coach any argument. Instead, his attention was on her. He didn't even appear to hear one of the players comment that the ball the Cub player hit must have been one of the controversial new "juiced" balls.

"I'm sorry about your losing out on the shutout," Elizabeth said, as he drew her into his arms.

He kissed her soundly to the applause of the players in the dugout, then took her to one side.

He hugged her to him. "I wasn't interested in having a no-hitter when I'd just made the most important pitch of my life."

She started crying again.

"What are you doing to that woman? She's always crying," one of the players called out as the Cardinals took the field in the top of the ninth with the score still tied.

It didn't help the waterworks any when Alec took an elegant jeweler's ring box from his pocket and held it out to Elizabeth.

"Open it," he ur[...]

She took the box fr[...] the lid and smiled while [...] down her cheeks.

"No wonder she's crying," [...] getting a look at the ring. "Y[...] skate, McCord. I think she oug[...] marrying you."

There was no way she'd reconside[...] to accept Alec's proposal of marriage. [...] any woman say no to a man who made [...] mantic gesture as the one Alec had made [...]

There, nestled in the velvet box, was a rin[...] seen before. A ring Alec had placed on her [...] before.

It was the ring from the gumball machine he[...] bought her at the pool when he'd been giving her [...] swimming lessons.

She'd proposed the first time. Insisted, actually.

It had taken her twenty-one years, but she'd finally gotten her man. She hugged Alec and covered his face with kisses. He held her tight for a moment and then returned to the dugout. She went back to her seat.

The score was still even—Cubs 1, Cardinals 1— when the team returned to the dugout moments later. But that all changed with the first batter, who hammered one out of the ballpark.

The Cardinals won and Gio, who was now seated beside her, cheered.

...ball fan,''

Sleep...

...ak dinner if you

...'n Shake, cele-
...ing the opening

...k dinner,'' Gio
...e a cheapskate.''
...rger,'' Alec said.
...ive dining estab-
...night.'' Alec fed
...ey drank in each

...er decision
How could
...such a ro-
...er.
...s she'd
...inger
...d

..., '' Gio said, going on com-
...c and Elizabeth were paying him
...bit of attention. ''I'm going to be best
...at your wedding. You can tell Nicholas and Tristan they can be ushers, but I'm going to be the best man.''

''Why? Because you want Ms. Greatbody to see you in a tuxedo?'' Alec asked, hitting the mark.

''Well, I do look great in a tuxedo. And playing in a rock band hardly gives us much chance to wear one.''

''You'd better be careful, Gio,'' Elizabeth warned.

''Why?''

"Well, you never know. Ms. Greatbody might think you look rather 'groomish' in a tuxedo, and next thing you know, you'll be saying, 'I do.'"

"Now, there's no call to get downright nasty, Elizabeth," Gio said, polishing off the last of his steakburger platter. He thought better of ordering dessert. There was only so much googoo eyes one man could stand to witness, even if Elizabeth was his sister and he loved her.

"I can take a hint. I'm leaving," he said, picking up the tab. "I'm paying tonight. You're not getting off this cheap, Alec."

They both waved Gio off without looking away from each other. They couldn't seem to keep their hands or their eyes off each other. Having found one another at last had a powerful magic all its own.

"My place or yours?" Alec whispered.

"How about the Ritz Carlton, cheapskate?"

"Cheapskate?"

"Well, you did get off cheap on my engagement ring, you have to admit."

"That was my grand romantic gesture," he insisted, running his finger along the line of her jaw and stealing a kiss.

"I thought proposing to me in front of fifty thousand fans was your grand romantic gesture," Elizabeth said, when they broke the kiss.

"No, that was sheer lunacy. Is there a full moon? I don't know what I was thinking. Well, that's not exactly true. I figured if you had any heart at all, you wouldn't say no."

"I wouldn't have said no if you'd passed me a note during the seventh-inning stretch. I've been waiting for you to ask me to marry you *again* all my life. I love you, Alec."

"And I love you."

"Does that mean we're going to the Ritz?"

"Okay, since it's a special night. But I'm going to have to start watching my pennies."

"I plan to continue working, Alec. You don't have to support me."

"But I want to. And I'm planning on retiring after the season is over. I've had an offer to coach high-school baseball. If I take it, my salary is going to be greatly reduced."

"But why are you retiring? You're still . . ."

"I know, but I want to go out while I'm on top of my game. And besides, I need to keep an eye on my . . . *my wife*. No more of those romantic dinners with dishy chefs." He gave her a stern look.

"You're jealous, I think. You *are* jealous, aren't you?"

"Damn straight, woman," he agreed as he grabbed her hand and tugged her along outside to the car. "Now that I've found what's been right under my nose, I haven't any intention of losing you."

"I haven't any intention of letting you," Elizabeth said, her hand on his thigh. "To the Ritz Carlton—and hurry."

"What's the rush...? We've got the rest of our lives together," Alec teased, dawdling.

Elizabeth moved her hand farther up his thigh and squeezed.

"Elizabeth!"

"What?" she asked, all innocence.

"Watch out for cops," he instructed, putting the pedal to the metal.

Postscript

"ARE YOU SURE YOU didn't get a rotor-cuff injury to your shoulder on purpose?" Elizabeth asked Alec as they relaxed in the private plunge pool off their suite at the glamorous Sandals resort on St. Lucia.

"I would have if I'd known how fabulous this place was. It's a shame I can't enjoy the windsurfing and waterskiing."

"I think you've done all right enjoying the king-size bed, whirlpool, and gourmet restaurants."

"Yeah, guess I have at that," he agreed. "Speaking of which, I hear a four-poster bed calling...."

"Alec, shouldn't you rest your shoulder?"

"I intend to," he said on a wicked laugh. "You've convinced me there are advantages to letting a woman be on top—"

"Alec!"

"Oh, don't get all modest on me now, Libby. I like it when you're a brazen hussy."

"Don't call me 'Libby,'" she insisted, following him out of the plunge pool and into their suite.

Alec laughed, handing her a robe to step into. He stood behind her with his arms wrapped around her as they stared out into the dark midnight, listening to the waves crashing into the half-mile stretch of crescent-shaped beach in front of the hotel.

"The week has just flown by. I wish we didn't have to leave in the morning," Elizabeth said on a wistful sigh.

"We don't."

"What?"

"I have a surprise for you," Alec said, taking her hand and pulling her back inside to sit on the bed. "Wait just a minute."

"What is it?" Elizabeth demanded, impatient as usual as she watched Alec pull a newspaper from his suitcase.

"Gio overnighted this newspaper to me and it arrived this morning. I've been waiting for the right moment to spring it on you."

She grabbed the newspaper from his hand. "What is it?"

"Turn to page twenty-two," he instructed.

"But this is..." she objected, then began scanning beneath their picture....

McCord–Bonetti

Elizabeth Bonetti and Alec McCord are to be married July 4th, 1995, at the Sandals resort on St. Lucia. The bride is the daughter of Angela and Anthony Bonetti of Arlington, Texas, and owner of the Bonetti Travel Agency. The bridegroom is a graduate of Boston College.

He is a professional baseball player, pitching for the St. Louis Cardinals.

"Alec!" Elizabeth squealed, tossing down the newspaper.

"It's okay, isn't it? I know we planned to be married on Valentine's Day, but I can't wait—"

Elizabeth threw her arms around his neck and kissed him soundly.

When they came up for air, Elizabeth began to fret. "Oh, my gosh, I've a million things to do. I need—"

Alec shook his head no. "You have nothing to do. Sandals is taking care of everything. They told me love is all we need. They arrange everything, including tropical flowers, champagne, wedding cake and a sunset cruise."

"You did all this when I was snorkeling and you were supposed to be resting, didn't you?"

Alec just winked at her.

Elizabeth began to giggle. "So then you really want to marry me in the morning?"

"I do."

Epilogue

The following New Year's Eve—Boston

THE BARTENDER EYED the three men in tuxedos curiously as they lined up in front of him. "What can I do for you, gentlemen?"

"I'm afraid you've already done it, Fred," Nicholas answered in a voice normally reserved for cross-examination. Tristan and Alec leaned forward, pinning the older man with accusatory stares.

Fred shifted uneasily. "And what is it you think I've done?" he asked coolly, folding his arms across his chest.

"Sold us some of your best champagne, for starters," Alec answered.

Fred's shoulders relaxed as he hid a smile. "Some folks would call that a favor."

"That depends on whether or not advice came with the champagne," Tristan stated smoothly.

"Advice? I never give advice," he assured them.

Alec looked at his buddies. "We need to refresh his memory."

"It was one year ago tonight," Nicholas told him. "We were three bachelors enjoying a night out on the town."

Fred stared at them, scratching his chin thoughtfully.

"Alec was a little grumpy because he'd been stood up," Tristan observed.

"You and Nicholas didn't even have dates," Alec reminded him.

"It doesn't matter. Any way you look at it, we were three guys without women," Nicholas said.

"And not having any luck finding any, as I recall," Fred mused, recognition finally sparkling in his eyes.

"Which is why you suggested we try advertising for a date. Run an ad in the personals and meet a real knock-out, a *fantasy* date," Tristan drawled sarcastically.

"I said that?" the burly bartender asked innocently.

"You did."

"And did you advertise for women?"

"We did," the three men answered soberly in unison.

Fred's brow wrinkled. "That was a little risky, wasn't it?"

"What? Advertising for a date or taking advice from a bartender?" Tristan's question produced a belly laugh from Fred.

"From the looks on your faces, I can only assume the personal ads didn't get the expected results. There's only one thing to do," he declared, then set a bottle of champagne on the bar with a thud. "This is on me."

"That's not necessary," Nicholas protested.

"Yes, it is. If something I said led you to getting hooked up with some pushy broads..." His voice trailed off as the cork from the champagne bottle exploded with a pop.

"Something you said led to us getting married," Nicholas corrected him.

Fred's eyebrows shot up. "You're married?"

"Yup. All three of us," Alec answered proudly.

"Then why are you here instead of out there?" Fred gestured to the ballroom across the hall where the New Year's festivities were in full swing.

"Because our wives are in the powder room," Alec answered.

"And they're probably going to be there for a while. You see, Alec's wife has morning sickness... or evening sickness or whatever it is expectant mothers get," Tristan explained.

"So we decided to come wait for them in here. Besides, we wanted to thank the man responsible for us finding such three gorgeous women," Nicholas continued as Fred filled their glasses with the bubbly liquid.

Fred could only shake his head in disbelief. "You *really* found your wives in the personals?"

"Well, let's just say because of the personals we found our wives." Tristan exchanged knowing grins with his friends.

Alec raised his glass. "To Fred, Boston's number one bartender."

"To Fred," Nicholas and Tristan seconded, clinking their glasses against Alec's.

Fred nodded gratefully, then said, "So you haven't told me. Who won the bet?"

Nicholas took a long sip of the champagne and grinned at his buddies. "Why Fred, we were all winners."

Pamela Bauer

Fifty red-blooded, white-hot, true-blue hunks
from every State in the Union!

Look for MEN MADE IN AMERICA! Written by some
of our most popular authors, these stories feature some
of the strongest, sexiest men, each from a different state
in the union!

Two titles available every month at your favorite
retail outlet.

In February, look for:

THE SECURITY MAN by Dixie Browning
(North Carolina)
A CLASS ACT by Kathleen Eagle (North Dakota)

In March, look for:

TOO NEAR THE FIRE by Lindsay McKenna (Ohio)
A TIME AND A SEASON by Curtiss Ann Matlock
(Oklahoma)

You won't be able to resist MEN MADE IN AMERICA!

Bestselling Author

JoAnn Ross

Delivers a story so exciting, so thrilling, it'll have you begging for more....

Legacy of Lies

From the haute couture world of Parisian fashion to the glittering lights of Hollywood, Alexandra Lyons will find fame, fortune and love. But desire and scandal will shatter her life unless she can uncover her legacy of lies.

Look for it at your favorite retail outlet this February.

<u>MIRA</u> **The brightest star in women's fiction**

MJRLOL

HARLEQUIN®

Deceit, betrayal, murder

Join Harlequin's intrepid heroines, India Leigh and Mary Hadfield, as they ferret out the truth behind the mysterious goings-on in their neighborhood. These two women are no milk-and-water misses. In fact, they thrive on

MISCHIEF & MAYHEM

Watch for their incredible adventures in this special two-book collection. Available in March, wherever Harlequin books are sold.

MOVE OVER, MELROSE PLACE!

HARLEQUIN®

Temptation®

Secret Fantasies

Do you have a secret fantasy?

Reporter Darien Hughes does. While celebrating her thirtieth birthday, she spots a gorgeous man across the crowded restaurant. For fun, she writes about this "secret fantasy man" in her column. But Darien gets a shock when "Sam" shows up at the paper! Enjoy #530 NIGHT GAMES by Janice Kaiser, available in March 1995.

Everybody has a secret fantasy. And you'll find them all in Temptation's exciting new yearlong miniseries, Secret Fantasies. Beginning January 1995, one book each month focuses on the hero or heroine's innermost romantic fantasies....

IS BRINGING
YOU A BABY BOOM!

NEW ARRIVALS

We're expecting! This spring, from March through May, three very special Harlequin American Romance authors invite you to read about three equally special heroines—all of whom are on a nine-month adventure. We expect each soon-to-be mom will find the man of her dreams—and a daddy in the bargain!

So don't miss the first of these titles:

#576 BABY MAKES NINE
by Vivian Leiber
March 1995

Look for the New Arrivals logo—and please help us welcome our new arrivals!

Once in a while, there's a story so special, a story so
unusual, that your pulse races, your blood rushes.
We call this

orrowed Time is one such book.

athleen Welles receives a most unusual offer: to sell one past day in her life for a
million dollars! What she didn't realize was that she'd be transported back in time, to
he very day she'd sold—the day she lost her true love, Zachary Forest. Can she right
er wrongs and reclaim the man she loves in a mere twenty-four hours?

#574 BORROWED TIME
by
Cassie Miles

Available in March, wherever Harlequin books are sold.
Watch for more Heartbeat stories, coming your way soon!